SEASON

The Girl on the Ferry

The Girl on the Ferry

j. d. Reid

Wolfe Island Press

Printed and Bound by Createspace, Charleston, SC.
Book Layout © 2017 BookDesignTemplates.com
Cover Design by Terry Belleville: terrybelleville.com

The Girl on the Ferry/ j. d. Reid. – 2nd ed.
ISBN: 978-1544678115

Mary Alice Marsh

CONTENTS

Publisher's Note 11

Forward by Freya Anna Bergman 13

8 AM Sunday, July 8th, 2012 21

Preface by Freya Anna Bergman...............................21

Sunday Morning 26

10 AM Sunday, July 8th, 2012 29

Preface by Freya Anna Bergman...............................29

On the Ferry 32

Monday, July 9th, 2012...37

Preface by Freya Anna Bergman...............................37

The Email..40

July 10th and 11th, 2012 43

Preface by Freya Anna Bergman...............................43

Nothing Happened 44

Thursday, July 12th, 2012...45

Preface by Freya Anna Bergman...............................45

Coffee Rendezvous 49

Friday, July 13th, 2012...59

Preface by Freya Anna Bergman...............................59

Nothing Happened 80

Saturday, July 14th, 2012 81

    Preface by Freya Anna Bergman 81

    The Spray 88

    Family 97

    Going Pee 108

    Becalmed 111

    Her Grandmother 112

    Anchorage on Hickory 117

    How Many Boyfriends? 122

    The Scar 126

    Marshall's Education 128

    Family Love 130

    Evening Approaches 133

    Sunset Kiss 141

    The Stars Above 143

    Believe in God 146

Sunday, July 15th, 2012 149

    Preface by Freya Anna Bergman 149

    Desperate Times 151

July 16th through 19th, 2012 157

    Preface by Freya Anna Bergman 157

    Intervention of Fate 157

Friday, July 20th, 2012 165

    Preface by Freya Anna Bergman 165

    Meeting at Ferry Dock 167

Saturday, July 21st, 2012 171

    Preface by Freya Anna Bergman 171

    Showdown 172

Sunday, July 22nd, 2012...181

    Preface by Freya Anna Bergman.......................181

    Nothing Happened 185

Sunday, August 26th, 2012......................................187

    Preface by Freya Anna Bergman.......................187

    The Denouement 193

    Marshall's Place 195

Last Word by Freya Anna Bergman 203

One Last Thing More 209

Addendum 211

In Memoriam..215

In Memoriam..217

One More Last Thing 219

    Preface by Hilary Freya Patterson.....................219

    Marshall's Joke...219

Acknowledgements 223

About the Author..225

Author's Note...227

Soup and Sex 227

About the Cover...227

Publisher's Note

Before this book could come to press, Freya Anna Bergman, a most high-spirited, loving, and exceptional woman, died in her sleep in her home at Niagara-on-the-Lake, Ontario. She was 97. After reviewing the manuscript, which was submitted only days before she died, it was decided to keep it in its original form with as little editing as possible. The reader will note there are large rambling prefaces and longer footnotes, and the prose shifts between first person and third since there were, in the end, two authors. The original intent was to have a professional writer translate Freya's memories of her lifelong friends, Leslie and Marshall Davenport, the parents of the well-known and widely admired philanthropist and leader within the aerospace industry, Geoffrey Davenport, into a more traditional form, one that could be enjoyed by the Davenport family for generations to come. It did not quite turn out that way. Freya herself took up the pen and the project transformed into something with a much wider scope. There is something to be said for spontaneity. The love and wisdom that pours from these pages is why we decided to keep it in its original form and it is why, after obtaining Geoffrey Davenport's permission, we collectively decided to make it available to the public. There is, we think, something to be learned as well as experienced within these pages. As Freya says, "Life is not just about you and I, dear reader; it is about *all* of us."

Aseem Zahin Ansari,
Chief Executive Officer, Wolfe Island Press,
Wolfe Island Ontario, Canada.

Forward by Freya Anna Bergman

I like to think that what you are about to read is a painting; a painting, in words, of a fleeting moment in time. It is a love story or, rather, a story about the nuanced interactions between a man and a woman that ultimately led to a love that lasted until, first Leslie, then Marshall, passed on into the great unknown, that *undiscovered country* that makes cowards of us all. That's *Hamlet*, by the way; you can look it up. Marshall could quote the *great bard* at will, which of course drove me, as well as others, quite mad. Leslie, on the other hand, would just smile and sometimes roll her eyes; but that is the way she was, so open, so accepting of others. She loved Marshall, of course, more than her life. She loved me too, which I could never really fully comprehend even though there was never any doubt that she did for whatever reasons she might have had.

That fleeting moment in time I am referring to was not especially singular; it happened over a period of days. I count six, in fact, with a week or so of what I call intermediate days that connected them. If you are expecting a lot of steamy sex, irrational passion, hearts that fall into disarray, forget it. What you will find instead is the first days that led to a lifetime. You may wonder what all the fuss is about; it was just a conversation, after all, between two young people becalmed in the middle of the St Lawrence River on a fine but windless day in July, telling each other about their lives, their hopes, their fears, and their expectations. Still, if I have ever seen true lovers in this world, it is they, and, as you well know, to find a love that lasts is rare. Many fall in love but love often vanishes, often surrenders to the mediocrity of daily existence, and often degrades lives to the mere convenience of living together. Of course, there is divorce. Couples divorcing themselves from one another were common enough in my day and even more common these days, as I understand it. You wonder why young people get married at all with such statistically poor chances of success. Hope, I suppose; hope that leads to the expectation that they can beat the odds.

There are winners and losers, which does not take away from the fact that *someone* has to lose, does it?

I like to think of myself as liberally minded and so I am not just talking about men and women; I am talking about women and women, men and men as well. I am, for instance, a woman who prefers women. I may now be a dried-up old bag, but I still feel the same. It is not that I do not *like* men; it is just that I do not *prefer* men. Even so, no matter how you look at it, no matter who is involved, their sex, their religion, their so-called best intentions, having been in love and losing it is a sad matter indeed.

If you cannot learn or, if having once learned you simply forgot, why the two of you fell in love in the first place then the foundation upon which you began your lives together may crumble ultimately and you may find yourself as alone as you began. This is true even though the room within which you stand may be crowded, and even though the one you once loved may be lying right next to you. That sounds a bit much, I suppose; perhaps it is a bit overly dramatic on my part. Perhaps I should talk only of what I know and I know this: I loved once in a way that almost frightened me but somewhere along the way I believed I had lost that love and I do not know why. I am already older than ninety percent of the population, most of the people I have ever known are dead, but I still do not understand the ways of the heart. There is something to learn, even at my age, so it seems. I have been taking notes, if you are not. After all, love, lasting love, is what we all strive for and hope for in our youth, and even in our old age; what we don't realize, and nor can we when we're so often blinded by the turmoil within us, is how mysterious is the source, and how rare. Still, if there is something to learn within these pages, you, dear reader, must find it within.

Whether or not I have learned anything at all throughout my long life, I have to admit that relating this tale of love to you has helped me in some fashion. Not that I believe I need help in any way, shape, or form, but I do feel a great deal more clear-headed about things. As stated above, I am no longer a young woman, and somehow over the course of the years I have perhaps become unnecessarily cynical about some things: politics, God, the future of humanity, the insidious mediocrity of life, people in general. The list is longer than it need be, and I fear that my cynicism is a reflection more of myself than of the world. In fact, that is true and I am sorry for it. I often wish my heart were stronger and I had more courage, more sticking power, but I am as I am and there is nothing for it really. I often wish I had Leslie's strength. Things are changing, though; my life is at an end, my love has gone, and I still ache within but I find I am smiling more. Just when you think your life is over, it begins again. I do not know who said that but someone must have.

As mentioned above, the moment to which I am referring spanned only a few days and was quickly over. One does not often even realize how important or significant a sequence of events might have been until much later, perhaps years later, and only if one looks back. Some do not look back, I know. My personal belief is that if you do not know from where you have come, how do you know where you are going? Therefore, I look back. Still, Leslie and Marshall rarely spoke of those days or brought out the few photographs they had to remind themselves of them; they didn't have to, I suppose. However, I do absolutely know these events formed the fabric and glue that held their hearts together as a couple for more than six full decades, a span of time of togetherness and love that not many can claim. More important, it was not just duty, or habit; it was love that held them together, a love that catalyzed in the very first days of their meeting.

It is difficult for a cynic like me, and perhaps you, dear reader, to believe, I suppose, that a mere conversation, even one spanning a week or more, could be so pivotal in the future lives of a couple. The current theory of how all this supposedly works is that biology brings lovers together. That is, raw desire and not family planning through conversation. Sex and desire, and lots of it, is normally the catalyst of love. When those fires are quenched, or at least when sex is understood to be available and therefore not something to pine for, that is when the relationship really begins to blossom. At that point, sex becomes more about intimacy and giving and not so much about taking.

Love is ephemeral. Big things kill love, small things, just about anything can turn the ephemeral nature of love into disinterest and sometimes into a deep dislike as couples demonize one another in the process of creating reasons for throwing aside someone they once loved; but get past that and intimacy, love, and commitment continue. That is why "practical" people stay engaged for years before they finally take the plunge into unqualified commitment. We have all seen that: let the fires burn down and then we will see what happens, and so on. But one cannot help but wonder in a situation like that if it's not more about convenience and habit, too much time "on station" so to speak, than love. People can fool themselves, given enough time together. This is not so, in the case of Leslie and Marshall. Their commitment to one another began immediately after these events and lasted for a lifetime. One year later almost to the day, they were married in St George's Cathedral, in Kingston, the oldest standing Anglican church in Ontario.

I wrote what you are reading now as well as a few comments and footnotes, and I added the Addendum at the last minute; but of the rest I must claim that I employed a ghostwriter. I would have preferred a female voice to help me, but the agency sent me a male. There was nothing I could do, I'm afraid, and I hope it is all right. If the reader should detect a male presence in the narration of the greater story then all I can say is that circumstances were such that it could not be helped, and I'm sorry. He is very young but seems intelligent enough. It is fair to say he did get the job done, and I do believe he did manage to put down in words the *sensibility* of what I dictated to him. He did not miss a thing as far as I could tell, and the tale *does* go on a bit. I know I drove him crazy, always correcting and adding this and that to what he imagined was complete. I do realize I have a tendency to go on a bit. You, dear reader, will just have to put up with it I am afraid. At this point in my life, I am beyond the ability to change the habits of a lifetime. Still, I must admit it has done nothing for my relationship with the young man. I probably will not see very much of him after this and it is too bad; I did, ultimately, rather like him.

The truth of Leslie's and Marshall's lives, the written down parts, the letters, the photographs, the papier-mâché version of their lives, was not particularly exciting or memorable; no one will ever write a history of them, except for me, of course. How does one sum up a life? God, I do not know: they were good, they were productive, and they loved and were loved in return, earth to earth, ashes to ashes, dust to dust, and so on. I cannot summarize their lives; no life can be rendered through the mere application of the written word. There is just too much that can said about any one of us. I know this much, though: they met; fell in love; married; had three children, two girls and a boy; leading to six grandchildren, four girls, two boys; all of whom are well-adjusted and have become productive members of society. Not bad, really.

I know this as well: they died and, as previously arranged, had their remains cremated and their urns interred side by side not in Kingston where they spent most of their lives, but in Niagara-on-the-Lake, where they spent the latter part of their lives together. Incidentally, their funeral services were in the *second* oldest Anglican church in Ontario, St Mark's, in Niagara-on-the-Lake. I mention it only because it seems like an odd coincidence to me. It is otherwise of no particular importance and no doubt means absolutely nothing. Still, I should add, now that I have brought it up, that Leslie and Marshall were not particularly religious. They only went to service at Christmas and Easter, and those especially beautiful spring mornings when one simply must go.

From a historical perspective, it could be said that Marshall was the more notable of the two, although I do not like the word *notable*; it is just a relative term and does really mean a great deal. *Notability* flies away very quickly whereas character does not, and Marshall had character, lots of it. At any rate, he rose to become a successful playwright and novelist and, ultimately, the director of a relatively famous festival that puts on 19th century plays for tourists in the summer season in Niagara-on-the-Lake in southern Ontario, more noted now for its wines than the still on-going festival. None of his works are read today, unfortunately; perhaps they should be for they dealt with all the big questions in life: life and death, is there a God; subjects which, sadly, today have fallen out of vogue. Many of his books can still be found on the shelves of most libraries but for how much longer it is hard to say; even libraries in this age of abundance must shed their load occasionally, particularly if a title has not been checked out to any great extent.

Leslie already had her PhD in Sociology and Psychology by the time she met Marshall. She became very successful as well, authoring a number of important papers on the subject of Emergent Societies, referring to what was termed then as third world countries but known today as simply part of the world. She ultimately obtained full tenure at Queen's University in Kingston and was a member of the faculty there while Marshall wrote his plays and novels. Incidentally, they completely shared the responsibility for raising their children even though Marshall was home most of the time. Leslie insisted on that and saw Marshall's literary career as important and as significant as her own. She was very athletic, too. They both were, in fact, as were most of the children; except, perhaps, their rather diminutive young son who was particularly inept at sports but who now, by the way, leads one of the largest aerospace firms in the United States. Incidentally, Geoffrey is also a member in good standing of the Canada Council for the Arts, and not only because the Canadian component of his company is largely responsible for the larger part of the funding of said council.

It was Geoffrey who commissioned me to write this very short and very particular history - so you can blame him and see how far it gets you. ...Actually, I do not know why he asked me really. Perhaps he was humoring me by giving me something to do in my last days, I don't know. Of course, he knows I know everything there is to know on the subject of his mother and father, so perhaps that's it. Another reason just occurred to me. Perhaps, in part, it was because *he* wanted to know more. I never thought of that before. The early lives of one's parents are generally a mystery to the children they will ultimately leave behind. At any rate, it is no small responsibility; and no one's about to write a memory of me, nor you most likely, dear reader. As Geoffrey explained it, a written history is rather a bit more than having one's life captured solely within the crackling pages of a faded photo album. Of course, I realize that a book can accumulate great layers of dust but that does not change the fact that if some future reader wants to pick up the text, he or she will be able to do so, thanks to this effort. It is an honor to be asked by Geoffrey of all people to undertake such a task. He never does anything lightly, that man, and I do so not wish to disappoint him. I shall endeavor not to.

I do not often visit Geoffrey and Anne in Colorado, it is just too far away, but when I do, he invariably has me over to his office to show me about. I do rather like it, he and his staff simply faun over me. During one particular visit, I stood up from the chair that he had just sat me in and looked closely at a framed photograph that was hanging on the wall, displayed in such a way he could easily study it from where he sat at his desk. It showed Leslie and Marshall, impossibly young, on the deck of *The Spray*, hanging onto the rigging as if their lives depended on it, the sky behind them effortlessly blue and the water of Lake Ontario dancing in the sun. They were smiling as only the young can smile. She was dressed in white, in a long-sleeved shirt, and hat and sunglasses, beautiful, trim, and fit; he was also in white, dressed in a t-shirt and shorts, longish hair by today's standards, brown in color, rich in texture, tall, deeply tanned, and handsome.

Life is funny sometimes. Odd points, places, and times connect when one least expects them to. I recognized the time and place. It was, indeed, a long time ago, and there has been a lot of water under the bridge since those days. I almost wept when I saw it I was so overcome. I felt the guilt too. I had not felt it for years but there it was still. Even though I have been forgiven a thousand times over, it seems only yesterday that I almost tore from the person I loved the most the one person she needed the most. Even so, how can one ever know what followed, or what was in their hearts, as the day in that photograph unfolded? No one knows but me. It is not a mystery that I should do so, for I lived it as well. What I did not experience firsthand, I learned from the only one who could possibly have told me, Leslie. She told me everything the night I suddenly panicked and dragged her down to Toronto only to tell her I loved her, as if she did not already know.

As she entered my small apartment, I could see immediately it was too late and I completely fell apart and I wept. I am still weeping, even though I could then, as I can now, recognize the joy she owned. I was, and am, jealous; insanely jealous, but also immensely pleased, of course.

FAB, Niagara-on-the-Lake, Ontario, November 12th 2080.

8 AM Sunday, July 8ᵗʰ, 2012

Preface by Freya Anna Bergman

One should always begin at the beginning. Of course, there is no beginning, at least, not in the sense of a specific instance of time where one can unequivocally say that this is when the mystery of love began. However, one can define the exact date they first met, not knowing until later what would unfold after that pivotal moment. It was July the 8ᵗʰ and it was a Sunday. The fact it was a Sunday is clear enough for the two of us took the morning ferry over to Wolfe Island to ride our bikes, and we always went on Sundays and never on Saturdays. I drove up from Toronto on the Friday; we always had dinner out on Friday night and then slept in on Saturday morning. I recall the bells of St George's sounding through the streets, mixing with the sounds of traffic and the summer wind, and the deep rumbling of the ferry as it reversed its engines and pulled into the jetty. We rode our bikes from Leslie's apartment near the university, which was only a short distance from the ferry terminal, packing small lunches and a few things to drink. We would get most of what we needed on the other side. Leslie had promised the singularly most wonderful sticky bun I would ever have in my life. I was not at the time certain what a sticky bun was, but I can assure you she was absolutely correct. Even today, once a month or so, I include a sticky bun with my breakfast; that's over sixty years of sticky buns, and that morning was the first morning I had ever heard of them. It is funny how different experiences in life can converge. For a long time, nothing of import happens, and then suddenly everything happens; in this case, one of the most pivotal moments in my friend's life, and in the second the beginning of my lifelong passion for sticky buns.

I do digress. I am afraid I am terrible for that, or good at it, depending on your perspective. The editor has not given me a word count and so, if it sounds okay to me and you do not mind awfully, I will just continue and hopefully I will not go too far off the main subject as my heart and mind sometimes jump about. I realize you have been warned earlier, this is just another friendly reminder.

At any rate, sixty years after, I can turn to my bed in the small apartment I now find myself in and see her. She swings her feet off the bed and places them on the floor, saying quietly to herself as she does so, "There... another morning," and then standing, noticing bright sunlight and blue sky through the window, again saying to herself so quietly I can barely hear her, "Thank you, God, for this wonderful morning."

It sounds hopelessly romantic these days, I know; religion, the belief in God, going to church, is just so passé. Who talks to God these days, for God's sake? These days the most prevalent philosophy of living one's life is to merely, live for the moment. That's me, anyway. I live by the moment, hour by hour, and minute by minute; at ninety-six, there is a high probability that I could drop dead any second and so I sometimes feel I cannot afford to do anything else.

At any rate, Leslie was not really the religious type; she said things like that, and believed in them too, but only because it was simply the right thing to do. It was the same at the end of her day as she lay back in bed. She'd say, "Thank you, God, for today," and a moment later whisper, "Good night, then," as if God were somewhere in the room. It was a little much for me I am ashamed to say. Once when we shared a bed in that small apartment in Uppsala, I heard her pray as she does and I asked her why. "You should always give thanks," she said, turning her head on the pillow to me. "Look how good we have it." That was Leslie, a nice person, thoughtful, kind, generous, loving, and beautiful, too. God, I loved her. The fact she is dead means nothing. I love her the same today as I did then and I always will.

Returning to that July morning in Kingston; that is, we are now in the present of the story. It is sometimes difficult for me to recall, exactly, where I am when I allow my mind to drift like this, so please bear with me. ...It is funny how you slip into old habits of memory and place so casually. At any rate, I am beneath the covers with only my face showing... Hah! You would think we were truly were lovers! We slept together in Uppsala and we slept together in her apartment in Kingston, but with all the same rules. It was what we did when I visited. We slept in the same bed but were not lovers; I just loved her, and she me. I am thinking of that morning… it is as if it were yesterday. I watched as she put her feet on the floor, stand, and stretch, silhouetted against the window. She glanced out through the window to check the day and then headed to the shower, and came out moments later. On the way back across the room, she caught her reflection in the mirror, stopped, and turned so that she could see herself full on. There was a moment as she studied herself and then she allowed the towel to fall. It was not something she did regularly. Leslie was not a vain person by any stretch of the imagination. She was no different from any of us in that regard. Occasionally we catch a glimpse of ourselves, our real, physical, selves, and we stop, and turn, and look, and inevitably, and inappropriately in my opinion, cannot resist passing judgment on ourselves. It is typically true of young woman of whom so much is demanded and so much is unrealizable. It is also true of old women like me, who have yet to accept the full ramifications of our ineluctable fates. I do not have much further wisdom to offer other than it does help tremendously if one removes all body-length mirrors from the premises. Hah! I love a joke. I hope you do!

Leslie was then, and so she remained her entire life, a beautiful woman. She was very athletic, strong and tall, and perfectly proportioned. She could not help but think her body as too large; it seemed like a man's body to her. Other than her breasts, of course, and the lack of that certain appendage, so she joked. Actually, she never joked about it, I did; it was *my* style and not ever hers. Leslie would not say anything that suggested anything at all crude, even if her mouth was full of it, as she said. I am sorry, that was perhaps an unnecessary allusion but one which I could not hold back. *Please* forgive an old woman who has still, I like to think, a penny's worth of *esprit*, or something like that, remaining in her old bones. I don't think of men's appendages very much at all, really, and never have. I do not know why I suggested I ever did.

The memories and the feelings that go with them occasionally surface and I do recall a time when real blood did course mightily through arteries that are not half collapsed. Once, again in our apartment in Uppsala, I was lying in bed, eyes half open, watching her climb out of bed. My heart quickens thinking of it even now. She removed her nightgown and stood briefly before the mirror and I heard her say, just below the audible range, whispering to herself, her voice, carefree, teasing herself, "There you are; is that you?" and she laughed and answered her own question. "Who else would she be?" She stood back studying her reflection, which was as clear to me as it was to her, but seen differently, I am sure: blonde hair styled closely cropped, her face very feminine, tapered, with high cheekbones. She ran her hands over her breasts and over her flat stomach and along the contour of her hips until her arms were pointing straight down. It was an athlete's body: she biked, hiked, swam, and went to the gym twice a week; still, she hated her body, I knew. She could barely look at it, and I watched her turn away from it while I could only look. "It's a curse, then; I'm cursed," I heard her say. She sighed, stepped back, and threw on her chemise, sweeping it about her shoulders, placing one arm in at a time and quickly tying it about her waist as the sun shone through the fabric, making her seem like an angel dressing. I almost said something but as she turned toward me to head to the kitchen to prepare tea, I quickly closed my eyes and pretended to be still asleep. I did not like pushing in on her privacy too far. It was bad enough we shared a small apartment, and shared the same bed too.

She would inevitably compare herself to me, and in those days I was short, petite, and had a classic figure. I'd like to point out that I am Swedish, if you have not guessed already, and I look every part of it with my blonde hair that used to be long and hang down the extent of my back. Stepping out onto the curb, whether it be Uppsala, Stockholm, or London, I could feel men's eyes follow me as I walked down the street; not that I cared, but it is still nice to be admired even if the those who do the admiring are not, in themselves, particularly admired in return, physically, that is. The perfect body, to me, was, of course, Leslie's; she was six foot two and absolutely drop-dead gorgeous. She remained that way for all of her life since, from the day she was born, she exercised and ate right and never let herself go. Unlike myself, I am afraid to say; by the time I was fifty, I had cut my hair short and was looking somewhat matronly. Now there is a real joke. I have never been anything like matronly and nor would anyone ever think so. Leslie never mentioned the changes my body underwent and always had something nice to say about what I might be wearing on any particular day, my hair, or my skin. It was those involuntary glimpses in the mirror that ultimately told me of the truth; that and the bathroom scales, those insidious inventions that should be relegated only to physician's offices and meatpacking houses.

On reflection, I wonder if I was not suffering at fifty what Leslie was suffering in her early twenties. Marcia, that dear sweet girl, Leslie's oldest, who is now at least thirty years older than Leslie was in the days I am describing, visited the other day. She looks a lot like Leslie but not to the same degree as Alice, Leslie's second oldest; and then, most particularly, Hilary, Alice's daughter. The resemblance there is, frankly, quite unbelievable, and almost scary. My heart skips when I see the child sometimes. It makes one almost believe we can be born again, which I realize is an absurd notion and one should not believe in it. Still, one cannot help but feel that way. At any rate, Marcia had come by to visit, as she quite often does, and on this day brought along a set of photos that she had extracted from 'the archives,' so she said. She held a little cube in her hand and the photos, newly imported into the device, stood up in three dimensions; I could see all sides. What they can do these days, it is simply amazing. There was a recreation of me from those "matronly days" and, I hate to say it but it is true, I looked damn good! It was a shock, really. I do not ever recall at any point during those years feeling good about myself. Of course, you can tell from my age I am well past the matronly stage; I am in the decrepit stage, if you must know, the morbidly decrepit, I might add. I am, in fact, a wizened little nothing; the only good thing is I am no longer overweight. Hah! There is always some good in everything.

Oh, one more thing before I hand you over... While I was recovering from the delight and shock of seeing a version of me from years ago, Marcia, so much like Leslie in character as well as physically, leaned in close and hugged and kissed me just as Leslie used to, cupping my face in her hands, kissing my cheeks, and my eyes, and finally my lips. Perhaps she had seen her mother do just that. She said, "You were so gorgeous, Auntie Freya; just look at you!" It took a while, I must say, before I could speak again and then lift my head up so she could see I was not crying. The simplest things, I can tell you, is enough to turn an old woman on her head.

So here it is, the first morning of the beginning. I am sorry it took so long to get here. There is just so much more to say than I imagined. What I have forgotten to mention, I am certain will be revealed in what follows, which, by design, are merely the bare facts of what transpired on that early Sunday morning. I give you, dear reader, my fellow author and partner in crime. Please be patient with him. He knows absolutely nothing really.

Sunday Morning

Leslie Krueger stepped to the window and pulled back the blinds. Sunlight poured in about her. She closed her eyes against the sun, feeling the warmth press against her. She smiled and opened her eyes. The sky was blue, not a cloud in it. She wrestled with the latch and opened the window to let the summer air drift inward. It had rained the night before, the scent and freshness mixed up in the air, almost like spring. She opened it wider and breathed in, and opened it wider again. She settled against the frame and looked out. The park across the street was particularly green, and the leaves had a vibrant sheen. The morning breeze lifted them then let them fall gently back into place. She could hear the sound as they lifted and fell. The dryness was out of the grass – it would feel cool and soft on her feet. She liked that, walking across the rich grass without her shoes on. She'd often kick her shoes off on the way home, holding them in one hand with her pack slung over her shoulder, setting out with her head up, conscious of the glancing beams of light between the high leaves of the tall maple and oak.

She stepped back from the window. It was going to be a good day. She and a friend were riding to the Island today. They'd take the ferry and get some ice cream at Ernie's and some sticky buns at the bakery. They'd ride as far as they could, right to The Foot at the very tip of the island. There they'd eat their lunch and take the path down to the water and take a quick swim – although her friend could not swim. The water was deep there. She'd probably just sit on the shore and watch. Leslie, though, was a strong swimmer. One day she might swim to the small island across the channel from The Foot; it was only about a mile, she'd have no difficulty. Not this time, though, and maybe never unless she could find someone to go with her; instead, she'd just swim out a few yards and luxuriate in the cool water. She loved the sensation against her flesh. It felt like silk.

It was time for her friend to wake up. She knocked on the bedroom door. She knocked again and heard her friend turn in the bed and acknowledge. Her friend's voice was still thick with sleep. "Minute."

Leslie paused. The response had been atypically truncated. Her friend normally would have responded with long words and convoluted sentences, all articulated with an acquired English public school accent, despite the fact she was Swedish. She decided to push her along and called again through the closed door, "Minute?" She heard in response the ruffling of the sheets. "I did say a 'minute' did I not, and a minute it shall be. Just give me a minute!" Leslie smiled. That was more like it. It was a long way from their school days in Uppsala and a lot of water had passed under the bridge since those days, and yet some things never changed.

She moved to the kitchen and began to prepare her breakfast – tea, yogurt, some fruit. It was a short ride to the ferry terminal from her apartment near the university. They'd be there in minutes so there was no rush. With the bikes, they were almost guaranteed to get on. Not so with the cars. Sometimes the lineup of cars was so long, it took several hours long to get across. The boat was always jammed this time of year.

Carrying a small bowl of yogurt in one hand, she drifted into the living room and selected some music on her iPod, turned on the amplifier, and set the volume up. The sound filled the small apartment. If that didn't wake her friend, nothing would. She had selected a rocked-up version of "Into the Black" by Neil Young; it was playing all the time in those days. The sound was rich in base and exceptionally crisp in the mid-tones and higher. The window curtains drifted back with the sound the volume was up so high. The sound system was the first item of luxury she had bought after she moved into the apartment; after that, she bought her Subaru.

She had a lot to be thankful for, she knew; many couldn't find jobs □ but still, she'd worked for it, slaved for it, in fact.

Her friend opened the bedroom door dressed and ready to go; she looked a bit odd with her hair all askew while dressed in the tight-fitting clothing, ready to bike. Her friend laughed, waved, danced with the music across the short distance to the washroom, and shut the door behind her. Leslie turned down the music. "If you're not out in twenty minutes, I'm leaving without you!" she shouted. She could hear her friend laugh. She returned to the kitchen, stepping into the light pouring in through the window. The light was almost blinding. It reflected off the tile floor and bounced off the walls. She could hear the day picking up outside □ more traffic, people coming and going. She quickly finished her yogurt and began to sip her tea. The day beckoned. "Five more minutes!" she shouted and laughed.

The future had not always been so bright. Her hand involuntarily lifted and touched the scar behind her ear. It reached up into her hair where it was mercifully hidden. Never mind that. She walked again over to the window and looked out. There was so much promise but there were touches of gray out there too. It didn't ruin it; it just placed an edge of shadow about everything. You're floating on air one moment then slipping down a slope the next. The world you see is painted by the heart. Who said that, she asked herself. She couldn't think; it was true, though.

The bathroom door opened and Freya stepped out. "How many more minutes do I have?" she asked, throwing her long blond hair behind her and tying it. Leslie stood in the light from the window, brilliant and scattered about the room. The shape of her, intensified by the tight-fitting top and shorts she wore for biking, turned in the light.

"None – you're out of time." The vision laughed.

10 AM Sunday, July 8th, 2012

Preface by Freya Anna Bergman

I always liked Marshall, right from the start. I would never admit it to him, not for years, but there it is even so. Ultimately, I told him how much I loved him and he told me the same, and, of course, we both cried. His eyes were wet, I could tell, so do not think he did not when he did. Not that we were ever lovers, that is a ridiculous notion; I felt no more sexually attracted to him that to my dead father. It was just that we ended our days loving one another, it is as simple as that. It is a notion that some people simply cannot understand. Why that is I do not know. Some seem to require a reason for loving someone but I do not a need a reason to love Marshall, I simply do; he deserves it. He and Leslie may be dead but that is not the end of things. It is not as if I have stopped loving them, for heaven's sake, which is equally as absurd.

However, in those far-flung days, I detested Marshall horribly. The irony is I would not have felt so strongly if he had not been so irresistibly likeable. It was his easy manner, I suppose, and the loose way he carried himself, walked, and moved his limbs so easily and casually and with such fluidity. His athleticism did that for him, but more than that it was his attitude. "He was one relaxed dude," to use the vernacular of those days. Marshall was more like I would have liked to be, relaxed, easy going, and patient... particularly patient. I continue to exhibit none of those attributes, however. I am a very impatient person and though I do not feel so inwardly, I am told I can be somewhat intense, even now. It is one of those long-lasting disappointments in my life that I cannot emulate in myself what I most admire in others. Still, I have some good points so I am not completely depressed about such things. I suppose, by now, I have come to accept who I am. I must say it has taken a while.

At any rate, Marshall was not in any way, shape, or form, a one-dimensional man; he was, like most of us, many-sided and full of contradictions. But he did have the ability to look you directly in the eyes, smile, and carefully and easily say whatever it was that was on his mind in such a way that you understood him completely. You may not agree with him but you liked him instantly. Geoffrey is exactly the same. Perhaps it is hereditary; after all, one just does not inherit physical characteristics but personality as well. One sometimes wonders how truly unique we really are; we are all the same, really, depressing as that might be to some. I cannot imagine who I inherited the greater part of my personality from, possibly my mother. I cannot say I knew my father well enough to know what attributes he might have passed my way. It was his intelligence, probably; my mother was never all that quick.

Speaking of intelligence, Marshall was also one of the most intelligent men I have ever met, which is a slightly annoying attribute, I must say, since he was very difficult to argue with and was invariably right in whatever subject we happened to be throwing back and forth. He could effortlessly quote the Bible, Dante, Milton, Shakespeare, Keats, T.S. Elliott, Cummings, Shaw, Thus Spoke Zarathustra, even, to his American friends, major passages from the US Declaration of Independence. On the scientific side, his big hero was Charles Darwin but, besides Darwin, he could quote Gould and Dawkins, and on the physics side, Hawking, Feynman, Newton, and, on occasion, *Galileo Galilei*. He did not mean to be snobbish about it at all although many thought of this affectation of his as snobbish. He always wore a small smile as he extracted the passage from some labyrinth within his mind. Still, it was boring, and weird really, when he decided to 'let loose,' as Leslie described his habit to try to fit to any occasion the right quote from some illustrious, normally dead, personage. It was his photographic memory that gave him the ability. Very witty, too, he was on occasion; more on that later, if I can remember to render a few anecdotes; but now is not the time I am afraid.

How odd it is, though, that as my mind dwells on the man that came before the son, I can stand in the son's office and talk of the not-yet-realized man, his father. The memory of Marshall I hold in my mind is immediate. I sometimes feel as if I want to nudge that memory of him, to tell him even before he steps upon the path of his life where that path will ultimately lead him: to

Leslie, his daughters, and his son, his writing, Niagara-on-the-Lake, all of it. What would the physical, that is, a stand up, talking, version of my memory of Marshall say, I wonder. Would he laugh and shy away? Perhaps never call Leslie back? I do not think so. He was not that type of man. He most certainly would have dropped everything and sprinted along that path while whatever uncertainty he might have held in his mind rushed to catch up, and perhaps never would.

The first time I saw Marshall he was exactly as he was in the photograph on his son's office wall: tall, thin, wiry. He stayed that way most of his life. He never acquired one of those rounded bellies most men seem to carry about with them. I cannot help but smile at the sight of thin men, narrow, slightly bowed shoulders, thin arms, and thinner legs, carrying about them a balloon- sized object about their middle as if they're pregnant. Big men with big guts, on the other hand, I expect of the breed. They disgust me as well but not quite to the same extent. At any rate, Marshall did not suffer from that particular malaise of aging, or inactivity blamed on aging. He also kept his hair. It turned from a luxurious brown to a very dignified almost pure white, which no doubt helped him, in no small way, land his position as director of the Niagara-on-the-Lake dramatic festival. He looked the part as well as spoke the part, which, of course, helps in any competition of that sort. He was simply perfect for the job. An ugly man never reaches a position such as that.

I should add that Marshall also liked to tease Leslie in a gentle sort of way. It was the way they interacted with one another, this gentle teasing that went back and forth between the two. I have to say I found it rather irritating at times though. I think Marshall knew that so he never really poked at me. We had this understanding, he and I. Even so, when he approached Leslie on the ferry that morning I could have killed him. He was a man, after all, and at the time I did not like men particularly, particularly when they were approaching my best friend and, in my mind, my lover. Still, it is uncomfortable for me to think I might have been a little put out he did not approach me first. At first, I imagined he had made a mistake but as his eyes fastened on Leslie, I knew he had not. It was my vanity, and I was very vain in this days. I am equally uncomfortable with the notion that I might have had something to do with why men in general seemed to keep their distance from Leslie, but it had nothing to do with her I can tell you; it was all me. In those days, I could cause a man to turn on his heel and run in the opposite direction; all it took was a particular look. Marshall was somewhat immune, I suppose. He had a great deal of confidence in himself. He knew what he liked and he liked Leslie. Not even I could get in the way of that. At any rate, after Marshall approached her on the ferry, and particularly after she emailed him back, I definitely wanted him dead. I hate to think what would have happened if my wish had been fulfilled. Fortunately, God has designed us in such a way that none of us can get what we most desire merely by thinking about it.

On the Ferry

Something, some sound or other, made Marshall Davenport turn; funny how that is, he mused later, trying to explain it to Leslie as well as himself. It is always the unexpected that turns one's head and opens one's eyes. The average, the mundane, is just that; and there was nothing mundane or average, or expected, about the woman he saw that very bright Sunday morning as he waited to board the ferry.

Her natural beauty was what was so unexpected, he decided, it was as simple as that. There was no other reason. When she caught his eye, she was walking up the ramp onto the ferry, pushing her bike ahead of her, following a friend. She was taller than just about any other woman, or man, boarding the boat. She was wearing her helmet; her long-sleeved upper garment molded over her shoulders and stretched tight over her chest, leading to her skintight shorts, the type worn by bicyclists. He just about fell over, she was so striking. He shouldered his pack and quickly followed her onboard but by the time he reached the car deck, a semblance of better judgment caught up to him. He maneuvered so he could see her better. She sat on the bench on the upper deck next to her friend, another woman with a much smaller frame than hers. It was the first time he gathered how big she was – not big in terms of heavy, or weighted, but big in terms of tall, muscled, and fit. Her proportions, shoulders, arms, breasts, tight waist, hips, long legs, were exact, perfect. He intended to talk with her. The sheer physicality of her meant it would be unlikely she would feel accosted by yet another male admirer; after all, she could probably beat the crap out of him. He held back but not because of that. He held back because he wanted to watch her and study her without being seen, to see if he could gather more about what she was like without necessarily having to embarrass himself by talking with her, and then, if it didn't work out, walking away as if nothing had happened. If she turned out to be an athletic 'grunt' – more pushups, more Pilates, than brains – then she wouldn't be for him. Her body, though; her body just didn't quit. He could barely take his eyes off her.

He climbed the ladder to the upper deck and cautiously took up position only a few feet from where she and her friend sat. She was turned so he couldn't see her face but her blonde hair was thick, short, fashionably cut. She had a long neck, very feminine. There was a noticeable scar behind her ear. She was talking to her friend; her hands, beautiful, feminine, were expressing what she meant and felt. She was someone who felt a great deal then. He tried to listen but the wind kept him from hearing. He felt like a voyeur, and a trespasser. One does not take photos of someone without asking and he wasn't asking, he was watching, taking photographs with his mind.

He waited for her to turn toward him. It took seconds, less than ten, and when she did, he pushed off the rail, walked right up to her, and stood directly in front of her, blocking her view of the lake. He was abrupt and forthright.

"Do you mind if I speak with you?"

He stopped her in mid-sentence, her hands frozen in mid-gesture, about to make a point. She stumbled over what she saying, not finishing it, and looked up to see a young man, tall and wiry, likely strong, a runner perhaps, she imagined. He was deeply tanned, dressed in a t-shirt and sandals, brown hair unruly but not long, and the beginnings of a beard on his chin and face. Not bad looking, but it was his intensity that struck her the most, his focus. She didn't know what to say and so remained silent and hoped he would say something else.

"I'm not selling anything, and I'm not here to convert you or anything like that – I just want to talk."

Her friend nudged her.

"About what?"

He opened his hands, palms up, and shrugged. "Well... What's your name?"

"Leslie. ...And yours?"

"Marshall."

Her friend leaned forward and interrupted, folding in a measure of practiced cynicism and ice. It seemed to Marshall that he had stepped on an unexpected hornet's nest. He turned to her, puzzled, and noticed Freya for the first time.

"She's the nicest person in the world," Freya lashed out at him. "She hasn't got a boyfriend, and she's available almost any time except for today. We're on a bike ride today. I've come all the way up from Toronto and this is our time. So leave her your card and maybe she'll call you back."

He looked at her with some wonder but immediately began to apologize. "Of course, I'm sorry, but this is the only chance I will ever have." He shrugged as if to say, what am I supposed to do, but did not add that. He noted that most of the men on the deck were watching her and not Leslie. It was the first time he noticed how beautiful Freya was. He was surprised he had not noticed it right away. He stood confused for a moment as Freya sat back and rolled her eyes.

Leslie recovered and nudged Freya hard with her elbow. "Freya!"

Marshall turned again to Leslie and addressed her with an earnestness that surprised both her and Freya. "I'll be perfectly honest with you – I was watching you come on the boat; I saw you talking with your friend. I like to think I am a keen observer of humanity, and what I believe I saw in you prompted me to come over and speak with you."

Leslie shook her head at the incredulity of what he was saying. She felt the beginnings of a nervous knot in her stomach. This is a first; definitely a first, she was telling herself. "Well, what would that be?" she asked him.

He brought his hands up and again used them for emphasis. He looked directly at her and waited for their eyes to meet. "Your friend confirmed it but I saw it right away – you are a good person, gentle, kind – it was the way you moved your hands, your careful words, even the way you looked out over the lake – and besides, you're very beautiful for all that." The words had rushed out of him. He seemed to have surprised himself. He stood back, shook his head in wonder, and smiled. He could have made the list longer, Freya thought at the time; his script needed a bit more work.

"I am not beautiful – but I'm glad you think so."

"I have never heard such bullshit in all my life!" Freya injected.

"Freya!"

It was most certainly bullshit, Leslie thought, but the way he said it had grabbed her. His sincerity rained off him. She turned back to him in apology. "I'm sorry but my friend's right, I'm busy today. ... I just hope it's not bullshit?" She had inadvertently added an inflection to her voice, making her reply sound more like a question than a statement; that and the fact she had not meant to say what she had. She should not let him know she was impressed, she knew, or interested. Men usually didn't speak to her like this. For a moment, she thought it might be a joke played on her somehow by Freya; but looking at him again, and glancing at Freya, she decided, no, it couldn't be.

"It's not."

She uncharacteristically blushed as if she had been caught out.

He was about to reach for her hand but caught himself and stood back. "Please listen to me," he implored. "It's not bullshit. I meant everything I said. I really want to get to know you." He glanced up and quickly over his shoulder. They were almost at the island. It was the fastest ride he had ever experienced. He had spent it watching her, he knew, while he could have been more fruitfully using the time to get to know her. "I see the ferry's about to make the island," he said, turning back to her. "There will be a mass exodus soon. As your friend suggested, I'll leave you my card... Not much of a card... It's the receipt from the book I just bought. ...All I need now is a pen..." He searched his pockets and came up empty. Ironically, it was Freya who reached into her pack and handed him one. He glanced at her with some surprise. "Thank you," and returned to Leslie. "My email address..." He wrote it down. "Email me, if you want to. Coffee, or something;

The Coffee House on Princess or Tim Horton's by the ferry; wherever you want... No pressure at all." He shrugged and added almost in apology, his words running together, "I'd ask for your number and call you but calling on the phone makes me so nervous that I never do. Email is preferred. I won't ask you for yours, I'll give you mine."

He handed her his receipt on the back of which he had scrawled his email address. Later she'd look at it and note it was *Of Human Bondage* by S. Maugham – twelve dollars. She knew exactly where he had bought it – the old second-hand bookstore on King Street. She often went there. When she pointed it out to him much later in their relationship, she asked, "Why that book?" and he'd answered, "For a fragment of life I have not yet experienced... Besides, twelve bucks, masterpiece, how can you go wrong?"

"Fine, thank you." She put it in the side pocket of her pack, thinking then that she'd never call him, she'd never find the nerve. "We gotta go."

She stood, turned, looked up, and found herself facing him. He was looking at her directly, studying her. He was as tall as she was, slightly taller perhaps. His eyes were gray like hers. They were exceptionally clear; their clarity startled her. She broke contact, stepped back, shouldered her pack, and put on her helmet. She turned to say, "See you later," but he had already gone. She saw the back of him by the ladder, two hands on the rails, sliding down – that's hard to do, she thought, and imagined herself doing the same.

Funny how these things are, Marshall told her later; I jumped down the ladder and reached the front of the boat just before the ramp came down. I looked back and saw you looking down at the scene □ the people, the cars, and the shore-side crowd waiting for the boat to empty so they could come aboard. I know you couldn't make me out in the crowd, and I saw you smile.

"What was I smiling about, then?"
"The world."

Monday, July 9th, 2012

Preface by Freya Anna Bergman

I understand that emails, as they once were, are gone the way of laptop computers, DVD players, and the old Internet of which vestiges I know remain. Everything nowadays is linked in through your so-called PAD, your very own 'Personal Augmentation Device,' which to me sounds very much like something related to personal hygiene: don't forget to change your "pad," dear. Not for me, I tell you; I am not about to be "plugged" into the world, literally, as young people are today. Do they not consider or care anything about their personal privacy? Alice, Leslie's second child, and very nice she is too like all the children are, told me just the other day how you can actually walk into a store and have your PAD tell you what you bought or even looked at the last time you were in that particular store. It would then make recommendations based on what is on sale as well as your preferences deduced from what you have purchased in the past. I was aghast. I also understand your PAD can autonomously register your heart rate as well as your fluid intake, and tell you if your boyfriend is lying or not, or what he's feeling at the moment by measuring the galvanic response of his skin as he snuggles up to you or, more likely, slips his hand down your blouse. I know perfectly what men are thinking, and I do not need my undergarment preferences known by the world! The world can be, and often is, a frightening place and I have no desire to make it more so.

At any rate, I digress again, I am sorry; it is a nervous habit and I expound when I am anxious. I am anxious because I am somewhat apprehensive about the next little bit that will, unfortunately, reveal a major faux pas on my part. There is nothing like the truth, although there is no such thing as 'truth' in this world except for, perhaps, in mathematics, and that is yet another Marshallism by the way. The truth in this case is that I rather sinned. I don't like or even understand the concept sin; it implies a

fixed notion of what is 'good' and what is 'bad' and I don't think
there is. The notion of sin is very Catholic, I fear; and I am not a
Catholic. Still, a rather prominent Catholic rather summed it up
nicely; he said, "The sin is in the omission; it is in the turning
away," or something like that. Good and evil are not *things*; they do
not exist outside us but are sourced from within us, is the short
summation of the concept. I believe we have the freedom to
choose what is good and what is bad, and I did something very
bad. Not a 'thou shalt burn at the stake' degree of sin, but I still
cringe as I think back on it, which perhaps makes it not the most
noble thing I have ever done. The admission is I hacked into
Leslie's email account. I am not proud of it but there you are. I
felt compelled to do so, given what I had witnessed that morning
on the ferry and the fact that, subsequently, Leslie simply could
not stop talking about him. To hear her speak over and over of his
accosting her in the way he did, inferred to me, at least, that she
felt that, what was in all other respects a nonevent, was, from her
perspective, the greatest thing that had ever happened to her. I was
still finishing off my very first sticky bun and marveling about it as
she began to pester me with questions about what I thought of
him. Was he as good looking as she thought? "He seemed very
intense, didn't he? I have a feeling he's highly intelligent too." I
choked on that one. "How the hell do you get that?" Her answer:
his eyes. I knew then that Marshall Davenport spelled trouble.
There was no doubt whatsoever, and the fact she carried on all the
way to The Foot and back was unequivocal proof. Even while she
was swimming, lying back and quietly sculling, she even shouted
out over the open water, "I wonder what he sees in me." I rolled
my eyes so far back in my head, I felt I might topple into the St.
Lawrence. There was no explaining it to her: "He likes your
breasts, dear!" I shouted back. "The delicate side of your
personality I don't believe he would have any indication of yet!"
"Oh, Freya!" She always said that when she was exasperated with
me, but I was exasperated with her as well and could not really
stop myself from teasing her.

She came out of the water and stood over me, dripping
cold water onto me as I squirmed fruitlessly to get away. She left
me nowhere to go on that rock-faced shoreline but to fall back

into the water. "You're just jealous," she said and sat in the sun to dry off; we had not thought to bring a towel.

"You would think you were in love or some such thing the way you carry on," I said, trying to keep the petulance out of my voice. She was right, of course; I was insanely jealous but had not yet realized it so her suggestion irked me. "Like a little school girl," I added.

She laughed, glancing quickly at me but otherwise staring out over the lake to the far island. "I am in love. I am insanely, crazily, stupidly, in love." She sighed. "I can hardly wait to see him again… Ah, love is such sweet sorrow…" She sighed again and then laughed aloud.

"You certainly know how to get under my skin, Leslie. Please stop, if you don't mind."

She smiled and shrugged. "I just like the attention, that's all. It happens to you all the time, but not to me."

"Right."

There is some irony here, which, of course, I did not realize at the time. The first thing is that we were only about a nautical mile from where a week later the two of them would hash out a lifetime; and secondly, Marshall lived only a short distance away from where we sat talking about him like little school girls. It is a wonder he didn't hear us. We rode past the road that led to his place on the way to The Foot and back. When I realized the first almost two years later, a cold shiver flew up and down my back with the thought that our lives may be susceptible to fate after all. Perhaps we do not necessarily hold our futures exclusively in the palms of our hands. I know it cannot possibly be true, of course, but it did feel that way at the time.

It was an easy thing to do, to hack into her account. I knew her password, and then, like now, whatever you send from your phone or laptop is recorded on the main server. I did not log into her laptop or her phone, I logged into the main server and there it all was. I am not proud of it. As it was, most of the traffic was between her and I, the rest was concerned with bill payments, overdue library books, the acknowledgements of recent purchases, and so on. There was nothing that night but by the next evening, after she had gone to work and no doubt mulled it about in her head all day, I saw what she sent him and his subsequent reply; and from then on, I kept a pretty close tab on whenever and whatever they communicated. I followed them, too, at a distance so I would not be seen. What a sinner I am, and knew I was at the time. When Leslie, my best friend, and the one person I truly loved in the world, thought I was two hundred and fifty miles west in Toronto, I was, in actuality, only feet from her. That, dear reader, I am not particularly proud of; but there it is anyway, out in the open.

The Email

Leslie hesitated over the "Send" key. Her heart was beating in her chest. There was a small trickle of perspiration running down her back; sending the email might open up a whole can of worms she'd rather not open. He would almost certainly get back to her – or maybe not; maybe he had forgotten about her by now, it had only been a brief conversation after all. She pressed the key and it was gone in an instant. Her heart sank and simultaneously lifted. No recall capability; she knew it was possible to recall an email but she did not know how. She found her hand was shaking. She went to the "Sent" folder and found it on the top of the list. She opened it and read it again.

> *Hello Marshall,*
> *This might teach you not to give out your email address so easily. Anyway, I'd like to carry on with our conversation if that's possible. The Coffee House on Princess and King, Thursday after work – about 6PM – is good for me. You can call or email, it doesn't matter.*
> *You are completely wrong about me by the way.*
> *Leslie.*

"Damn!" She slapped her forehead with her open palm. "I forgot to include my phone number!" She thought for a moment about resending it with the phone number included this time but then decided against it. He could email and then she would give him her number. Then another horrible thought struck her and almost made her sit back in the chair: had she spelled his name correctly? Were there two 'l's or only one?

She stood up from the computer and moved about the apartment, walking back and forth as she burned off her nervous energy. She turned up the music and paced some more. In less than three minutes, she heard a chime and caught the message banner, opening then closing on her screen. She jumped to the computer. It was from him. She opened it.

Leslie...

This is a surprise – I was about to make it my business to haunt the ferry until I saw you again. Thursday is good. I'll be there.

I'm not wrong.

Marshall.

July 10th and 11th, 2012

Preface by Freya Anna Bergman

Leslie could barely sleep thinking of their up-and-coming rendezvous. I cannot speak for the Marshall of those days but from what I know of him now, I imagine he slept very soundly indeed. He was very clear-eyed and always possessed a great vision of life. Like Leslie, however, I did not sleep well at all. The panic that would eventually overcome me was slowly building and I did not know what to think. I waited for more emails between the two but there was nothing. I went to class on Tuesday, and then again on Wednesday morning, but after that there was no point; no matter how hard I tried, I could not concentrate. It is perhaps again ironic that I was experiencing the same consuming anticipation as Leslie, but of course for completely different reasons. She feared he would not like her and that, on second glance, and in the context of the coffee shop, the longer shadows, the different way she would be dressed, he would realize how physically large she was and back politely out after a quick coffee, taking back all he had said on the ferry.

She was such an innocent. I loved her so. Her physical size and the effect it had on men was a recurring concern of hers that was completely unfounded, at least to a point. Most men had to look up to meet her eyes and that, in of itself, goes against the male instinct to dominate everything about them; "Brouhaha!" and all that. Men can be very Neanderthal, as we all know. Of course, she was not intimidating in personality; there was no one sweeter.

On the other side of her concern, though, Leslie worried that *she* might not *like* Marshall. If that were the case, it would be very disappointing, and quite likely lead to a rather awkward situation in which she just might have to inform him on the way out that there was absolutely no point in continuing. That, I know, she had been forced to do on more than one occasion previously; and I know that she could not sleep afterward then, either, mainly due to a misplaced sense of guilt. She has such a good heart but she has to realize that it is all part of the game. If you win at tennis, do you feel guilty, I asked her once. No, you do not. I drew the parallel for her and it did help, or so she said. Still, I know her so well; she has such a strong but tender soul, not so easily bruised but always thinking of the other.

For my part, the very opposite concerns kept me awake. They were concerns that stopped me from going to class and stopped me from being able to eat properly. Simply, I was afraid that she was going to like him and that he was going like her. In fact, there was after a while no doubt in my mind that that would be the natural outcome of their rendezvous. After all, after approaching her on the ferry in the way he had, he knew enough about her already not to be easily put off. For her part, it was not every day that someone came up to her the way he did; that alone was saying something and would no doubt convince her to not let him go so quickly. That and the fact he was, indeed, a handsome and charming bastard, as I said before.

Nothing Happened

Absolutely nothing of importance happened, or was even considered, between the 10th and 11th of July.

Thursday, July 12th, 2012

Preface by Freya Anna Bergman

I must offer an editorial correction to the above. I fought to have something more added but it was not to be, it seems. At any rate, it is not true that nothing happened between Wednesday and Thursday. I practically tore myself apart that is what happened! Of course, Leslie was absolutely beside herself! That is what you get when you have a male member of the species trying to relate the inner hearts of women, I suppose. Perhaps one cannot describe such things in our modern prose, highly utilitarian as it is. Surely one can at least make an attempt and draw on one's imagination to give the reader some sense of it, though. I am almost ready to give up, I must say. This may be my last entry. From now on, I will leave it to my male counterpart to describe the facts of the case in his typically one-dimensional fashion.

At any rate, I cannot do that, and you know as well as I that I cannot, and on Thursday I could positively not stand it anymore and took the train back up to Kingston. I do not know what was in my mind but I knew I could not stay in Toronto while Leslie was taking a step in a direction that could only spell disaster. My heart was in my throat and my stomach twisted into a tight knot. I had been sick twice, once in my apartment and then again on the train. I was a wreck, I do not mind saying so. Thinking of those days now, and when I think of who I was and what I ultimately became, my heart still flutters and my stomach twists. I should have told her I loved her long before and, of course, that was what I was intending to do, if only I could get there soon enough.

As the reader might imagine, it is not a simple thing for a woman to inform another woman that she loves her, particularly if the other woman may not be aware of the feelings the other might have. Simply put, the greater part of my anxiety was that I did not know how Leslie would receive the news. The shock for her would be great, and she may not be able to handle it. There was some part of me that wanted to forget the whole thing, play it out as a friend would and not a lover, and then disappear. I would disappear and die, that is how I felt at the time: I wanted to run away as far away as I could possibly get and then die. No, no, not die, that is not right, not even in retrospect is that correct. What I wanted was for her to *believe* me and *accept* me, but I feared she would not, and that is why, without resolution, and consumed by dread, I was sick and shaking. I kept repeating to myself, "*I should have told her, I should have told her*"; immediately followed with, "*You could not have! You could not have!*" I was torn, simply torn apart. I just had too much to lose. I could have lost Leslie, and there went my world.

I took a cab from the Kingston train station downtown, got out on Princess Street, a block down from where they were to meet, and walked up. I was an hour early. I scheduled myself for the red-eye back to Toronto at eleven that night. It should be enough time, unless she took him back to her place and then I would not know what I would do: go home and cry most certainly, or jump off the LaSalle Causeway, given how I felt about that possibility. But she was not like that, I reminded myself, and I rationalized to the point where, in some ways, I actually felt sorry for Marshall. He was about to get a grilling, I was sure. Still, it was those first steps along the plank that so unnerves one. I could barely breathe nor stop from throwing up on the sidewalk, except I had nothing left in me. My whole body shook with the trauma of the whole thing. This is not pleasant to talk about but it is true even so. One does like to think of one's self being so ill or debilitated that one cannot think clearly.

I watched events unfold from the Sports Clothing Store across the street. I was inside the store, playing with the clothing on the rack, flipping through the garments, pretending to look at athletic sportswear, pulling one out occasionally, holding it up then putting it back, while all the while watching the street for Leslie. He arrived first. He was five minutes early. He was taller than I remembered but just as skinny. I wondered what she saw in him. It came to me that perhaps I could walk across the street and attempt to dissuade him of his interest in Leslie before she arrived. What could I say, though: that we are gay lovers and that he has no idea what he was getting into, and he is trespassing? No, it would not work, I decided; he would see through me immediately. I am a good judge of character and I already knew that he was too observant of human nature for that. I do not mean me; he did not understand me, or even think of me at all. I mean, Leslie; he understood her well enough already to know she was not a lesbian and, as such, he would immediately see that I was and then know my true purpose. Still, it might work, I reasoned. Besides, if I did nothing, I was simply a voyeur without a plan. So there I was, running off to Kingston without so much as understanding why I might be doing so, with no plan at all, puking on my new shoes while simultaneously wringing my hands in thoughtless desperation.

Still, I had not come all the way from Toronto, I reasoned, just to watch. I felt a deep coldness within me and my heart was pounding, pushing the blood through as I tried to decide: was I, or was I not, going to cross the street to confront Marshall? My legs felt weak and there was a possibility I might even collapse with the pressure I felt I was under. God, wouldn't that have been horrible. I made a move to walk out. I headed toward the door but then once again changed my mind. A clerk asked if there was something he could help me with. I shook my head, returned to another corner of the store with a similar view across the street, and once again pretended to browse as the room spun about me and my legs nearly buckled. I knew the clerks were watching me, no doubt speculating on what I might be up to. I was a shoplifter, they probably thought. They stayed in the background, not taking their eyes off me. I could not leave the store. I would be seen. Marshall would recognize me, certainly; and Leslie... God, if I bumped into her. I did not want to antagonize the store clerks in case they asked me to leave and Leslie could come by any moment. I felt I had no choice but to remain where I was, smile, and hopefully put their fears to rest. God, if they could only have read my mind, they would have called an ambulance.

Leslie arrived a few moments later. She walked right past the store and stopped briefly at the corner. She stood only five or six feet away and if it had not been for the pane of glass, she would have seen me, I am certain. She looked gorgeous. My heart almost stopped. She was dressed in a light blue summer dress, open at her neck and tied at her waist. I could not see what she wore about her neck but I thought I had glimpsed a flash of gold, which meant the necklace she had purchased earlier in the summer: a delicate chain of gold carrying a single golden pendant depicting a mysterious Mayan cartouche. I had helped her pick it out; it was what she should wear with that dress. It seemed and felt odd, that perspective of her, she not knowing I was close. I was intruding into her private self; I was spying and I knew it, and I felt a surge of guilt because of it. If I had made myself visible, suddenly springing from the store to stand beside her, she would have, of course, turned and greeted me warmly, if not with some amazement. Without me being able to give an answer as to my presence, she would simply accept the fact I was there and, undoubtedly, because she has such a good heart, invite me to join them without ever asking me any questions whatsoever. I would smile, of course, and pretend it was a mere coincidence we should meet, adding I could not, and would not, join them, as if it might be a mild inconvenience to me. I would then leave her with a smile and a careless wave, knowing I would have to explain myself to her later but not caring because that would be later and, by then, I would have all my excuses arranged. Not that she would believe them. She is not a fool. Invariably the truth would come out and I would be right back where I did not want to be.

None of that happened. I remained frozen and unobserved. I looked about. Marshall had already seen her. I watched him look up and place his hands behind his back as she stepped lightly across the street. They shook hands. I could scarcely believe it; I mean, up until then, I do not believe I had shaken a man's hand, ever. I am too proud for that. Besides, a woman should not do that. It is the way men greet one another, and should be reserved for them. I noticed, too, that she was almost as tall as he was and, surprisingly in the dress she wore, she looked almost petite, certainly trim. They each turned to the coffee-shop entrance. He stepped in close to her and, as she entered, he placed his hand very carefully on the small of her back to guide her. I felt a pang of jealousy for that simple touch that almost dropped me to the shop floor. My head spun, I could barely see; I was so full of that black dog I wanted to scream at them, run across the street, and fling open the door, declaring myself. I had not, up to that point, experienced that sensation before, not with such intensity; but I would experience it again later and I can tell you, dear reader, I would not wish it upon anyone. It is consuming. It turns you. At any rate, the door closed behind them and I thought I was going to be sick yet again but I was not. I held on and quickly left the store, showing them my empty hands on the way past and trying to hide the fact my eyes were filling with tears. I was undoubtedly as white as a sheet.

I did not linger in Kingston. I caught a cab back to the station and caught the next train and I was back in my apartment just after 1 AM on the Friday, completely spent.

That is my story up to this point. It does get worse I am afraid. If I thought then I was at the bottom, I was most certainly wrong. At that point, I had no idea what the bottom was or what it could be like. I know you're up to hearing all about it but I'm not quite certain that I'm up to the telling any longer, and that despite the fact it was over sixty years ago. In addition, I am aware that I seem to be telling more of my story than theirs. It is, unfortunately, unavoidable since I am, in fact, a major player in their story. I shall, however, endeavor to refrain from going over the top, as they say, in any further description of my involvement. I do feel that I did go a little above and beyond up there and, although I feel I might be requesting too many favors of you, dear reader, please, if you think I have gone too far, forgive me once again.

At any rate, it is time to let my accomplice in crime tell the raw facts of this part of their drama and leave my part out of things.

Coffee Rendezvous

Thursday came fast enough. She saw him standing outside The Coffee House as she waited on the far side of the street, waiting to cross. She sensed he had seen her, though he was not looking her way. She wondered if he was seeing the same woman he remembered. She was not as attractive, perhaps: her hair, or face, her complexion, or was she bigger-framed than he remembered, or was there something else about her that he had not seen at the time and he was already disappointed? The day was different, the place; her hair was not the same, and she was not dressed the same. She was dressed in what she normally wore for a night out in the summer months: a light cotton dress that reached to her knees, and practical shoes, all loose fitting and light in color. She wanted to impress him. This was her best.

Marshall had seen her immediately. He had watched her come up King Street, past the clothing store, and stop at the corner. She was the same woman he had seen on the ferry. His heart thumped in his chest. God, she was gorgeous! She was wearing a light summer dress that showed her form. He did not recall her hair being combed back and she was taller than he remembered but otherwise she was the same woman he had seen on the ferry, exactly the same. To steady himself, he placed his hands behind his back and moved off to the side to pretend he had not seen her as he reviewed in his mind what he could possibly say to her. He knew exactly what. She was the future; he had seen the truth of it at a glimpse. How to trust a glimpse: he must trust his instincts, he knew.

She approached. He was in profile, studying the menu on the storefront. He was dressed almost exactly as she had last seen him on the ferry: T-short, shorts, sandals – of higher quality, perhaps, but he was otherwise dressed fundamentally the same. He might have combed his hair, it was pushed back behind his ears and not quite as unruly. He hadn't shaved – it must be his look.

She touched his arm and he turned. "Hi there."

"Hi there."

"Do you remember me?" she asked and inwardly closed her eyes against her stupidity as she felt a rush of red climb up into her face.

His heart was soaring. She had touched him.

"Remember you? …Of course, I do – but do you remember me?"

"Of course." She inadvertently flattened her dress over her hips as she smiled.

"But you are more beautiful."

"I bet you say that to all the girls!"

"No." He laughed.

He was nervous. She could see he was nervous. He opened the door for her and she breezed past him. They had each been in there before and they each ordered a medium-sized coffee and, that done, found a table together in the back. She had tried to talk about the weather as they waited in line: "Very warm." He hadn't answered but had smiled and nodded as if he didn't know what to say; not a good sign, she thought, but she smiled and chatted briskly, trying to make the best of it as her heart began to sink with the thought that the downward slide had already begun.

He was listening to her chat, her voice softly rising and falling, making small talk, guiding him along. He could not get over the fact he was so close to her. He sat across from her at the table, straddling the chair. He could think of nothing to say; he was completely tongue-tied, which surprised him. Everything he had rehearsed since Monday night and up until the ride over on the ferry he had completely forgotten.

"I'm over-rehearsed," he said.

"Pardon?"

"I'm over-rehearsed. I seem to have lost my train of thought."

"I'm nervous as well," Leslie admitted, taking the lid off her coffee. She felt a film of perspiration threatening to break out on her forehead; next, it would be under her arms and along her back. She could not help her body from reacting like that; she hated herself for it. He'd notice; he was certain to notice. She had no idea why she was so nervous. She had stood up before hundreds of people to give a lecture or to present her case.

He tried to smile. "Don't be," he said and removed the lid from his coffee as she had. He leaned forward and inhaled the aroma. "Ah, French Roast...." He glanced up as he breathed in; "I love the smell... the richness..." He offhandedly pushed the cup across the table and she leaned over and inhaled as he had.

She sat back. "It smells like coffee."

He laughed nervously at her obvious response. "Of course." He recovered his coffee and replaced the lid. He found he could not look up at her. That's odd, he thought, and forced his eyes up, and felt himself blushing. "...So, your name is Leslie but what's your full name?" he asked.

"Leslie Krueger."

He pointed to himself with the cup, spilling some coffee on his shirt and on the table. "Marshall Davenport."

She nodded, "Hello," and smiled, glancing at him but quickly averting her eyes, then glancing back and commenting, "You've made quite a mess there."

"Don't I know it?" He reached for a napkin, wiped up the spill, and took the excess out of his shirt.

"That looks better," Leslie offered softly.

"Yeah… You're making me nervous now," he said, smiling up at her as he did so.

She shook her head quickly and tightly. "I can't help it," facetiously adding, without thinking, "You must be much practiced at this."

"No, not really."

"You seem very relaxed."

"Appearances can be deceiving," he said, reaching for another napkin to wipe up a missed part of the spill.

She nodded and smiled, her face crimson.

"I have some questions, if you don't mind," he said finally, after a moment and after sipping his coffee again, sitting back and finally looking at her.

She sipped her coffee. It was still too hot for her. "Sure."

"How old are you?"

"You're not ever supposed to ask a woman her age – but it's thirty-one."

"I'm thirty-four. Are you married?"

"No, are you?"

"No. Are you currently in a relationship?"

"No, how about you?"

"No…"

"Is your list long?"

He smiled thinly. "It goes on infinitely, I'm afraid – but you have answered all the important points, so…" and he pretended to tear up a piece of paper in midair before her, "I'm done with the list. From now on, we're pretty much on our own."

Leslie's heart dropped and froze. She misinterpreted him. "Does that mean we're done? Do I get to go home now?"

He instantly fell back in the chair, surprised. "No! No, I don't mean that!"

"Oh." She nodded. "Okay…" She had thought he was about to walk out and leave her there. Her face showed it.

"Whatever made you think that?"

She shrugged.

"I'm sorry. I didn't mean it to sound as if I was grilling you."

"That's okay. It shows you're organized, I suppose."

"I am usually very organized; but I should not have had a list, an imaginary list though it was."

"Okay."

"I was born here in Kingston," he offered, desperately trying to draw their conversation back in line. "I have not always lived here. I was gone for a while but came back."

She glanced at him briefly, asking, "You have traveled a lot?"

"No, not really – how about you?"

She returned to her cup and studied the rim. "No… Most of my life to date has been under the skies of Thunder Bay; and then, for almost half of my life, I was away at school."

"Where did you go to school?"

"Waterloo, and McGill; I spent a year in Uppsala, Sweden, studying Swedish of all languages, and, then, finally, McMaster in Hamilton where I obtained a PhD in Sociology and Psychology."

"You have a PhD in Sociology and Psychology?"

She looked up finally. "I'm afraid so."

"You're afraid so?" He ran his hand through his hair. "Jesus!" He sat up straight. "What are you doing in Kingston?"

"Post Doc, Queen's."

He passed his hand through his hair again and then threw his hands up and let them drop onto the table. "So, you're also brilliant? I had no idea!"

"You sound surprised," she began, stumbling. She had a PhD and she was stumbling. She had worked hard for it and she was no fool. She hardened and collected herself, anticipating a major fiasco between them and already thinking about sprinting toward the door. She said, very quietly, wondering even if he would hear, "Are you inferring a woman could not possibly be as smart as a man?"

He jolted back in surprise. "No – what makes you ask that?"

"Some men just do, that's all," she offered quietly. She looked at him full faced. 'It's a man's world out there," she said, harder. Freya must be wearing off on her, she thought.

He leaned forward. "I'm sorry…"

"It's all right…"

He dropped his head into his hands and looked out through his open fingers. "This is not going well, is it?" he asked.

She slowly nodded and reached for her purse.

He instantly sat upright, again shocked. "You're not leaving, are you?"

"That's what you want, isn't it?"

"No!"

He waited for her to sit, carefully watching her do so. She sat without looking at him but she quietly smiled and let him see that she was smiling. "Okay, then… Maybe we should start again."

He shook his head and tried to recover. "I started off poorly."

"We both did."

"You've been on dates where the man has walked out on you?"

"It has happened."

"That's fucking insane!"

She glanced at him and away.

"I'm sorry that happened to you."

"Well…so far today no one's walked."

They both smiled and looked up and their eyes met.

"Let me tell you the truth then," Marshall offered.

"Is there such a thing?"

He remembered what he wanted to say and he said it. "Sometimes in life a door opens and you see the future. Last week on the ferry a door opened and I saw it clearly."

"What did you see?"

"I saw you."

"How did I look?"

"Gorgeous, as beautiful as ever!"

"I'm sure – who else did you see?"

"I saw myself."

"There's no doubt about that!"

He lifted both hands in surrender. "Okay, okay! I know it's bullshit – well, not entirely bullshit…"

"It's bullshit."

"I know, I know! But I did see something in you. It's not a joke, it's not a line, it's not bullshit, it's the truth, and the only truth I have!"

"I feel like I'm being played."

He noticed she did not reach for her purse, which he took as a good sign. "Has this happened to you before?" he asked.

"Absolutely." She smiled sardonically. "Men… what can you do?"

"Alright, alright… I don't know how to convince you of the truth here."

"There's no truth here."

"Oh no, there is, there is!"

"There are a thousand girls out there like me. Look again, maybe."

He vigorously shook his head back and forth. "Oh, no! No, no, no, no…!"

Leslie shook her head in bewilderment and leaned forward. She pressed her point, speaking aloud and clearly, "You don't even know me!"

He also insisted. "Like *hell* I don't – I would not be sitting here otherwise!"

Leslie stared at him blankly.

"Please believe me," he said.

"Why should I?"

"Because life and love is a mystery and we are part of it."

Her eyes opened in surprise but then she nodded slowly. "You are a very unusual man," she thought. She almost stood and left but said, "One more time then."

He fell back with a sigh of relief. "Good…" He took her hand away from her cup and held it gently and carefully.

"This is the truth, then; this is why I am here: My name is Marshall Davenport. You're the girl I saw on the ferry. You are as beautiful as the first time I saw you. I'd like to get to know you, if that's all right."

"…Okay."

She knew her face was flushed red, she couldn't help it, but that, she agreed, was the truth.

"You won't be sorry," he added.

"Oh, I will!" She laughed. It burst out of her but she quickly held it in check. "I think you are very weird!" she said, watching him blush, and recovered her hand. She smiled at him and let him see she wasn't going anywhere.

"I'm not always this weird," Marshall offered.

"Well, you're going to have to prove it!"

The ice was broken and what remained of the tension between them dropped away "It's not bullshit, by the way," he once again added, settling back again.

"What isn't?"

"That Life and Love is a mystery…"

"Hmmm…"

They each laughed then, fully and openly, and together.

Their conversation opened and as they settled, they went on to talk about what they liked and didn't like: movies, books, food, scenery, politics, religion, and beautiful places to travel to, forgetting as they did so all about their earlier acrimony. The more they talked, the more she fell into their conversation and liked him. He lived on the Island; his parents had passed. What do you do?

He shrugged. "I am a man of the world; I study the world."

She laughed and assumed he was unemployed – not so odd these days. "What did you graduate in?" She could tell he was educated.

"Paleontology"

"Ah, that's why…" He laughed, not denying it. He didn't tell her until later that he also had a degree in history as well another in English literature but, by that time, there was nothing about him that surprised her. There was hope after all. They stumbled upon the subject of sailing, something they both loved to do. He had a boat. "Of sorts," he said; and, hesitating, wondering if it was all that great of an idea, she finally agreed they would arrange to meet on the weekend. She could hardly believe it. After all the ups and downs, she had not only survived the date but this very decent, handsome, a little bit eccentric perhaps, guy was going to call her back – more than that, they were going to go sailing. Unbelievable, really.

Also unbelievable was that they almost closed the place. They didn't leave until they began to stack the chairs. He walked her back to her apartment four blocks away and outside shook her hand again. She was not about to let him kiss her; it was too soon. After shaking her hand, he backed away at the same time she turned toward her door.

"Saturday morning, then?" he called, turning her around. "I'll meet you on the other side?"

"I've already said yes. I will be there."

"Goodnight then, Leslie."

"Goodnight, Marshall."

She turned but then glanced back. He was walking backward along the sidewalk, watching her. "You'll miss the boat!" she called.

"I'll miss it then!" He entered the light cast by the streetlamp, threw his arms up, and then let them fall. "I had a great night!" he shouted.

"Goodnight!" she shouted back and turned away again.

She thought she heard his laughter across the distance as she opened the door, stepped through, and felt it sweep shut. She glanced back once again but he had disappeared. She glimpsed him running at the far end of the street in and out of the pools of light cast by the streetlights. He might make the boat yet, she thought, and smiled. She gathered her keys and took the steps up to her apartment. She could hardly wait to tell Freya.

Friday, July 13th, 2012

Preface by Freya Anna Bergman

Leslie told me that Marshall, so unlike him, tripped over himself once or twice on their first date. He began on the wrong foot, it seemed. In the opening salvoes, her heart sunk, she said, believing that what he saw the second time was not what he had imagined the first time on that light and breezy day on the ferry where the sun and flashing waters can turn a man's heart about. Telling me all about it months later, she perhaps imagined his intentions might have been realigned as the ferry dropped its ramp onto the far shore where the heart does not soar nearly as high. It is almost incomprehensible to believe that Marshall, of all people, should have been so awkward or misrepresentative of himself; he must have been very nervous indeed. It is, perhaps, unfair to criticize him so thoroughly when one considers that, by arranging to meet a beautiful woman like Leslie, he was consciously playing with fate, and potentially opening a door that could very easily lead to destinations he had no idea existed only the day before. It would make any sane person nervous. He claimed later, typically, that he knew exactly what he was doing and that, if anything, he was, perhaps, somewhat overly confident. But he was smiling when he suggested that so that I knew, that he knew, that I knew, he had been caught out on the matter and was therefore more like the rest of us mere mortals after all; that is, not quite so perfect.

I must admit that this day in particular was not originally on the formal list of days to be included in Leslie and Marshall's history. It was an intermediate day that simply tied one day to another without anything in particular happening that was new or otherwise noteworthy. My compatriot in this effort could only agree, but when I showed him this 'Yet another Preface!' to a chapter that did not, on paper or in his mind, exist, he blanched then turned the most scarlet red before opening his mouth and expostulating in his somewhat rough language, forgetting as he does all the proper nouns. He agreed to read it over but when done, he continued to insist we leave it out since, although perhaps interesting, it had absolutely nothing to do with *them*. I equally insisted that, indeed, the events, or the sentiment I should say, described within this little *Intermezzo*, if that's what I decide to call it, is very important indeed. It after all provides the reader with all the necessary emotional background of why I did what I did and how it was that Leslie could forgive me afterward. It has, I argued, everything to do with *them* because if I had had my way at the time, there may not have been any *them*! As you can see, I ultimately did get my way although there does remain some degree of rancor because of it. No matter, it is my book, and my friends', and neither are his. He *is being paid* after all for his efforts, and quite handsomely too! Hah! If one doesn't possess a sense of humor then one shouldn't have signed up!

At any rate, Leslie tried to call me twice the evening before, immediately upon coming in, then a few minutes later, possibly believing the first call would have awakened me while the second I was sure to answer. I was not even home yet. I was still on the train. The truth is I did not answer her calls more because my phone was in my purse than the fact I really did not wish to talk with her. Luckily, for me, I almost never hear my phone ring, or vibrate, or whatever while it is in my purse, so it saved me the trouble from having to decide to answer, or not to answer. I did not know she had called until I was home and I was not about to return her call then, and by the next morning I found I still could not return her call since by then I did not have it in me to do so. I went to class as scheduled, listened, but heard nothing of the lecture. The words came in and passed right through me. I was not thinking of Leslie, or Marshall, the unfairness of the world, or even myself. I was not thinking at all. My mind was numb, as my body, independent of my mind as it sometimes is, slipped through the familiarity of the day. I moved automatically about, merely stepping through the actions of the day: up in the morning, shower, missed breakfast, crossed the street without being run over, classes, smiling when required, listened to the lectures, and so on without a thought of what was going on around me or what was being said. I was emotionally numb and dumb. Occasionally, the image of his hand touching the small of her back would

THE GIRL ON THE FERRY · 61

surface and my heart would fly out of me as my stomach knotted and fell away. I could not linger there or think of that and so I forced myself not to.

I understand there is medication available that can place one in a state of numbness similar to the one I describe above; one feels like crying but cannot. The down side, no pun intended, is that one can neither weep nor laugh. The up side is that it mercifully dilutes the experience of being alive. I can only say that I would be only too willing to take such medication had it been available to me, despite what it might have done to my body and soul, if it would have saved me even a moment of the anguish I could not entirely suppress that day. Still, I know it is best to stand up and face one's demons, knowing equally that it is not an easy thing to do.

Later that day, I, of course, called her; not calling her would have been unacceptable, and a sure indication that something was seriously wrong. Of course I called her knowing she'd be teaching her class and unable to answer but she'd see my call-display number and know that I had tried to reach her, relieving me of some blame for not getting in touch with her right away. We finally made contact after the dinner hour as I sat in my living room with the lights out, the radio and TV off, and the red of the setting sun bleeding around the edges of the closed blinds. I could not stand the light; the light of day was depressing and so I had kept the blinds closed all day. I dialed, she answered, and from the moment I heard her voice, I knew I had lost everything. Still, I put up a brave front and spoke to her as friend would. I do suspect she could tell the difference, and knew, or suspected, that not all was right. She knew me well enough to make that assumption, certainly.

Leslie and I first met because she answered an advert I had placed looking for a roommate: "*Young female, congenial, easy going, studying at the university,*" was how I described myself; "*looking for female roommate of similar age and interests to share accommodation*" completed the advertisement. Three girls responded and, typically, one male, who could not resist the possibility, remote as it might be, of sharing a tight space with a female that would no doubt lead over time, at least in his mind, to some orgasmic relationship. They each called the phone that was in the hallway just outside my apartment since I could not support a phone in those days and nor could anyone else who lived in such a pension as I. I decided to have the three us, and not the male, meet, ironically, in the coffee house around the corner from the apartment so that from there we could go up and see.

The first I interviewed was Leslie. She was waiting when I arrived. I knew it was Leslie at a glance. I do not know how that could be but it was true even so. I had provided a description of myself so she would recognize me but she had offered no description of herself. She was tall, athletic looking, and the way she was dressed indicated she was not Swedish and was likely an American, or even English. She turned as I approached and smiled. There is more and more irony here, and it is perhaps why when Marshall approached Leslie on the ferry something within me wrenched for, like Marshall, my first glimpse of Leslie told me all I needed to know. I was instantly in love with her. I did not realize that at the time of course. It is only in retrospect that one knows such a truth with such certainty. If I could point to any instant of time when my love for her was first sparked, it would be then. It is not common to have that happen but it does happen. What I saw was that not only was Leslie beautiful, her smile showed that she was also *kind*. I can think of no other word but kind: she was a *kind* person in that she liked and cared for people. I could see it at once. Other adjectives that could be applied include caring, sympathetic, generous, gentle, thoughtful, compassionate, benevolent… all of which I saw within her at a glance, and all summarized in the word *kind*. No fool, either, I discovered quickly enough. I dwelt on her beauty though. It was my age I suppose. I was at an age when one focuses more on the physical than the spiritual. There was no doubt about it, though. In the vernacular of the days, Leslie was, in my mind at least, '*hot.*' I did not even bother interviewing the others; she was in. I was so excited I practically tripped over myself as I showed her about. I cannot get over it, really; I was just like Marshall, or Marshall was just like me. Possibly that is why Marshall and I eventually got along so well. I don't know though. It's only a theory and I hate to admit it really.

It is indeed amazing, though, what one can tell at a glance. I do agree with Marshall on that. I also realize, of course, that first impressions can be deceiving, and that one can, '*smile and smile and be a villain*'; but sometimes the heart just knows, and seeing Leslie for the first time, my heart knew. I remember it now exactly: I shook her hand and then asked her if she would like to see the place and we went up. On the way I asked her if she was going to school and I learned she was in Sweden to learn a bit of Swedish, which I thought odd because not too many came to Sweden to learn Swedish. No one cares except for the Swedes and they do all they can to learn almost any other language but Swedish, and focusing on English than any other. She was an American, I thought, but she quickly told me she was Canadian. The apartment was exceedingly Spartan, I told her, wondering how her North American sensibilities would take to it.

There were two rooms, the main room that included the living room, a pullout bed, a small desk by the window, and also the rather sparsely outfitted kitchen with nowhere to sit to eat other than the pullout bed. Then there was the bedroom, more like a closet, actually, in which were a double bed, a dresser, and a single window that opened to the street below. The bath was down the hall and shared by three other apartments, all with female occupants, fortunately, or unfortunately, depending on one's perspective. I expostulated upon it, saying we could do with a few more men about but only because men are generally brief in their ablutions, while most women tend to linger upon them, often occupying the one lone bath for ridiculously inconvenient and protracted lengths of time. It is one of the few truths about women where men just might possess some superiority. I laughed. She laughed along with me and I blushed, feeling positively good about myself. She had that way about her. She always made me feel good about myself, even if there was no particular reason for her to do so. I have said it a thousand times before and I will say it ten thousand times more, "God, I loved that woman."

During the tour, I explained that, since I was paying two thirds of the rent, I would get the bed and she the pullout in the living room. It was ridiculously cheap rent, even in those days, and for her as well as me it was perfect. She said as much. Besides, it was only for a short while, several months at most, until the winter term began and there would be more apartments opening after those that had not made the first term went home. She took out a few brand new crisp Kroner from a hidden pocket on the side of her pack and gave me the down payment, and I folded the bills, shoved them into the front pocket of my jeans, reached up, and shook her hand to settle the deal. Her grip was strong; it rather lifted me right up off the ground. I commented on it and we laughed and then went back down for a coffee where we talked most of the morning away. It was a rather nice pack, if I recall; bright red with lots of pockets and straps and an all-weather cover. I got one for myself right away with her down payment.

A few months turned into twelve. We never did look for a better place, the rent was too good and we got along so well. Eventually we shared the bed, mainly because the pullout was almost unbearably uncomfortable. Leslie, of course, then insisted on paying half the rent. She obviously did not mind sharing the bed and, of course, from my perspective, it was absolute heaven on earth. I quickly came to learn that her body, her heart, her kindness, her sense of humor, and her intelligence, made her singularly the most beautiful person I had ever known. I was not 'out of the closet' as the world now refers to letting one's sexual preference not be a secret, but I certainly knew my orientation.

Of course, I tried very hard not to let Leslie know of my predilection, knowing instinctively it would ruin everything between us. I played the role as expected and, like all women of our day, and to this day too I suspect, we sat in the street-side cafés, pointing out the better looking and preferred members of the male species all the while giggling to ourselves as we imagined what he might look like with his shirt or pants off. We rarely imagined them fully naked, though, but with enough clothing removed to leave no doubt as to his manhood. We talked, and laughed, and imagined like that together. It is perhaps somewhat revealing, or perhaps it should have been, that, although I was constantly being accosted by those same dream-state men, I was also invariably dismissing them with the wave of my hand while Leslie sat back with a lifting smile, saying in her new Swedish, "Next time, Freya, wave them my way!"

Men generally gravitated toward me rather than Leslie because I had the so-called 'classic' figure: petite, big-breasted, a nice round bum, wonderful skin, clear-eyed, all the major curses that can inflict a woman. I was Swedish, after all, and looked somewhat like my namesake; at least so I was told over and over again by the men who asked my name and I felt good enough about them to tell the truth. It was completely boring, really, and all so predictable; all men are. However, I do believe that all the men who stepped up to me first could also see that Leslie was beautiful; Marshall, as I had, saw it at an instant, so I am validated, I think, in saying so.

As I intimated before, there was something about her in those days and even on the ferry that summer morning that perhaps could intimidate a man. It was the almost overwhelming physicality of her, yes; but it was also her unflinching honesty and integrity that was reflected in the way she turned and faced any man who had courage enough to approach her □ and usually over my shoulder or behind my back and after I had asked them to scoot. Some made the attempt, of course, but they ultimately either walked away after fruitlessly trying to impress her, or she simply waved them away as I had, declaring them boring. I laughed at her. "How are you any different from me?" It bothered me and delighted me at the same time as I realized that although she wanted to find someone, she was not *desperate* to do so. In fact, given the times, I believe she would have found it rather inconvenient if someone like Marshall had been about. I really do not know what would have happened if he had been. She would have waved him away with all the others, I suspect. Timing in a relationship is everything.

Of course, and oddly too, sex, for her, was out; men can detect that predilection right away as, of course, can I. That alone might explain why that there was not one single man that made anything more than a casual effort to get through to her. She was uncompromising and she no doubt imagined that I felt similarly, which, of course, was not true. I wanted sex. I craved it. I even had the person I wanted desperately to have sex with lying right next to me night after night; but I could not, and could not for all the reasons I mentioned above. I loved her, and I would forego sex with her if it meant keeping her by my side. Sex with anyone else was also out, although I suppose I could have snuck it in somewhere while Leslie was not watching. Still, I could not do that since I would see it, if she would not, as a betrayal.

I was, at first, astounded at her rather old-fashioned and somewhat priggish attitude that in retrospect was not so different from my own. At the time though I would roll my eyes and laugh, not at her but at the idea that someone should be *so reserved* in our modern day. She would watch me say this and then smile and then shrug her shoulders, in effect saying that is just the way it is, no doubt wondering why she did not see me jumping from bed to bed but too polite to ask. She nudged me once. "You're more like me than you admit." I did not deny it and blushed with the truth of it, I think. She prodded me, and I knew she was testing me, when she said, quite out of the blue, "I'm holding out for love," but in that determined and focused way of hers that told me I had better speak truthfully if I was going to say anything at all. I wisely decided to say nothing but waved her comment away, not wanting to be trapped into saying something I might later regret. *"You have found love, damn it! She is sitting right across from you!"* I thought, but would never think of saying.

    I recall sharing a bottle of wine with her one night. It was a warm night, the stars were out, it was late, the crowds had mostly dispersed, and the bottle was almost gone. She emphasized, pouring another bit into her glass then the remainder into my own, "I will live loveless until love finds me," in a forlorn, almost resigned way, but glancing up at me as she poured. She was no doubt under the influence but that is how the truth sometimes comes out, and so it gave me no measure of hope that if she found love with me, and she knew that I loved her equally in return, then perhaps one day we could be together, and not just as friends. My instinct told me that she, like most hot-blooded women, craved sex; and, more important, that kind of intimacy that can only be achieved through sex, at least when you are young, and we were young. The difference was she knew her mind, and her mind, and not so much her heart, ruled.

    God, I loved her. I would lie with her at night and watch her sleep. I would listen to her breathing and consciously synchronize hers to mine. Sometimes my hand would wander across the short distance between us and touch her arm, or her hand, or the curve of her hip, and, nervous that I might wake her, I would slowly withdraw it. The best part was I would then slip down into a deep sleep, knowing that when I awoke, she would be there. I must add, too, that Leslie always wore to bed a knee-length cotton nightie embroidered across the front with a string of bright red miniature roses. It was very old-fashioned of her and not just prudish. I, of course, had to maintain suite. I bought a blue one that was almost identical. We could not have a naked woman sleeping next to a fully pajama'd woman now, could we? Not that there is a great deal to a cotton nightie, it barely conceals what is beneath; but it is a covering, and a boundary. Anyway, I could not tell her how I felt and I feared very much that she might find out. If she did, I would lose all of it. I simply could not risk that and so I behaved myself. It was very difficult. Somehow, I was able to overcome my temptations. I do not know how, really.

Irony piles upon irony. Of course, everyone imagined the two of us as vapid lesbians; after all, we shared the small apartment, we slept in the same bed, and we both, equally, so it appeared on the surface, seemed to eschew men; in Leslie's case hardly on purpose but that was beside the point and hardly mattered. The only good thing was that Sweden is not the United States nor is it Canada, and, simply put, no one cared, or seemed to care. Our lives were free and carefree. In most respects, it was the best days of our lives, mine certainly. I should not speak for Leslie; in fact, I know they were important days for her but not to the same degree as they were for me. Her best days lasted more than sixty years and they were all with Marshall.

Leslie and I did, obviously, get along marvelously. My mother lived in Stockholm and we went there on occasion to see something of the big city. We took the rail to Copenhagen and the ferry across to Holland and Amsterdam, and from there, Paris, and Munich, and then back to London, and we even took the Chunnel as it had just opened. We spent only weekends in each city since that is all the funds we had. It was wonderful, though, interesting, and exciting. Besides Swedish and English, I spoke French as well as German quite fluently and therefore felt quite at home on the continent. Indeed, I had been to all those places before but Leslie had not and I lived the first time experience again through her eyes and sensibility. It is true; I saw them all anew. It was a new world I glimpsed through her eyes: richer, more varied, without the taint of cynicism for which I was, and still am, well known. She always said I was her tour guide and always thanked me profusely for accompanying a 'gawk-eyed tourist' as she referred to herself; but, in fact, it was she who guided me. My eyes were opened as much as my heart and I saw the world in an entirely different color.

We slept in pensions, sometimes sharing a bed. There were students aplenty, and, of course, male counterparts that followed us about and tried to sneak us into their beds, or get us drunk on cheap wine and hope we went voluntarily, albeit under the influence of alcohol. It was not to be, though; I made sure of that. Leslie, of course, followed suite and, indeed, was wonderfully defensive of me since I was normally the primary target. Not that she had to *beat* anyone up but there was never any doubt that one did not cross the line while she was present. I did not care what they thought of us, and nor did Leslie, it seemed. The rumors that followed us about were true, of course, at least as they pertained to me. After a while, one begins to believe in the myth and I began to think of us more and more as a couple and in the same fashion as what was claimed by others.

Once, after a few too many glasses of cheap wine, I almost reached out to her as we lay down together. I was so close, I was so determined, so much in love, and so certain she would accept me; but in the end, I once again could not muster the courage. I wondered, and still do on occasion, that, if the alcohol could have made her forget for a moment, then perhaps she might have accepted my advances □ under the influence of the wine, I say again and I hope you understand why I can suggest such a thing given what has happened since. At the time, though, I dreamed of the possibility even though I kept my burning hands and arms to myself even as my heart leapt in my chest. I remember lying next to her and closing my eyes, the room spinning about me from the wine. I can feel the warmth of her close by, smell the wine and the cigarette smoke in her hair. I feel like screaming, but I don't. Once again, I cannot handle the possible rejection. Hah! I am almost sick from the fear of it! Besides, what did it matter? I was with her day and night; we shared the same bed, what else was there? I knew what. I just could not say, or suggest, or do, what.

These are, I suppose, horrible and revealing things to admit, particularly now that I am an old woman and 'the Auntie' after all. I am not the same now that I was then, so one might argue there is no point in revealing an old truth once it becomes no longer true. Besides, nothing really *happened*, nothing *measurable* to any degree; it was all just *within me* and therefore not historical, and perhaps therefore not relevant. Still, we would never have ended up where we did if I had not been true. I do not think so, anyway. The truth is, and I don't mind saying this for all to know, Leslie may be passed on, cremated, and buried, but I love her the same today as I did in those carefree days, and with as just as much passion. Here is another admission. I know she loved me too, she made certain I knew. As smart as I like to think I am, it took me a while to understand that, and where her love for me fit into both of our lives. I did not understand it until years and years later, when she very carefully and lovingly explained it to me.

More background is necessary, I am afraid. I hate to look too far back into the past but, as it is said, we are the product of our past. I take that to mean the genetic material we share equally between our mothers and fathers as well the environment that modifies our behavior. As such, I am the product of an illegitimate relationship. My mother was Swedish, my father English; and I lived apart from them both, although I took my mother's maiden name. Of course, once again, most want to know if my mother was that famous actress with whom I share the same last name, as well as Swedish citizenship. I can say here, and for all time, that it is definitely not so, although I do carry, or, I should say, I used to carry, some of her natural beauty and do have what I believe is a superficial resemblance to her that is often remarked upon, facetiously quite often I have to admit. Even so, we liked to make light of my last name, and Leslie and I watched all of the Rossellini films, and of course *Casablanca* as well as *Murder on the Orient Express*. Leslie used to say it was uncanny to see me up on the screen but she would always laugh as she said that and I knew she was teasing. Still, in my most delusional moments, I felt I did indeed possess a number of similar traits. I am Swedish, after all, and quite attractive at that, even if I should say so myself. On occasion, I would catch myself peering into the mirror searching for the resemblance, but catching myself out I would laugh and scowl at the mirror as I tried to chase away my vanity. As I grew older, the resemblance did drift, of course, even though I could still turn men's heads until I was sixty or so, and even after. It does make one feel good to be admired, though it never went anywhere of course.

At any rate, my arrival on the scene ended my parent's affair. My father returned to England and my mother went home to be looked after by her mother. For my very first years, my maternal grandmother raised me, as my mother went back to work as soon as she could. There was no tenderness between my grandmother and I. I was, quite frankly, even in liberal Sweden, an embarrassment. My father, despite the fact that he was married and already had two children, was a decent sort and helped defray my costs. I recall the checks coming in and my grandmother tearing them open, never satisfied that it always seemed to be the same amount. Shortly afterward though, I was often the owner of a new dress, or a pair of shoes; and at Christmas, there was always something under the tree for me from him.

He obviously thought about me in those early days even if he spent no real time with me. More than once, he wrote that I was often in his thoughts. I imagine it was because his real marriage fell somewhat short of his expectations. The reason no doubt is that, looking back in his mind to where he had once stood, or slept I should say, he turned to thinking of my mother and then, by association, me. Would it have been better for him with my mother? I used to look at her and then a photograph of him that I kept and could not decide. They were quite different people; not just male and female, which is different enough, but they also had quite a different perspective of life: the importance of this or that, who won the war, the need for justice, and the type of justice they sought in the world. Big things like that separate people and often cause wars on the scale of societies and nations. Of course, that is not the way it always goes; as the man and woman interface, opposites often attract and so perhaps they would have got along just marvelously, one never knows. There was some original attraction after all. In the end, though, the reason for my father's attraction could have been nothing more elevated than my mother's breasts, which were, because of genetics, the same size as my own. In the end, though, I know nothing at all really, except for the obvious fact that when my mother announced to my father she was pregnant with me, he ran.

When I was eight, my mother married and I was sent off to London to attend a school just a few miles from my father's family home. I know it does not seem right, and it was not right, but I was never invited over to his home. It would have been a bit much, I suppose. There might have been some explaining to do to his wife and children although I do believe his real wife, Margaret I found out later, knew all about my mother and me. My father implied that he had told them right away, and that they all understood and were sympathetic. If they did not know at first they did eventually because I told them. When I was sixteen, I wrote Margaret a letter. *"Dear Margaret, You don't know me but..."* I never did get a reply. It is not surprising that I did not, I suppose.

My life student life was one of extreme loneliness. I feel those same echoes of loneliness today now that Leslie is gone, and Marshall too. I saw my grandmother and mother on all the holidays and even my father would stop by at the school to check up on me and to ensure all was well, as he said. That was before I was sixteen. After I was sixteen, at the public school, he visited more often. The letter I had sent had something to do with that, I am sure; he never said so though I sensed a degree of relief in him that had not been present before. It was as if the letter had settled things once and for all. I hope so, anyway.

I never did meet Margaret, or my brother or my sister. I did see some photos once. They were not a particularly attractive family. Margaret had blonde hair like my mother; she was big-breasted, and a little jowly. Her face was flat and uninteresting, and very English. My brother and sister looked like him, really; there was not much of her in them. I do not recall their names and it hardly matters that I do not, not any more. My father told me all about them though: slovenly, jaundiced, spoiled, overweight, self-serving, not particularly ambitious, and, worst of all, academically challenged, stupid in fact. I laughed when he said that. He said it all once; it just fell out of him, out of frustration, I suppose. Anger, too, because Margaret had left him. By the way, my father's last name was *Snodgrass*. How can one support a last name such as Snodgrass? It is simply ridiculous. That is the English for you, I suppose. God, I am glad I am not *completely* English.

At any rate, my father, despite his rather irregular family, was a handsome man but a bit portly by the time I was old enough to note such things, and always immaculately dressed, with his hair combed precisely to the side. Nice enough, I suppose. He would kiss me on the forehead in greeting and then again on departing. I never lacked for anything; there were always sufficient funds to ensure my education, arranged outings, my clothing, medical expenses, and whatever else might pop up deemed necessary for my continuance. There were others, however, who recognized that I spent most of my time alone and took me under their wing, no doubt feeling sorry for the abandoned child, as it were. They often invited me along on their family outings, or simply over for dinner. I was not the only child in such a position; there were a number of us who found ourselves abandoned in the English school system, a particularly British tradition that I understand is not quite so prevalent in our newly hatched "youth-focused" society. It was common enough then that I was not that much of an oddity. Perhaps if I had been poor, I would have gained a lot more sympathy. At any rate, my early schooling is why I am Swedish at heart and temperament but English in grammar and etiquette. Many claim, once they hear of my Swedish heritage, that I have a clear and distinct Swedish accent layered over my English accent, but I find that hard to believe. I asked Leslie and she said once that I spoke as if my mouth was full of marbles and with not just a little twist of pretense thrown in. I was a little chagrined but there is some truth to it. I speak more or less with an English accent then; or I speak as I speak and that is all there is to it and I do not apologize one way or the other. I forgave Leslie, of course; it is absolutely impossible for me to remain angry with her for long.

I should speak of my mother. She was a beautiful woman and, although I do not think my father was attracted to her solely because of her intelligence and wit, she was no fool. She was a bit slow sometimes and was never all that quick at figuring things out but she had a wonderful command of English while my father spoke only a spattering of Swedish. I learned to speak English from my mother in fact, which made the transition from being Swedish and living in Sweden to being Swedish and living in England quite a bit easier. My mother felt guilty for years about sending me away to school but could see no alternative; it was by far the better arrangement as far as she was concerned. I hardly blame her; she had a life to live, after all, and I knew, even at that tender age, I did not fit well into the life she was trying to build for herself. She was not a selfish woman but I was a mistake, though she did everything she could for me. Of course, I was also my father's child. That and the fact my grandmother became ill and was no longer capable of looking after me meant that I was going, and that was all there was to it. "It is for the best, Freya, you can see that, can't you?" I remember my mother saying, silently crying but carefully turning to me to ensure I would notice. She was like that.

My grandmother died when I was in Second Form. She was not a particularly likeable woman but she did her duty by me, which is about all I can say about her. I did not really love her. I did love my mother, though. I could really never decide how I felt about my father. Sometimes I felt I loved him; sometimes I detested the fellow, but mostly, as a daughter is expected to, I did love him, I think. Like my grandmother, he was dutiful. He must have loved me to some extent although I could never really get it out of him, and so it is only a supposition really.

The first person I truly loved, of course, was Leslie. I have not stopped loving her since our first days together. She was, and remained throughout our entire lives, everything to me. I do not know why that should be so exclusively so. I was, as I have stated over and over, physically attracted to her but I had been, and have been subsequently, physically attracted to others without the same depth of feeling. I love her, I believe, because it is clear to me that she loves me, not in the way I had once hoped, perhaps, but because she loves me for who I am and, quite often, despite who I sometimes can be. She has always, always, always been a true friend and a lover in the purest sense in that regard.

I did not really know Leslie's parents; I met them only once. She dragged me all the way up to Thunder Bay to meet them. What I recall are two people very much different from Leslie. Neither of her parents smiled nor laughed in my presence; they must have, of course, I just cannot recall. We sat in their parlor and talked of our time in Uppsala, Leslie's plans, and mine. We had roast moose for dinner, a first for me. It was delicious and tasted very much like a very rich roast beef. Even though he was

well into his seventies by then, her father was still one of the
largest men I have ever met. He was big-boned and well over six
foot four it was said, and I certainly believe it. His hands were the
size of my head and his biceps much larger than I could put both
hands around had I attempted to do so, and I certainly did not.
Her mother seemed a rather diminutive woman, neither large nor
small physically. She was very reserved. She said little the whole
time we were there; but each time she did speak, there was
inevitably some reference to *Our Lord,* which I found somewhat
disconcerting. I spoke German to them for a while. They were
very surprised, delighted even, that I could speak their native
tongue. We spoke for an hour about the family history, the
grandfather who had been in the German army throughout that
very complicated and brutal period called World War II. I must say
that Leslie seemed a bit remote from them. There was no overt
affection displayed in my presence, although I could tell they were
certainly concerned for her welfare and paid close attention to all
she and I had to say. My mother, despite her new husband, who
never fully accepted me, would always greet me at the door with a
hug and kiss and often, as she got older, with a tear. I do not think
I would have liked my mother to be like Leslie's mother.

It is hard to imagine how Leslie could have been the
product of the two people who were introduced to me as her
parents. Leslie was a lovely open woman; there was nothing lovely
or open about the two I met. There was some physical
resemblance, particularly with the mother. I hate to say it but one
wonders if her father was indeed her father. I never had the nerve
to ask. There was a suggestion, made by Leslie, once again sipping
wine late into the night, that there was a possibility he was not.
When I jumped on it and demanded she tell me more, she said
only that she sometimes felt sorry for her mother and often
wondered just how much love there was between them, a state of
affairs that Leslie vowed would never happen to her.

"Sometimes it is unpreventable… Life goes on: you
change, they change," I offered quietly, inadvertently taking sides.

"I would walk out the door."

It is a testament to Marshall that she never walked out the
door on him. He worshipped her and it was hard to imagine that
their relationship could ever have devolved as she claimed her

parents' relationship had. There was never any doubt as to their love for one another, not ever; that is why I am writing this history.

Now this is completely irrelevant but I think it necessary to add for the sake of completeness, if nothing else. My mother died at the age of ninety-seven from complications due to pneumonia. I had just seen her a month before but I flew over for the funeral. I was seventy-four at the time; one old woman saying goodbye to another. Leslie came with me since she knew my mother well, and I needed the company. My father died in a twenty-six car pileup on the A1 just outside of London; he was sixty-three years old and killed instantly, as explained in *The Times*. I did not go to the funeral but sent flowers; a large arrangement of chrysanthemums, the same as my mother preferred. I arranged a similar but much more extensive arrangement for her funeral. I also donated a small sum to his pet charity, Doctors without Borders, and never did receive a thank you for either the flowers or the donation. For my mother I donated to the Alzheimer's Society, since, by the end, she was beginning to suffer from that horrible disease. With respect to Leslie's parents, first she died and then he. One day she simply did not awaken; she was seventy-five. *Our Lord* took her I suppose. One feels she might have actually requested passage, deemed fitting, and the door subsequently and rightfully opened to the Kingdom into which she passed. He died when he was eighty-four, four years later. Leslie called him every Sunday at 9 AM sharp and one Sunday he did not answer so she had the neighbors go over. They found him dead at the kitchen table, his dinner before him untouched. He been there for almost a week and it was not just the autopsy that told us that; he was about to tuck into a dinner of fish, trout in fact, which meant it was a Monday.

It is, indeed, perhaps odd as well as a little sad, how one's passing is marked in the memory of others. I wonder how I shall be remembered. I know how Leslie is remembered, and Marshall too for that matter, and not just by little old me.

I say all of this because one must understand the background and history Leslie and I shared up to that point. After the year was up in Uppsala, we were, of course, the best of friends. I graduated after three years of European History and she felt she had learned enough Swedish to get the general idea. It is not an easy language to learn, and far enough away from English that she did struggle with it. She could by the time she left speak enough to get by.

When it came time for Leslie to return to Canada, I contrived to follow her back. Contrived is perhaps not the correct word; perhaps *arranged* is better. I did not hide my plans from her nor did I keep from her the fact that I'd applied for graduate studies at the University of Toronto. She knew I followed her. I suppose she thought it was just part of my greater plan of seeing the world, and knew that I had not yet experienced Canada. She was glad I was coming; she was excited. The University of Toronto is world class, and the fact I had been accepted into graduate studies, albeit in history, was, well, a feather in my cap from her perspective. I was a very good student, you see, A Class all around. My father, perhaps recognizing a bit of himself in me, felt that I should go up to Oxford, as he had. I certainly had the grades as the well as the ability. He once said to me in the pretentious but melodious accent he had picked up from years of grooming in the highest public schools of the land that "Average students, if they're disciplined, and work hard, can often excel in many aspects of academia and, indeed, often do better than the lazy, but gifted, student. You, my dear, unlike my other children, are not lazy, and I believe, as do others, that you might actually be gifted. Write the exams, pass them, and I will pay for you to go up to Oxford."

"Can you say that again please?" I mocked his accent and pretentiousness while I related the memory to Leslie. She and I were sipping wine beneath the terrace on *Mont Real*, Leslie preparing for her new position and quite excited about it. She said I sound a great deal like him. I do not see it myself. At any rate, I hate to be facetious or mean; it was, in fact, the nicest thing he ever said to me. Anyway, I wrote the exams, gained admission, but went to Uppsala. I wanted to go home, I told him. Of course, home is not always the same as what one remembers and although I did well, I spent only three years there, perhaps wasting my time, as my father suggested, by studying European History, from the Swedish perspective no less. I achieved my admission to Toronto not only from the grades but also from the references I had made in Uppsala, as well my former mentors in the public school I attended in England: The City of London School for Girls, if you are curious and want to check. My name, as far as I know, is still up on those brass plaques they put up to honor students who graduate with honors. I have never checked since I have never gone back; perhaps I should. They are not all bad memories there.

When I told my father I was heading out to Toronto to pursue graduate studies in Canadian history, there was a long silence at the end of the phone line before he said, and I am not mocking him, believe me: "Don't you know, my dear, that Canada does not have a history?" I begged to differ but laughed for I felt it was somewhat true. Now, of course, I know it is not; we all have a history, some of which we can admit to, the remainder perhaps not. Canada's history is somewhat benign and might be construed by some as being, well, boring. I do not find it so, but some do. In fact, if I was to be judgmental at all, I believe Canadians should feel proud of their history. Boring in the sense of a history could be construed as a good thing. The 'not boring stuff' usually refers to revolutions, war, pestilence, and pogroms for the people, none of which Canada suffered within her own borders to any large extent, not by world standards at any rate.

Of course, my father could have meant that Canada has no history simply by the fact it has only been a nation for a very short period of time, just over a hundred years or so. I do not think so though; he meant what I first thought he meant, with a sense of superiority over those poor colonists whom he believed continue to 'hue wood and draw water' as a means of survival. Smug, he was at times, very British. I do not believe I have ever met a Canadian who would have put up with him for more than a minute or two before they politely turned away. Canadians generally prefer Americans to their British brothers and sisters, although they often have little nice to say about Americans, despite there being very little difference between them culturally.

At any rate, I blew it somewhat; for all my highly vaulted intelligence, I had no idea of Canadian geography. Toronto is a long way from Montreal where Leslie was to pursue her graduate studies experimenting with rats most of the time as I understood it. But we continued to see one other despite the distance; there was a train, as ridiculously expensive as it was, and still is, that connects the two cities, and we saw one another every two or three months or so. It was a bit different then, though. She was home while I was in a foreign country but that was not the least of it. The growing difference in our relationship sprung more from the fact she was almost completely absorbed in her studies. Not too many are capable of attaining a PhD no matter what the subject matter, and when they finally recognized the talent in Leslie, they simply dumped the work on her. She spent most of her waking days studying or in the lab with her pet rats and had very little time for socializing. Of course, I was also ostensibly absorbed in my studies as well, but it was not the same. As Leslie was dribbling the ball and dunking it, a turn of phrase often invoked by her son Geoffrey years later, I was wandering about the intellectual landscape jumping from history to literature, to philosophy, dabbling a bit in foreign relations, then back to history. I was bright, eager, curious of all things, and my father was paying the bills, which was the main thing. For Leslie, it was not like that at all. She was on a scholarship, the funding for which had a beginning and an end, which amplified her already prodigious ability to focus and get the job done and on time before the funding ended. Eventually, some high and mighty world-recognized brainiac recognized her talent as well as her hard work, and convinced her to leave McGill and work in his lab at McMaster from which, three short years later, she was awarded a PhD in Sociology and Psychology. Although I know what it *is*, I still don't know what it *does*. Whatever it can or cannot do for society, I do know that Leslie was highly regarded in the field. The best thing, though, was that at McMaster she was relatively close by and we saw a great deal more of one another, every other weekend or so. More on my academic pursuits later, perhaps, but suffice to say for now that it all turned out well. I did eventually graduate and ultimately found gainful employment organizing tour trips about Europe. There is nothing I do not know, or *should* know by now, about Europe and its history. I feel I may have forgotten more than I recall, which is usually the case after one graduates as I understand it.

We have finally arrived to where I want us to be; that is, the present, meaning the present in the context of our story line. So it is then that Leslie and I finally connected. The sun, if you will recall, was leaking into my darkened living room as I sat morosely on the couch, thinking of ways of disappearing into the greater ether. We skipped through most of all the normal preliminaries, she with her call-display.

"Freya?"

"Yes, yes, it's me."

"I've been trying to call you."

"About what?"

"You know, you were there □ that guy on the ferry... Marshall."

"Oh right! Yes, of course! How did it go? I'd forgotten."

"Forgotten?" And laughing, "Oh, right! You forgot!"

"Okay, I didn't forget. How did it go?"

"Great... We're seeing each other again."

There was a pause within which I could think of nothing to say.

"Hello... I said we're seeing each other again..."

"That's good."

"Good? Freya! What's gotten into you?"

"Nothing."

"...Something."

"I've just been busy, that's all. I don't feel so great."

"Oh, I hope you're feeling better."

"I've been writing this paper on the Fenian raids in Upper Canada in the 1860s. I've been working on it for over a month. There are some Kingston connections, too; perhaps we could visit some of them if I came up?"

"What kind of raids?"

"Fenian."

"Oh. Well, okay... But listen ... I'd love to go, really, but not this weekend. I'm going sailing."

"...Do you think that's a good idea?"

"You know I love to sail."

"I meant with a strange man."

"Strange? He's not strange. ...Well he is a bit, but not in the way you mean."

"You don't even know him."

"I know him well enough."

"My experience with men..."

"I know about your experience with men," Leslie interrupted. "But, Freya... I can look after myself."

"I know, dear, I know."

That's about it; nothing much, but it killed me. I spent the rest of the Friday evening sitting in the dark, sometimes logging into Leslie's email account to see if there was any more communication between them, but there was nothing else. I felt guilty but could not help myself as I checked over and over again.

Nothing Happened

Nothing of relevance or interest occurred on the 13th of July 2012. Why, exactly, we continue to include in this history non-verifiable and non-historical meanderings is beyond me. This entire chapter should be deleted. I would apologize but I didn't write it.

Saturday, July 14th, 2012

Preface by Freya Anna Bergman

Marshall's boat was named *The Spray*. He named it after the famous boat *Spray*, sailed single- handedly about the world by one who may arguably be described as the best sailor that has ever lived, namely Joshua Slocum. Marshall prepended the definitive "*The*" to the name as if to denote his boat as the one and only. I don't know why he did that but I do know there were, over time, at least four incarnations of the same boat, ultimately leading to a thirty-nine foot ketch not so dissimilar in design to the original *Spray*, in concept that is. The final version of *The Spray* was, of course, a modern boat of fiberglass construction with a full navigation system, including radar, as well as sails that were raised and lowered by a single push of a button. It was beautifully maintained over the twenty years they owned it with rich teak and mahogany rails and teak paneling below. It turned heads in any harbor it entered, particularly I like to think, with Leslie manning the wheel and their young girls, Marcia and Alice, sitting up on the deck scantily clad in breezy white t-shirts and ridiculously short-shorts that barely concealed the primary colored bikinis they wore beneath, Marcia in vibrant green and Alice in stunning yellow. Marshall would have been on deck ready to throw the lines across while guiding Leslie the last few meters to the jetty. Baby Geoffrey, of course, would have been in the cockpit with Leslie, with a lifejacket on and tied to the mizzen in case he should wander over the side, which he had on occasion threatened to do, not out of malice, but by mere stumbling.

That was an intentional pun, by the way; for those uninitiated in the vernacular of the sea, a '*head*' refers to the toilet, so '*turning heads*' has a double meaning... I would not otherwise mention it but I am somewhat proud of the nautical minutia that I have acquired over the years; it makes me seem rather saltier than I really am. At any rate, I am not much of a sailor, I am afraid. I did not know the difference between the head and my head until

Marshall explained it to me. But even with that advanced
knowledge of the sea, as well as knowing that the pointy end is the
bow, the opposite end is the stern, left is port, and right is
starboard, I was still not much of a sailor. Marshall insisted I know
these things before he would continue to allow me to come aboard
and, as I said, I am highly intelligent and I did learn, finally, all the
finer points necessary to join them on their cruises about the
Thousand Islands. I am certain Leslie would have waived these
rather austere requirements but Marshall was insistent, particularly
when I made light of his sailing ability after I heard how they had
been marooned, windless, the first time Leslie joined him.

There exists somewhere, probably now in one of those
photo cubes I talked about earlier, a photograph that shows me
on the aft rail of *The Spray*, one hand on the tiller and the other
holding a paper bag, the contents of which are not shown but
known to everyone who has ever heard the tale. I can tell you, dear
reader, since I have already told you possibly far more than I
should have, that the bag concealed a bottle of Pepto-Bismol, a
disturbingly pink and somewhat chalky substance used to settle
unsettled stomachs. It was the only way I could sail. Marshall often
said I could be sick even with the boat tied up alongside, and that
was partly true. It is a simple matter of association: my body, with
a mind of its own, would recall being sick on the last voyage, and
just stepping aboard was enough to trigger the memory and set my
stomach heaving. Of course, the bigger the boat, the better my
stomach fared. I had no difficulty in the larger ferries churning
back and forth between the continent and England, or from
Kingston to Wolfe Island and back. In general, the larger the boat,
the better I fare.

Well, that is not true, exactly; I was never able to
participate in a Caribbean or Mediterranean cruise despite the fact
that many of the ships are larger than many cities; some so large in
fact that many claim they had no idea they were at sea at all. I had
a morbid fear of them, though, which I can only attribute to a
combination of my days on *The Spray* and, perhaps more
significantly, to a rather unfortunate recurring nightmare. While
sitting at the captain's table with a number of other well-dressed
personages, I lose it entirely, lean forward, and vomit into a bowl
of pink punch with floating bits of ice and green mint, and all that,

which I immediately associated with a bowl of Pepto-Bismol. It was only a nightmare and I know it is silly, but after that experience there was absolutely nothing anyone could do that might convince me to place even a single foot on one of those cruise ships. I do not prefer all-encompassing luxury in any case; it makes me feel rather *spoiled* and I do not like that, so I do not think I am missing much.

Even so, some aspects of sailing on *The Spray* were delightful. An example might be the time we anchored off Grindstone. It was the third invocation of *The Spray*, a thirty-six foot Hunter, I think it was, and Marcia was about a year old. I know this because she was born in May and the trip I am referring to was the May of the following year. It was a beautiful day and *The Spray* was snugged up close to shore. A high stand of pine towered over us; I can still smell the summer scent as I sit here and write this, the memory is so fine. The resin heats and fills the air, you see. The scent reminds me of a woodshop with shavings all about where lovely things are built. It was near the end of day, anchor set, sails in, and so on. I felt lazy, lazy... I moved forward to sit on the rail to take in the sun and read my book. I happened to look down through the open hatch and there was Marcia, tucked up and sleeping the sleep of angels, her red curly hair spread out on her pillow. It was a small thing, I know. There are so many other things that one could have noted and remarked upon but that in particular remains in my mind. When I think of Marcia, and I do all the time, I often think of that day. She claims she remembers, but I doubt it. I have told her of it so many times she believes she remembers when, of course, she could not possibly have, she was so young. Leslie does not remember, I know; she smiles when I tell it again but it was just another moment for her, I am sure. Marshall says he remembers and I believe him more. Seeing Marcia laying there, I looked up, pointed, and made comment, while turning to see who would be about. Leslie was nowhere to be seen but Marshall was aft, tucking away the remainder of the mainsail. He looked up when I called and clamored forward. He stood beside me, looked down, and smiled, and gave me a quick hug and kissed my hair, which surprised me. He must have said something; I wish I could remember what it was he said but I seem to have lost it.

There are so many things to remember. It has struck me that I have possibly forgotten more than I recall. I sit back and think back on those days and all the days leading up to the present and wonder where they have gone and, sometimes, if they were even real. I look about me and see on the mantle in my small room a host of photographs to remind me. And when Marcia visits me, and Alice, and their children, I, of course, know those days were real and true. Neither Marcia nor Alice would be who they are, nor would their children be who they are, if those days had not been. Geoffrey, too, of course; and young Catherine. Geoffrey is a bit of an anomaly in that he's more of a phenomenon than a carefully blended soul crafted by love and attention. All Leslie and Marshall had to do in his case was to place him in the world, provide shelter, nourishment, and love, and he took over from there. His daughter Catherine is somewhat similar, I am told. I do not know her as well as I should but from what I have heard, she is her own delightful self.

I see Marcia the most. She comes on Sundays, in the early afternoons, usually accompanied by one of the children. Of course, they are no longer children; Elizabeth is over thirty, older now than Leslie was at the time of this telling. Elizabeth, an academic like her mother, will sometimes come on her own, as does Laura. Laura does not always come alone but sometimes brings along her latest man, who hardly seems like a man at all he seems so young. She is a concern for Marcia. She has the look men and, of course, boys like. She is petite, with big breasts, a pleasant face, pleasing curls, in about that order. Whomever she brings usually sits off to the side, undoubtedly craving to have poor Laura all to himself once again, the desperation to be anywhere else but here plain on his face. I am not particularly impressed with any of her boy-men, quite frankly, and I have told her so. "Your breasts are a curse," I tell her, "and that pretty face; you will never be without men but you will not be able to trust one of them." She laughs when I say that, glancing over her shoulder at her latest, who picks up when he hears the word 'breasts' but then quickly settles back into his stupor.

Alice drops by, of course, too; and even at sixty years of age still looks remarkably like her sister. They could have been twins, the two girls, spaced as they were by only two years; but personality-wise they are quite different. Marcia is levelheaded and focused, like her mother, while Alice is a dreamer and, not so focused shall we say; she is more like her father. I love them equally, of course. I like their husbands, too: Neville and Douglas, particularly Neville who can be quite a wit. Douglas can be a bit of a pain; he likes to think of himself as an artist or one with artistic leanings because no one, of course, can make a living being artistic unless one is of the caliber of Marshall, and he certainly is not. I heard him once refer to me as that *old lesbo*; I know it was a while ago, before he and Alice were married, and I have forgiven him for it, but it still rankles nonetheless. The fact *I am* an *old lesbo* has nothing to do with it, of course; I suppose I just do not like the impertinence.

I am forgetting about the other children, Robert, Marcia's youngest, and Eric, Alice's oldest. I have already mentioned Catherine, Geoffrey and Anne's one and only child. You cannot love them all but I certainly do like each and every one of the children. Robert can be a bit of a pain; he just graduated from McMaster as an Electrical Engineer and has a penchant for very ugly and very shallow, I think, young women. It is unfathomable. He can do much better and I have told him so. Eric, on the other hand, is a very shy young man who, at twenty-three, looks barely old enough to be left on his own never mind drive a car. He is very musical, like his sister. He plays the guitar. He has Marshall's flowing brown hair tucked in behind his ears and a scrap of a beard about his chin. You would think that Geoffrey would look like that but, no, Geoffrey, as usual, is his own self, taking the best of both his parents. He is tall, muscular, and blond, with eyes like his father's. His wife Anne is drop-dead gorgeous and she's an absolute pro at making one feel comfortable. She listens. It is quite a talent. She is well trained, I think. Of course, I do not know her very well because I do not see them very often. They live in Colorado.

The thing about Eric and his guitar: he and his band participated in an open-air concert at one of the wineries not too long ago. It was part of a wider effort these days to revive *good old rock n' roll* and hopefully have it replace what is more and more being referred to today as *angst music*, which is supposed to be poetic and romantic and all that but is really completely self-indulgent and completely boring. We all attended his concert. It was a laugh, and lots of fun, and I came away feeling quite astounded by the energy and sure talent in the young people. They seemed so confident of their future. The band opened with a piece from AC/DC, I think; and when it came time for the guitar solo, young Eric stepped forward. I could hear the surprise in the people sitting behind us and just ahead of us. He looked so young and innocent, not at all like the other musicians, who were all making an attempt at appearing as disreputable as possible, even though one could immediately see it was all for show. His electric guitar was slung low about his hips and the sound that came out was astounding and somewhat overpowering. The talent and confidence and the positive energy that issued forth from that guitar and that seemingly wet-behind-the-ears young man, threw the crowd. Two thousand people or more immediately jumped to their feet and applauded, whistled and hooted, and hollered, and the ones in the front and surrounding us began to dance in that wild abandoned way that the young have. It was something to behold and something that stayed with me for quite a while. Alice and Douglas went out of their way to tell me they told me so; Douglas, in particular, looked particularly pleased, as well as somewhat smug. I do not like him sometimes. Did I already mention that?

I forgot to mention Hilary, Eric's sister. It is outrageous that I should do so. She plays the piano and may ultimately be the best artist in all the family, beyond even Marshall; but it is early days, I know, and the future is hard to determine. The child is only sixteen. I have never seen a more beautiful child, not only in body but spirit, and not only because we share the same birth date, May 22nd. I know one should not love one child above another but I simply cannot help myself. I wish I did not, but there it is. She is Alice's youngest and, likely, the last of the grandchildren; from now on great-grandchildren, though one never knows. I saw Hilary just the other day. She came with her mother, and while her mother and I talked, sat on my bureau with her head back and long skinny legs hanging over the edge. She was watching me, her eyes shifting back and forth from me to the outside gardens. I could feel her eyes rest on me and I looked up. "I saw a photo of you the other day, Auntie."

"Did you, dear, now; which one would that be?"

"You were dancing with Grandma, slow dancing. You were very beautiful, Auntie; so was Grandma."

"As you are, my darling; as you are."

"I will write a song about you one day."

Hilary plays the piano, and beautifully, and brilliantly. She is a prodigy, really; many say so but one doesn't want to make it such a big deal in front of the child in case she decides to believe it herself. "That would be very nice, dear. I look forward to hearing it one day."

Her mother sat back and added, "That is very nice of you, Hilary."

The child was again looking out the window, a half-smile on her face. I knew suddenly what was crossing her heart; I felt I could almost read her thoughts. It was a revelation that shook me to my core and, with that, a course of tears inadvertently flushed upward and I had to look away. Alice squeezed my hand and then there was no stopping the tears; I positively burst out. The child climbed down off the bureau and joined her mother as they each embraced me, each believing, no doubt, I was weeping for my lost friend, Alice's mother and Hilary's grandmother, and their father and grandfather as well. It was not so. I was not weeping for the lost years but for the years to come. God, one small thing leads to another and the next thing you know, a universe is born.

I am ridiculous I know; back to the subject at hand, I suppose. This book, as I have said before, is about the binding threads that comprise lasting love. The thread I am talking about in this case is merely a conversation between two young people who are simply just trying to get to know one another. The two, Leslie and Marshall, talk about everything from food to family to previous experiences in love and even the existence of God; but as everyone knows, it is not what is said that is important but how it is said, as well as the implicit understanding that underlies what is being said. The reader might find it particularly boring since nothing of importance seems to happen. Still, it is a great mystery how nothing very much can come to mean so much more. I will let you decide on the significance, or lack thereof.

Oh, one last thing; you will see that this is a very important chapter. It is central to the entire story and, as such, I thought it necessary to add additional detail where necessary. However, because it enclosed within a single chapter, as it were, and there are, by design, no more prefaces within which I can add what is necessary to the greater script, I have decided to add, on the occasion I feel it necessary to do so, additional footnotes. My partner in crime is, of course, dead set against it, saying how ridiculous it is to have footnotes that are often more extensive than the actual body of the text. I have to agree that it is a bit unorthodox; however, that is my style and I will add whatever I feel is necessary whenever I feel it is necessary to do so. Besides, from what I have seen of the publishing industry, I doubt very much that this history of ours will ever make any particular list. It is, then, a record more for my own sake, as well as the family's, than for the mythical, perhaps unrealized, reader that might be you. At this point, I hardly care what you, the public, or the children, or those yet to come, might think. It is what it is, I am afraid.

I do apologize for my somewhat hardened attitude on this point but, again, if anyone should be reading this and cares as to the content, please, again, bear with me.

The Spray

Leslie walked down the ferry ramp leading to the Island. Marshall was waiting for her. He was standing at the far end, letting the others slip past. As she neared, he stepped into place beside her and led her up the hill. A short way past the shops, they turned into a small marina and there he introduced her to *The Spray*.

"This is your boat?"

"This is she."

"Does she float?"

He helped her aboard. *The Spray* was ready for sea, as he said. The stays and shrouds hung loose, some frayed in places, and there was a small ancient motor hanging off the stern, tipped up and turned on its side. The fiberglass cowling was missing, revealing the pull-wheel and the cord wrapped about it. The sails were in place, the jib on the forward deck, the mainsail hanging from the boom, ready to be raised. The hull needed a coat of paint and a new fiberglass finish-coat but *The Spray* was otherwise clean and well maintained. Leslie had brought their lunch – she opened the thermos bag and showed it to him. He lifted each individual item up and out to examine it: ham sandwiches, one each and an oversized bag of chopped veggies, which, as he lifted it up and out, raised a smile and an inquisitive glance at Leslie. There was a quart of lemonade to be shared and parsed out in the plastic cups she had also brought, red presumably for her, blue for him, all to be finished off with chocolate chip cookies, two each. He smiled as he zipped the bag back up and stowed it below. He showed her the water he carried: four liters – they might need it; it was going to be hot. He also showed her the head – never been used but in good working order, as far as he knew. He noted her discomfort. "Well, you could always… you know…," and motioned the concept of hanging her rear end over the aft rail.

She rolled her eyes but, recognizing his sense of humor, laughed. "You would have to be locked up down below before that would happen!"

Walking off the ferry had shown her the same man she had expected. It was in his smile and the casual manner he held himself. On the way over, she had worried he might not be there and had prepared herself to be stood up. It would not be the first time.

Even before the ferry made the jetty, Marshall had picked her out of the crowd on the lower deck, waiting to come ashore. She wore a hat pulled down low over her eyes and stylish sunglasses, and as the ramp dropped, he noted she wore a white, short-sleeved collared shirt and a pair of matching shorts leading to her long tanned legs. He could see she wore her bathing suit beneath and smiled. "God, she's beautiful," he said again to himself. As the ramp fell into place, he could see her look up and pick him out of the crowd.

"I'm only kidding."

"I'm not."

They upped sails and headed out, hull up, the nose of *The Spray* dropping into the first wave it crossed and then lifting up out of it before slipping down the far side of the next. The wind was coming off the lake, gusting to twenty knots. There were three-foot swells capped in white. Leslie hung on. She tried to speak, to appear interested and engaged. It didn't work. She could barely hear her own words as the wind whipped through the rigging. He was leaning forward, his ear turned toward her, trying to hear what she was saying, unable to but nodding along with her. She glanced up through the rigging as she babbled on for the third or fourth time what a beautiful day it was. It was taut and strained. She imagined the shrouds might snap or the sails tear under the strain. She finally shouted, "Are you trying to kill me or what?"

He laughed and glanced over his shoulder toward the shore. He motioned it would be a moment longer and, as *The Spray* cleared Ferguson Point, he turned off the wind and the boat instantly righted and settled. The noise was all but gone. He let the mainsail out, loosened the jib so it billowed outward, and *The Spray* began to run. They were heading up the channel, passed Brown's Bay, Brophy Point, McDonnell Bay, keeping them all to starboard. They cleared Oak Point, and Howe Island was starboard. Leslie glanced at Marshall and laughed quietly with the day and the pleasure of it, feeling good.

Marshall reached into his daypack and handed her a new container of suntan lotion and a long-sleeved shirt – one of his, clean, recently laundered – that was made of light, high-tech fabric to help with the sun and wind. "I don't want to see you burned to a crisp." It was loose fitting. She had to fold the sleeves up onto her wrists and the ends fell over her hips and over her shorts.

He rummaged below, handing her the tiller, and returned with a foldout seat for her to sit on and another for himself. He settled back, his feet stretched out, and smiled at her.

"Leslie… I knew you'd be called Leslie. You look like a Leslie."

"I do?"

"Most certainly."

"Well, I can't say that you look like a Marshall."

"I don't?"

"Nope."

"What do I look like then?"

"A Bert, a Doug, another Doug…"

He laughed and leaned further back, with his feet propped up and his hand resting on the tiller. "I'm putting you in charge of the jib – when I say let go or haul in port, I mean the rope on your left – use the cleat to secure the line; alternatively, when I say let go or haul in starboard, I mean the rope on your right."

"I know what port and starboard is."

"How about the quick release cleat?"

"That too."

"We're done then. Training is over. …Another Doug," he mused, smiling. "Shit, I hate that name…"

She laughed again. "Marshall's fine… I knew you were a Marshall from the first time I saw you."

"You did?

She laughed outright, throwing her head back. "Give it rest! Forget it! And no, I didn't!"

"Sure, Les…"

"Marsh…"

"It's Marshall."

"It's Leslie."

They each laughed.

They sailed up under a brilliant blue, with not a cloud to be seen. The sun was tracking high through the sky behind them. The lake, now turned to the St Lawrence, glittered like a sea of diamonds. She pulled her hat low, adjusted her sunglasses, and leaned further back against the rail. She turned her face up to the sun. A slow swell followed the wind, lifting the stern of *The Spray* and then setting it down gently as it carried through. She smiled to herself with the joy of it.

"May the wind always be at your back," Marshall said, placing over it an Irish accent, while watching her.

She nodded and glanced at him and returned to the sun. "Where did you pick up the accent? Irish, is it?"

"Right you are, darlin'."

She laughed. "You're about as Irish as I am."

"And what are you?"

"Canadian – of German descent, but I don't like to think about where I came from. I'm not that now."

Marshall smiled. "I thought so."

The Spray corkscrewed and dropped then lifted. Marshall hauled up on the mainsail and tightened up on the jib, *The Spray* straightened, and her speed increased. The river swirled out behind and fell, snow white, off the bow.

She leaned back, watching him. "You do this a lot I can tell."

"Aye, Billy; that I do…" He guffawed. She smiled as he continued, dropping the pretense and smiling with her. "All summer, whenever I can. It helps me think."

"What do you think about?"

"Everything."

She looked incredulous. "Give me an example."

"How about the seventeen-year oscillatory period of cicadas?"

She laughed. "What?"

"Every seventeen years, a particular species of cicadas break up out of the earth and enter the adult stage. For seventeen years, they lie in the ground and then, finally, by some magic trigger, they rise up and sing their hearts out. It's quite a racket, really; the men sing and the women come a runnin'. You can hardly hear yourself think – as you might imagine. "

"It sounds… well… unusual. You've experienced it?"

"In Maryland, two years ago… Over a period of just four weeks, they eat, mate, plant their eggs back in the ground, and die. It's truly amazing."

She looked at him strangely. He was opening up in a way she had not suspected. "I've heard of it but I never thought of it quite like that," she said.

"Every day I thank God I'm not a cicada," he said.

"There's that too, I suppose…" She waited for him to continue, and then asked, smiling, with absolutely no idea what he might say next. "What else then?"

"That's good enough for now… I don't want to spoil you."

She laughed aloud, watched him smile with her, and blushed slightly.

They carried up the channel, keeping closer to Howe than Wolfe. The wind caught the shoreline and pushed them along with it. *The Spray* came in closer to the shore; the trees were higher than the mast. The water was black and mirrored the trees as the wind pushed them along in growing silence.

"This is different."

"It is…" He pointed out the eastern most shore of Breakey's Bay, two miles away across the channel to Wolfe Island. "That's where I live."

She studied the far coastline – heavily treed with what looked like a stand of pine mixed with maple, and a cliff-like bank of layered limestone reaching to the water.

"Where?"

He pointed. She still couldn't find it. He handed her a pair of binoculars, shuffled beside her, and pointed. She aimed the binoculars along the length of his arm and studied the shoreline. "I only see a dock – a beaten-up old thing," she said. She could feel the cool closeness of him. He backed away slightly, giving her space, and she smiled to herself about that.

"That's it but take it easy with the dock; I built it myself. I pull it out in the fall and push it out in the spring. It's too shallow and too exposed to keep *The Spray* tied up there any time of the year."

"Where's the house?"

"It's in there somewhere. It's hard to see."

She glimpsed a small gray building with a green roof, and close behind another building, which was larger, also gray and also with a green roof.

"That's my barn."

"Do you raise animals?"

"No, it's only what I call it; it's actually my workshop as well as my study."

"What do you study?"

"I told you – everything. …I'll show you one day."

"Show me? You're going to show me what you study? That sounds exciting…"

He smiled as he accepted back the binoculars. "Contrary perhaps to your expectations, I may not be the most thrilling guy you've ever met."

"I have no expectations."

He sat back by tiller, folding back again, tucking it beneath his arm. "That's good."

Later she would discover he kept *The Spray* secured to a buoy in Breakey's Bay; he had sailed down to Marysville the day before to meet her there. She was impressed and surprised he'd gone to so much trouble.

"Do you live by yourself?"

"I live alone but I'm never alone."

"Hmm..."

"I read a lot."

"Ah... Do you go to work?"

"I work every day. I get up and go to bed with the sun – except for the winter, of course, when the sun gets up late and goes to bed early." He leaned forward to make his point, a notion flashing through his mind and enervating him. "I continually find it difficult to fully understand why the ancients didn't know we live on a great sphere," he continued. "Of course, we know that some of them did understand the mathematics perfectly well – Menelaus, Ptolemy, Hipparchus... so it's a puzzle."

"...I never thought of that."

"...You watch the sun come up and fly across the sky; you can see it follows an arc. It walks along the shoreline of Howe, moving northward in the summer and then, on the solstice, changing direction and heading south. It is highly predictable – they could certainly measure and predict it – but the angles are difficult, and they had no closed formed model to describe it; something we demand, but not them perhaps."

There was an undercurrent of perplexity in him. It had come out in the way he had described the sun flying across the sky.

"How much do we not understand I wonder?" she asked, following his tone.

"Precisely."

He surprised her; she had not quite expected him to be like this. She liked it though; there was nothing forced or overtly intellectual about the way he had described the motion of the sun. It had sounded and felt spontaneous and natural.

He was looking at her with renewed interest. "Tell me about yourself."

"If you don't tell me about you, why should I tell you about me?"

"I showed you my house. I explained the motion of the sun, to say nothing of the wonder of the seventeen-year cicada cycle." He smiled.

"For which I shall always be grateful – but none of that is about you."

He smiled and lifted his hands and let them drop, something she had seen him do before. "Okay, I'm unemployed; what can I tell you?"

She laughed but quickly dropped into a smile. "How do you live? How do you eat?" She continued to smile, waiting for his response.

"My parents died. I inherited everything."

That surprised her and her smile disappeared. "You were the only child?"

He nodded. "It wasn't a lot – but it was enough to let me do what I want. It was our summer cottage. I fixed it up so I could live there all year round."

"It seems a very isolating thing to do."

He shrugged. "Tell me about yourself," he repeated, changing the subject. "You're a smart girl I know, but I want to know more about your family – where you were born and all that."

"Not much to tell."

"I want to know anyway."

"Why is that?"

"One day I might write a book about you."

She laughed quietly. "My life is boring; no one will write a book about me."

"I could write a book about you right now."

"That's crazy!"

He laughed with her. "Go on, then..."

Footnote by Freya Anna Bergman

Marshall did of course write that novel; it is what made him famous. It was not literally about Leslie, of course; it was about life and love and loss and it was titled, *The Pattern of the Quilt*, inferring the patterns that make up our lives. It took him a year to find a literary agent, almost another year to find a publisher, and yet another year to be distributed; but after that, and after the critics looked at it, it took off, rising to the *NY Times* bestseller list. It did not make him wealthy, exactly, but it did place his name out there. There were about five hundred thousand copies printed or distributed as e-books, which is rather a large number, particularly in those days.

Of course, I have no conceit that this particular collation of words and phrases will ever be published, other than the few copies that will be distributed to the family. Geoffrey is a wealthy man, I have a lot of time on my hands, and so, between us, I do the writing, with some help I must admit, and he will have it bound and distributed; thirty copies or something of that magnitude he implied. Of course, Geoffrey is a man of principle and if this effort in some way does not measure up, I am afraid that will be the end of it, and possibly just as well. I absolutely detest reading those boring family histories, particularly the ones put out at Christmas, detailing in poor grammar but excruciating detail, the family's trip to Florida that year. To think that what we are writing here might turn out to be somewhat similar if one is not careful does lend a certain gravitas to the effort.

My assistant in this endeavor is not particularly pleased with this analysis, where we are and are not heading. There is not much chance he will be famous because of this effort. I think he has been hoping for more. I tell him if this book never sees the light of day, what does it really matter? *He is being paid,* I remind him again and again; although he still seems to imagine there might be some royalties afterward. Where he got the idea there would be royalties, I do not know. I emphasized that *I* am not being paid, and nor will I be rewarded with a rush of royalty payments once it is done. He is not talking to me these days and I do not know why exactly. He is a nice enough lad but a bit sensitive, I dare say. What did he expect, I wonder? I suspect that, like many young people, he might be somewhat delusional as to his own worth.

At any rate, Marshall's first novel was really his first foray into making money; up until that point, he had been either supported by his parents; his scholarships, which were substantial and quite a few in number; and then, after his parents passed on, subsisting on his inheritance. Even after they were married, he insisted he use only his own money while she used her own. He was a bit odd like that. Perhaps it was pride, manly pride, but I really do not think so. It had more to do with making it in life; that is, he felt it was important that he should succeed on his own, without help from Leslie. He was a proud man, then, yes, and, as I mentioned earlier, possibly one of the most intelligent men I have ever known. It is clear to me too that he needed Leslie; she focused him, I think, and gave him *reason* as well as *direction*. Prior to Leslie, he had been holed up on the Island, as beautiful as it is, caught up in his own mind and memories of his parents. She saved him, really. He often said that as he swept her up in his arms and planted a kiss on her lips. I did not know why he said that until I look back now and can understand him better. One should think about others more often, I think.

It was typical of him to lift idiosyncratic pieces of knowledge from some depth and expound upon them, as he had with Leslie on the subject of cicadas and the trajectory of the sun; he was an endless source of information like that. He was a walking *Encyclopedia Britannica,* although expressed solely within the context of his own interests, which were somewhat eclectic I must say. He published three other novels after the first, all to do with 'God and Eternity and the Meaning of it All.' Each told with humor and lightness, I should add, so one does not think his novels read as if they were sourced from some stodgy old reverend pushing out his favorite philosophy for us to yawn over. It is very much Marshall in the pages of the books he wrote, and I hope you are beginning to appreciate who that man was and what he was like. His third novel was short-listed for the *Booker.* He should have won that year. I have no idea how the selection process works but the committee, or whatever it is that finalizes the decision, entirely missed the point that year it seemed to me. It is a common problem with committees as I see it; they often come up with quite *average* decisions.

Family

"Well…"
"You have German heritage."
"With a name like Krueger, I really don't think so."
Marshall smiled, watching her. "I thought so."

"Well, there's no denying it. It is important to know one's past but while in the present, one must always look to the future."

"I can only agree."

"With a name like Davenport, you must be English."

"Oh yes, quite right..."

"You sound Irish, though." She winked.

"I say, do you mind awfully if we come about just head? We'll run aground if not."

"Run aground, you say? That *would be* bloody inconvenient."

Marshall shifted the tiller and *The Spray* came up a few points across the wind. He hauled up on the sheets and gathered in the main, and motioned for Leslie to haul up on the jib until *The Spray* was close hauled, hull up slightly, dipping easily in the slow swell.

"The wind is dropping," Leslie offered as *The Spray* settled into her new course.

"I dare say it is."

"Okay, I get it; you're heritage is English."

He laughed, as she did, and they each settled back as *The Spray* headed into open water, riding comfortably.

"What a gorgeous day," Leslie said for the thousandth time.

"It is that."

She was watching him closely. He glanced out past her over the mottled surface of the river and then back to her with a half-smile, waiting for her to continue.

"My grandfather was a big man..." She indicated how big he was by opening her arms. "It's hereditary...," she said, lifting her hands and showing him, and then quickly placing them back in her lap. "When he came to this country, he went to Fort William, now Thunder Bay, to work in the lumber camps."

"Fort William and Port Arthur were amalgamated into Thunder Bay in 1970 – what's with the hands?"

"How do you know that?"

"Honestly?"

"Honestly."

"You told me you came from Thunder Bay and I looked it up."

"My history interested you so much?"

"Well, I didn't know too much about you at that point and, well, it was one of the few tangible pieces of knowledge I had, so I looked it up."

"Hah!"

"Well, keep going then," Marshall persisted. "I'm taking notes."

She shook her head and laughed, he again joining her until they both settled, eyeing one another as Leslie considered continuing, already saying more to him about her family than she had told anyone, even Freya.

"My grandfather was perfectly suited to the lumber industry," she slowly continued. "He could split a log this round." She wrapped her arms about an imaginary tree with the tips of her fingers touching. "All it took was a chop or two of his axe. God, he was a big man... You should have seen him." She sat back, catching her breath. "I take after him... as you can see."

"No, I don't see. You're beautiful: athletic, maybe – but not big like that at all."

She laughed, looking up, hearing the sincerity in his voice. "You know how to charm a girl – I have his hands." She again lifted her hands to show him.

He leaned forward, reached for her hand, and held it. "Hmmm... I see what you mean...."

She jerked it back. "Don't make fun!"

"Not surprisingly, these are woman's hands," he said, smiling. "I know a thing or two about hands, and those do not belong to a lumberjack."

"You know a thing or two about hands, do you?"

"I do indeed."

"Such as?"

He again reached for her hand and she allowed him to take it. He lifted it up for her to see, and turned it to each side, separating the fingers, folding each in turn into her palm, and then held her closed hand in his. "The human hand is comprised of twenty-seven bones," he said. "There is a thumb and four fingers." He opened her hand to show her. "The palm..." He ran his fingers over her palm and turned her hand over. "The back..." He carefully placed it on her knee and settled his hand over it. "It is connected to the wrist..."

"Is that so?" She recovered her hand. "I could have told you that."

"Ah, but the hand, and a woman's hand in particular because it is so delicately shaped, is an instrument of beauty, and far more besides. From tool making to the ability to play the piano, the hand coupled with the mind makes us who we are as human beings. You have beautiful and creative hands, Leslie; do not ever think you do not."

"And I see you have a way with words as well as a tendency toward the poetic."

He sat back and smiled. "You think so?"

"I do."

He laughed, his laughter settling quickly into a smile. "Tell me more about your family then," he again prompted, not letting go.

"I have already told you more than I have told most."

"So what's wrong with that?"

"Your turn is next."

"Okay."

She reluctantly continued but opened up as she went on. "I was born on a cold and snow-swept February morning – 1982, if you need to know..." She hesitated, watching him, uncertain if should continue, but then did. "Nothing much to note other than my grandfather, German; parents, German; and I am German. I was born in East Germany. My grandfather came here because he surrendered to the Canadians at the end of the war. He was in Holland. In the meantime, he had completely lost track of my grandmother; he didn't know whether she was alive or dead, but here's the funny thing... Twenty years later, my mother, just recently married to my father, doing some research, discovered through the Canadian government that my grandfather was alive and well and living in Thunder Bay. That is what opened the door for my mother and father. My father didn't meet his father until he was nearly twenty-eight years old. My grandmother had been without her husband for the same period of time."

"They didn't remarry in all that time?"

"Nope"

"Why is that do you think?"

"They married right in those days, I suppose."

He frowned. He thought her response might have been facetious but it was hard to tell.

"I was two years old when we emigrated from East Germany."

"Do you speak German?"

"Yes, still. I learned my English at school. My grandmother never did learn it. My parents still have some difficultly. My grandfather, though, was quite articulate, although always with a heavy accent."

Marshall nodded as she spoke and as *The Spray* cleared Howe and veered into the wind to carry her out into more open water. The wind was just off her stern quarter and propelled her along at a slow but steady gate.

"That's quite a history."

"Your turn."

Marshall laughed and shrugged. They drank some water, shared the lemonade and one of the sandwiches before he would give her any of his history, and she didn't press him. They cleared Wolfe Island and he pointed out the old lighthouse and called it Quebec Head.

"That's The Foot?"

"That's The Foot."

"I bike there quite often. I swim just off that point."

He pointed out the smaller islands: Arabella, Hickory, and Ant; eastward, the low lying buildings of Clayton, New York, clustered on the shoreline; and north, in the distance, the white dome of the water tower and the church spires of Gananoque.

"You've lived here your entire life?" Leslie asked suddenly.

"Pretty much."

"When we came over, we lived in Thunder Bay with my grandfather and my grandmother. I lived there most of my life, until I went to school. I couldn't wait to leave. I positively ran from the place." There she was once again talking about herself; she could barely believe it.

"The bugs were that bad?"

"That's not the least of it!" She laughed.

"Parents?"

"Yep, and life there; I felt stifled. I was stifled."

"When you ran, where did you run to?"

"As far as I could: undergrad at Waterloo; graduate studies at McGill; PhD at McMaster."

"Oh yes, you told me – and Sweden."

"Did you study the history, geography, and demographics of Sweden as well?"

"Well, I…"

"I won't bother to ask you the name of the capital but do you know the population?"

"About nine million, five hundred thousand."

"You're unbelievable!" She laughed.

He was blushing and trying to hide it. "Why Sweden?"

"What does one do when one goes to Sweden except study Swedish, of course. It was the best year of my life."

"Why's that?"

She shook her head. "Oh, I don't know. It just seemed like it. I was free, I guess; and I met Freya."

"Who's Freya?"

"My best friend."

"The other girl on the ferry?"

"That's her."

"She's friggin' gorgeous – Swedish?"

Leslie smiled. "You noticed? …And, yes, she is mostly Swedish, although there is some English blood in her too as I understand."

Marshall smiled. "I only had eyes for you of course."

Leslie laughed. "You're such a bullshitter!"

Marshall's smile widened. "Why Queen's now?"

"I came here not four months ago as part of my post doc. It's the first real job I've had in my life. They don't pay me much but, hey, I have a nice apartment, and a new car – I can't complain."

"What are you driving?"

"A brand new Subaru Forester."

He laughed.

"What's so funny?"

"I'm also driving a Forester – but not so new. It doesn't leave the Island."

"Why not?"

"I'd be pulled over."

She laughed and leaned back, removing her hat, letting the wind play through her hair, her long legs stretched out.

Marshall glanced at her and then away, finally dropping his head into his hands. "God…" He sighed so she would not hear. He looked up seconds later, steeling himself.

She sat upright and put her hat back on, tucking her legs back under her.

"What's the matter?"

"Nothing – not a thing."

Footnote by Freya Anna Bergman

Yes, Leslie had a gorgeous body that could take one's breath completely away. I know all about the effect she could have; I was certainly not immune. If she had only known how visible and how beautiful she was, she might have been a little more aware of the effect she had on certain men, and Marshall in particular. She possessed a certain innocence in that way. Still, as far as I know, he did behave himself and never made any outward advances on Leslie without her inviting him to do so, either directly or indirectly. Of course, after a while, they simply hung off of one another as if they required each other for support. It was as if they could not so much as walk down the street without one being propped up by the other. That lasted just a short while, and then things returned to normal, thankfully.

One other thing I should mention about Marshall is that, at least in the early days, he was particularly prone to the use of profanity, such as *"That's fucking insane!"* or *"You gotta be fucking kidding me!"* or *"friggin'"* this, or *"friggin'"* that. Leslie called it "dropping the *f-bomb*." Of course, Marshall meant it in the lightest of ways. He was not mean at all. It was employed generally, used an adverb or an adjective, and very rarely as a proper noun. When applied to someone he did not particularly admire, he normally invoked *"Fucking asshole…"* a term that he never applied to women as far as I know. He was barely conscious of his predilection but he was not completely unconscious of it either. When he caught himself out, he would always apologize and Leslie would say, "I don't mind so much but please don't expect me to condone it," as only she could say, always trying not to tell him what he should or should not do, or say, in life. He stopped on his own accord. By the time they were married, I rarely heard him issue a single word of profanity and, in particular, the f-bomb. Only once, in middle age, when the cottage was infested by an invasion of red beetles did I hear him say, "How do you like that, you little fuckers!" as he sprayed and watched them fall from the wall in sheets. It was a small thing and I do not think he knew I was listening, or he would not have said it. Still, the f-bomb must have been upward in his mind for it to come out so casually and so easily like that. It is a tribute to the man, I suppose, that he was able to contain it in the way he did. I can only imagine what conversations went on within him though. I suspect some things are better left unknown; it is, perhaps, why we did not adapt over time to be able to read another's mind. It would have quickly led to the death of one or the other, not benefiting the species in any way.

Leslie is very conservative in her application of profanity although she did, on occasion, apply such words as, 'shit', 'bullshit', 'bullshitter', 'sonofabitch', and so on. Later in life, though, she made a conscious effort to remove all forms of profanity from her vocabulary, for the children's sake no doubt. Even then, she did slip sometimes with the odd "*damn!*" now and then, such as when she might stub her toe. "*Damn, that hurt!*" or 'I've been working on this paper at work; I just can't seem to get through it; *it is the damnedest thing!*"

Nor do I commonly invoke profanity in my dealings with life's adversities. Although I have to admit, I do reserve the f-bomb in the form of an adjective for those special people that, once in a blue moon, stumble into one's life. I also have been known to use the word 'asshole,' but more as a descriptive term rather than the noun that it is. I really do not think further examples are necessary; I think you get the idea.

About Leslie's family, I said it before and I am saying it again, the one thing that struck me about her mother and her father, the only members of her family I had the opportunity to

meet since her grandmother and grandfather had passed on by the
time I was around, was how different they were from her. How
can two austere, seemingly cold-hearted, deeply religious,
somewhat uninformed, not all that bright, isolated people give
birth to, basically, a saint? It is a puzzle to which I keep returning
again and again. There are so many puzzles in life and that is
certainly one has that has remained unresolved over the years. The
main thing is that I fear her father might have been a brute. It is
only a feeling I have and there is no basis of fact for it but listening
to Leslie describe him and watching the expression that crosses
her face as she does so, there is no doubt in my mind that he once
beat her. I also believe it was no accident that she flew through
that glass door and cut herself so badly; nor, in retrospect, do I
believe her when she flatly states he never sexually molested her.
But then again, a daughter might not, given how embarrassing and
humiliating the resultant fallout would be, admit to her friends,
even her best friend, that she was beaten or *sexually molested* by her
father? How can one talk about being raped as one traipses about
the mall with friends in tow, looking at the sales, trying on this and
that?

My father and I were not close but if he had ever done
anything like that to me, and if I had not immediately found some
way to kill him, I would have, at the very least, run away. I certainly
would not ever talk to him again. I like to think I would have had
the courage to report him to the authorities and take whatever may
come after that. The odd thing about it, though, is that Leslie
possessed abundant courage in all aspects of her life and so I
wonder, if he had ever assaulted her, why she never mentioned it,
not even once. She could have mentioned it to her mother, of
course; but if she had, it went no further than that. Her mother
would have known but the fear and the loss of security and home
might have prevented her from doing anything but letting her
husband know she knew and was not happy about it. The woman
I knew as her mother had none of Leslie's courage so it is a likely
scenario. In the end, the three of them might have decided to keep
it in the family and there it remained.

It bothers me, it really bothers me; but in the end I know
that I have no proof. It was just a feeling, backed up by not so
much what Leslie said of him but what she did not say, and I have

to remind myself that, in the end, Leslie loved him. I know she looked after him and often called him to see how he was doing as he sat alone in that small family home of theirs.

I have a particular memory that often surfaces in my mind. I was sitting in the car waiting for Leslie. It was raining; the car was idling, the windshield wipers intermittently on and off; I had the heater on full to quickly warm the car and take away the fog building up on the glass on the inside. Outside the day was fall-like and the house appeared dejected and lost amidst the broken granite and stunted spruce that, over the years of neglect and poor maintenance, had begun to encroach. Marshall was in the car with me, huddled up in the back, trying to get warm, 'ladies in the front' and all that. He saw what I was looking at, leaned forward onto the seat, and said, "That's what years of neglect and encroachment does for you," as if reading my mind. I could almost see what it would be like in the hours after we left, the old man sitting in the darkened house, rotting away as the timbers rotted. The image has stayed with me. I don't know why. I do know, though, that Marshall liked the man no more than me. He told me as much, without Leslie hearing, years before, when her mother was still alive. It was the first time we had met them. The day was much nicer, we were waiting by the car, and I asked under my breath, "What did you think?" He glanced at me and said quickly because Leslie was already running along the drive toward us, "They are both very strange – she's a rather pleasant strange but he's a fucking asshole."

Years later, when the old man died and we all showed up in Thunder Bay to bury him, I asked him again. We were standing in almost the exact same spot. "I haven't changed my mind from the last time you asked, Freya," he said, smiling in the way he smiles, knowingly. He looked about him; I wondered if he was looking for Leslie, ensuring she was not within earshot. It seemed to be the case for he turned to me and added, whispering, "Nothing has changed here, do you notice?" "I have." "Only years of neglect and the encroachment of time," he said, paraphrasing himself from years earlier, and I nodded, feeling the truth grasp me. I remember I shivered. "Yes." He did it on purpose, of course, emphasizing the patterns within our lives as well as our own inevitable fates.

Her mother, as I have said before, appeared to be a very subdued woman. I could equally apply reserved, quiet, introspective, inward, undemonstrative, as well as extremely religious, even pious; and, perhaps, beaten, one never knows. Physically, as I also said, there was some resemblance but the woman I recall was decidedly overweight and flushed of face, with darting eyes that rarely looked up, but when she did, you could see Leslie in them. She was nice enough, though. I remember once - and it was probably the last time I saw her alive and walking about - she served us biscuits with jam, thin slices of cheese, cucumber, saltine crackers, and tea, nicely presented on a tray as we sat in her living room. She set the tray down between us, poured and handed us our cup on a saucer, turning back quickly to ask if we desired any sugar or milk. It was the most animated I had ever seen her. It was also one of the few occasions we spoke when I did not hear a single "God bless" or an "Our Lord" mixed into our conversation, though I never really had an opportunity to talk with her to any great length, so what do I know of the real woman other than her affections of speech?

She did once say, though, in the midst of Marcia's graduation, I think, right out of the blue, that, and this is quite out of character and is, perhaps, a reflection of her true character, suppressed as it might have been, that throughout the wedding she had noticed how my *butt jiggled*. It took me a moment but then I realized she was referring to Leslie's wedding, and I was horrified. I was the Maid of Honor and stood next to Leslie up front in the great cathedral of St George's with two hundred and more sitting behind me, and it turns out my butt was *jiggling*! I imagine the pious were supposed to be looking up to heaven and not at my butt! I was somewhat nervous prior to and during the ceremony, I have to admit; but even so I wish she had not mentioned it. It was almost twenty-three years later and what did matter, after all? What was her point, I wonder? The day had otherwise been quite perfect and I had imagined all along that I had always looked my ravaging best. She somewhat ruined it for me, I am afraid; not entirely, of course, but after that I thought of her as the type of person who always somehow manages to place a dimmer light on things. Again, not like Leslie at all.

One last thing, and again going back to why Marshall was so good for Leslie, perhaps better than I would have been. He not only was a male, which, of course, was important, he also more or less matched her in intelligence and values, and they each held many common interests. But the most important aspect of Marshall that I believe completely turned the tide was the simple fact that he was *fun*. Leslie needed a sense of fun in her life, and he gave it to her. Of course, he loved her madly and that, in and of itself, goes a long way, although it is never really quite enough, is it? I like to think that I possess all of Marshall's finer attributes, except the male part of him of course; and I do like a bit fun but fun has had to *come to me*, rather than me *creating* it all on my own, that is the way I am. Anyway, I do not believe it was a real factor in Leslie choosing Marshal over me. Leslie is simply not gay. I perhaps sound bitter but I am not; I am just a bit sad still. I do love Marshall. He is wonderful.

Going Pee

The wind began to drop. It was barely a flutter across the deck. The river, too, was calming. Marshall tightened the sails and change tack to catch as much wind as possible.

"You know something… I've really, really got to go pee; I mean, really, really, really got to go."

"Well…"

"I've looked down there … and there's no way!"

"I won't look."

"It's not that. I'm just not going down there and sit on that thing. My knees around my ears… forget it!"

"I was hoping you would."

"Why's that?"

"I gotta go too."

"What were you going to do?"

"When you were down there I was going to stand up and… you know. There's only one way then."

"What's that?"

As she asked, the wind dropped, sails sagged and fluttered, and *The Spray* lost way, her nose dropping and her mast suddenly righting.

Marshall rummaged about under the seat and pulled out what looked like a large canvas bag. "A sea anchor – we'll still drift but not as fast." He looked up. "I gotta go pee about as bad as you so I'm motivated." He tied a short line to the anchor, opened it, and threw it overboard. "There you go…" He handed her a line, which he also found beneath the seat. He tied one end to a cleat and handed her the other. "There you go… drop over the side and do your thing. When you're done, I'll haul you back in."

"I wouldn't normally do this but I really got to go!" She quickly removed her hat and sunglass, his shirt and her shorts, climbed up and, with the line loosely tied about her wrist, threw herself off. She surfaced right away.

"Hah, wonderful! The water's gorgeous!" She swam out on her back and a short distance out she threw back her head and sculled in place. "What a relief! Hah!"

Marshall threw himself in after her. He swam further out, away from her – he was a strong swimmer, like Leslie. He pulled up and, like her, lay back. "Ah, the small pleasures of life!"

"You don't have a rope!" she called after him.

"But you do…"

"Yeah, but it's mine!"

He laughed and swam over to her. He neared. "Ah… A warm spot! You didn't happen to pee here did you?"

"Yes! Yes, that's exactly the spot!" She laughed.

"Argh!"

The Spray had picked up a gust of wind and was already drifting away; the line was almost all taken up. Marshall swam up to Leslie and grabbed the rope, which was now tight and slowly dragging Leslie along.

"You forgot to take down the sails!"

The wind dropped immediately, the wind spilled out of *The Spray's* sails, and she wallowed.

"See, what did I tell you? No worries."

"You were supposed to stay onboard until I was done!"

"You looked like you were having such a good time, I couldn't resist."

The wake from a far unseen boat caught up to them, a low wall of water that lifted them up then passed. They watched *The Spray* ride up and down the sides, her mast momentarily careening across the sky as her rigging rang against the aluminum mast. *The Spray's* bow turned and the wind filled her sails but then immediately dropped off. They swam back and hauled themselves in. Marshall was first. He reached up, grabbed hold of the rail, lifted a leg up over the side, and was in. He turned immediately and offered Leslie a hand but she refused. She hauled herself up as he had, one leg up and over the rail, but, unfamiliar with the technique, pitched head first into the cockpit. He helped her turn herself about and sit, and before she could speak, gave her a towel to wipe her face. She had lifted some skin on her elbow and her knee and it hurt though she said nothing about it.

"Whoa!" She breathed a sigh of relief. "A ladder would have helped!"

"My very next acquisition."

She caught him looking at her. She quickly looked for his shirt and put it about her and, once over her, put her arms through one at a time. Marshall searched about below and came back with some bottled water and some ointment for her scratches. He handed her one bottle and took another for himself. "Hide if you wish. You are a beautiful woman."

She shook her head, felt herself blush, and accepted the ointment. "You're not too bad looking for a guy…" She shot back but meant to say, "You mean not too bad looking for a guy," but the words had become mangled. She applied the ointment, grimacing with the slight pain, and then opened the bottle of water and drank.

"I notice how you cover yourself – you're very careful."

She shook her head and shrugged again. "I don't even think about it."

"Now that's another lie." He smiled.

She threw her head back and looked at him straight on. He returned her stare, one for one. She smiled first and he followed. She drank some more of the water as he did and looked out over the wide and very still surface of the river, now the same color as the sky, a light blue.

Footnote by Freya Anna Bergman

It happens all the time. Anyone who has gone swimming with another invariably accuses the other, at some point, of having peed in the water. "You peed!" "No I didn't!" "Yes, you did, the water feels warm!" and then laugh, swim about and away as if in disgust, the other throwing their head back and laughing, particularly if they did pee. It never changes. We're all the same. Frankly, it is why I rarely swim, particularly with another in close proximity, and never in a pool. I also cannot see the importance of this particular incident but Leslie, when we were finally over our differences, could only talk on and on about it. It was as if Marshall had quoted *Moby Dick,* or some such masterpiece, as they swam about, heads back, feeling the waves drag over them. I have said it is the small things, but only the reader can decide, I suppose, the importance, or lack thereof, of their mutual experience of urinating in the St. Lawrence River.

Becalmed

The wind stayed down and *The Spray* became becalmed. Marshall had drawn in the sea anchor and had set all sails – but there was no motion other than the slow wallowing of the boat. It was oddly quiet, only the random jangling of the rigging against the mast and the flapping of the sails as they folded and folded again under the influence of eddies of wind that climbed up from the nearly still water. Every sound seemed unnaturally amplified, even their conversation.

"It was not predicted on the Marine Forecast I heard this morning. Steady winds, 20 to 25 knots from the east all day was what was predicted."

"That's what they all say."

"I'm not kidding – I wouldn't strand you in a boat with a guy you've only met once before."

She smiled so he would know she wasn't concerned. They sat quietly and comfortably without saying a word.

"Day after day, day after day, we stuck, nor breath nor motion; as idle as a painted ship upon a painted ocean."

"You're just full of that stuff, aren't you? What was that from?"

"The *Ancient Mariner*."

"Huh, I knew it."

He smiled.

Footnote by Freya Anna Bergman

For the record, Marshall had not memorized the entire *Rime of the Ancient Mariner*, only from, "All in a hot and copper sky, The bloody Sun, at noon," to, "Water, water, everywhere, Nor any drop to drink." He did that small part, however, quite splendidly.

One other thing, dear reader: please note how this footnote is of the correct form and, more important, so I have been informed, it is also of an appropriate length. I shall endeavor to make any other footnotes that I should find necessary similarly to the point.

Her Grandmother

She looked out over the water – perfectly flat. "I didn't tell you about my grandmother." There she was volunteering information about herself again; she could hardly believe it.

"No, you didn't."

"A hard, unsmiling woman; the war, extreme poverty, and not having a husband, but mostly time did that to her. She'd sit in the back of the kitchen in her rocking chair – we still have that chair; my mom's holding it for me until I can take it. Anyway, she'd sit in that chair, sunlight through the window laying across her work, day in day out, knitting away; socks and sweaters for everybody. She never spoke English – never even tried; it was too late for her, she said. "There, I hope they keep you warm," she'd say in her high German, handing over yet another pair of socks – which, by the way, always fit perfectly. I don't know how she did it; she never measured my feet. I still have dozens of those socks, and maybe half a dozen of her sweaters. I don't wear any of them

anymore, but I keep them in my dresser drawer." She caught her
breath and turned to face him. "Is your grandmother still alive?"

"No – but I have her chair. I kept it."

"Ah, well, then, you know what I mean."

He smiled and nodded.

"She didn't sit like that and knit, did she?"

"She did, in fact."

"Ha... Who's to know? We're all the same in the end."

"We are that... but she had nothing of your grandmother's
history."

"Tell me about her," Leslie asked, realizing only then how
little he had said about himself and his family.

"There isn't a lot to say... nursing sister in World War I,
married the man she brought back to health, followed him back to
Canada. It is a pattern in our family – fate bounding us about. My
mother, my grandmother's daughter, was a nursing sister in the
next war. She, too, married the man she brought back to health
and the two of them returned to Canada after the war. My father
used to say he went to war and came back with a wife and a limp.
My mother used to say she came back with a limp... It was a
family joke."

Leslie laughed, continuing to watch him carefully, the
expression on his face, his smile, his eyes.

"Tell me more about your grandfather," Marshall
prompted.

"My grandfather... I already told you he was a big man...
but he hardly ever said a word. He'd just nod, say what he wanted
and what he meant, and never repeated himself. You didn't dare
cross him – he had that about him."

"Tough guy."

She nodded. "Tough guy... You felt if you crossed him,
he'd grab you in those big hands of his and crush you." She held
an imaginary object. "Tube of toothpaste – squish! ...Busted out at
both ends, that's what you'd be. I felt that way, anyway."

"Did he ever beat you?"

"Never, and not my grandmother, as far as I knew. I never
saw him kiss her either though, or show any outward affection.
They each found God and prayed a lot together, I remember that,
at the kitchen table, holding hands. My father beat my mother –

but only when he was drunk. Fortunately, once he found work, he wasn't drunk as often. Now, neither he nor my mother drinks very much at all. Not that my mother ever drank to any great extent, just a sip of wine now and then."

"Have your grandfather and grandmother passed on?"

"Yes they have."

"Your father sounds like an asshole, I have to tell you."

"You sound like my friend."

"Freya?"

"Yes, Freya, that's what she said, and I suppose it is true; but he's still my father. They always had God and Jesus, or whatever, in their lives; you'd think that would be enough, wouldn't you?"

"What do you mean by that?"

She shook her head. "I don't know." She shook her head again. "I don't think they loved each other, from what I saw anyway. It was a cold place, my home. I could hardly wait to leave. They were more like roommates that have come to accept each other's bad habits than husband and wife. I have sworn to God that will never happen to me, and if it does… if circumstances are such that…" She looked up. "Do you think your parents were in love? Were they some of the lucky ones?"

"Yes, I do – I think so. When my mother died, my father…" he shook his head with the memory, "…couldn't handle it."

Leslie leaned toward him. "What happened?"

"My mother died of pancreatic cancer – and my father… well, my father just dropped dead four days after she died. The autopsy said it was a massive stroke and that he was most likely dead before he hit the ground."

"Four days! Oh my God, that's awful! And you were left by yourself?"

"Exactly by myself… I was the only one left. After all that history, after all that time – I have boxes of pictures of old aunts and cousins – there was no one left but me. Quite remarkable, statistically speaking, that is, but true nonetheless. Friends, of course; they had lots of friends, and colleagues, and so on. There was quite a crowd at their funeral."

"Hold old were they?"

"My father was seventy; my mother, sixty-five."

"Ah, same age as my parents. Still kicking, though. My grandfather died when he was eighty, my grandmother when she was ninety."

"You were close to her, I can tell."

"How can you tell? I haven't said anything."

"It is how you say, grandmother; it is in the inflection of your voice."

Leslie sat upright. "Ha," and looked away.

Footnote by Freya Anna Bergman

Marshall has a gift for drawing people out. He rarely talks of himself but loves to hear others talk on and on about their own lives. He would lean forward in that earnest way of his and one could not help but spill one's guts, so to speak. He would have made an exceptional psychologist or a psychiatrist, particularly in these days when most people just want to talk about themselves all day long. Of course, I cannot place Leslie in that crowd. Everything I learned about her I determined only over a period of time, piecing her life together across months, and then years of conversation. It was very unlike Leslie to reveal so much of her life at the first sitting like that. He surprised her, I think; it was his compassion, his interest in, not just her, but those surrounding her. It was also his natural intelligence and, more important I think, his kindness. Yes, I think that is what sold her originally, that and his somewhat understated sense of humor. He was very much like Leslie, in fact.

Marshall's inquisitive mind, his idiosyncratic knowledge, the poetry he quoted, would make many believe him to be perhaps somewhat pretentious, but he was not. Everything Marshall said was said with a deep unaffected sincerity; one simply knew he spoke what he meant and believed in what he was saying. In short, one could tell he was speaking from the heart. One also knew that his genuineness was equally mollified by a lightness in spirit that suggested that even the truth could be laughed at, and that often life can be taken far too seriously. He was perfect for Leslie, absolutely perfect. I think she would have seen that right away but would not necessarily have believed it until it was proven to her time and time again as their relationship developed. Even so, by this time in their conversation, I would say the fire had been lit and was not just smoldering.

One other thing I have noted in the retelling is how similar their backgrounds were. I do not, of course, mean the specific details but more the direction. They were both the only child in the family; they were both academically driven, and, by the time they met, they were both, for all intents and purposes, orphans. Marshall certainly was, and Leslie was orphaned in the sense that she felt very much alone in the world. Her parents may have been living but she was segregated from them by all things in life that matter if one wants to remain close: distance, belief, temperament, and education, and those shared memories of love that are so vitally important in binding people together. I know she felt alone, she told me so; and I suspect Marshall felt the same, alone on the Island as he was, living amidst the ghosts of past summers in their summer cottage, now his home.

Finally, it is only just beginning to dawn on me the importance of Leslie's grandmother in her life. Of course, she had to be; her grandmother was her mother's mother and, ostensibly, the second closest person to her while growing up. I recall Leslie talking about her, and she did once mention the socks and sweaters but I do not recall ever *seeing* the socks or the sweaters, or gathering their importance to her. It was something she kept from me but told him right away. It just goes to show, I suppose, the direction her heart was already beginning to lean. It does bother me somewhat. It should not I know. It was, after all, almost a thousand years ago. I feel stupid now, as if I let Leslie down in some way; Leslie and her grandmother both, that is. I believe her name was Gerda - Gerda Charlotte Kreuger - but Leslie only knew her as Oma. "Thanks for the socks, Oma." "Speak German, child." "Vielen dank fur die socken, Oma." "Sie sind herzlich eignelanden, Leslie, kind."

Anchorage on Hickory

The Spray was wallowing. It was midday; the sun was high in a cloudless sky. There was no canopy and the sunlight was intense, there was no getting away from it. The cuddy would be suffocating. Their conversation lifted and fell back and slowed with the heat. Finally, in a lull in their conversation and without explanation, Marshall climbed to his feet and dropped the motor.

"We're heading back?"

"I would, except for one thing..."

"What's that?"

"I don't have enough gas to get us back."

"What kind of backup plan is that?" she asked flatly.

"Hey, with the price of gas, I can't afford to keep the tank full."

"What are you doing now?"

"I'm going to look for some shade; I know where there is some... We have enough gas for that."

He started the motor after a full pulls and turned *The Spray* about, not bothering to take down the sails. As they flapped back and forth under the false wind, he handed the tiller to Leslie and recovered first the mainsail, tying it in bundles to the boom, and then the jib, which he collected on the foredeck; all the while *The Spray* puttered along under Leslie's helmsmanship. Done, he took the tiller, swung *The Spray* toward Hickory, and opened the throttle. They were over a mile out so it took some minutes.

"I think the lack of gasoline may not be our only issue," Leslie stated.

"Why's that?"

"The clanking sound coming from the motor, the white smoke pouring out the back, the fact you have the throttle wide open and I can swim faster."

"I take your point... points, that is."

"Yes, 'points' is plural."

"But have some faith."

"Oh, I have faith."

He managed *The Spray* along the coastline of Hickory, keeping well off and away from the shelf of rock, and then turned them into a small sand-bottomed bay across from The Foot, about a mile off. They anchored in merciful shade close to shore.

"Told ya," Marshall teased.

"Lucky, I would say."

"My middle name…"

Marshall set the anchor, secured all the lines, and folded the tiller back in place.

Leslie breathed in deeply and sighed, letting it out slowly. "I can smell the warmth in the forest and the pine resin," she said, looking about. "It smells so fresh. It's such a relief."

"You're easy to please."

"You're the first one to say that!" she said, waving his comment aside. "Not even Freya says that about me."

"She doesn't know you then."

"Ha!"

Once completely secured, they immediately opted for another swim. Leslie was first in. She dove off the transom in perfect form, slicing into the water and not surfacing immediately but pulling herself along beneath the surface with long and reaching breaststrokes; an angel underwater, Marshall thought, watching her until she surfaced a distance away. Marshall followed, diving off the bow and cutting into the water as she had, but he was quickly up and swimming in strong strokes away from *The Spray* as it slowly swung about on its anchor.

Leslie called out, cupping a hand about her mouth. He was a hundred feet away, at least, on the far side of *The Spray*.

"Are you peeing again?"

"What do you think?"

They each laughed.

"What about you?"

"Oh, I'm not telling!"

"You stay right there! I don't want any of your pee in my water!"

"Too late! The current's going your way!"

They laughed again, swam toward one another, and met half way along the length of *The Spray*. Reaching her, Marshall surprised her and kissed her for the first time. She laughed and kicked away.

"Your face is flushed red like the sun has been at it," he said, clearing his eyes and pushing his hair back, treading water only feet from her.

"Yours is red from something else!"

She laughed again and kicked back further, rotated about and swam out. She swam with strong strokes, her head down, then up, in synchronized breathing. She swam half way across the small bay and ducked down and then up, turning to see how far she had come. The high forest reflected in the silver, golden, and perfectly still surface of the bay. *The Spray* had turned on its anchor while Marshall had remained where she had left him, now alone in the midst of the bay with *The Spray* at an oblique angle from him. He waved. She waved back and pushed off again back toward *The Spray*. It was an easy swim; the water felt warm and delicious. She touched the side of *The Spray* and rotated about, turning and floating on her back, her arms spread, looking upward at the cloudless sky, feeling the security and serenity of the bay as it wrapped about her.

When she righted, Marshall was already aboard. He had his t-shirt on; it was wet in places where he hadn't bothered to dry himself off. He was standing on the bow, holding onto the mainstay to keep his balance, watching her.

"It looks like you're having fun," he called.

"It's gorgeous!"

"It is that."

"I mean the water! This bay!"

"That's what I meant..."

As before, he offered to help her up and this time she accepted. He offered his arm, she grabbed hold with both hands, and he easily hoisted her aboard. She helped by lifting her leg up over the side and standing. He stepped back immediately to give her space, turning and then handing her a towel and then her shirt. He returned to sit on the aft rail, carefully balanced on the gunwale, rewinding a rope so as not to watch her as she dried herself.

'You can look now."

She, like him, was perched up on the gunwale. She had remained in her bathing suit, drying off in the light breeze that felt almost cool.

"I was just coiling the rope, don't want it tangled…" Marshall stuttered and, hearing what she said, muttered, "Well… Good then." He was beet red beneath his tan.

She put the shirt over her shoulders and her arms through the sleeves but didn't button it up. "This is a wonderful spot. How long do you think we'll have to stay here?" she asked.

"Until there's wind."

"When's that going to happen?"

He smiled and shrugged, looking up. "Never, I hope."

She laughed, enjoying the attention she was getting. "We'll starve to death, or die of exposure; all sorts of horrible things will happen."

"You can always swim across to The Foot and walk back to Marysville. It's only seventeen miles or so."

"I thought about it."

"You could catch a ride with a friend of mine."

"You would leave your boat?"

"No, I'll stay here. I'm the captain, I can't leave."

"I'm staying too then."

Marshall could have suggested they motor over to the government dock adjacent to The Foot and tie up there. He could have called Old Farmer Brown – he could glimpse the eaves of the farmhouse next to the old government dock. The old man would put her in his old Ford pickup and take her back to the ferry, the old truck clanking along Hwy 96, the front wheel bearings grinding in protest as he took the sharp corners. She'd be home in two hours while he'd stay with *The Spray* until the wind came up. He thought it through but said nothing of it. For Leslie's part, she too had noticed the government dock and had recognized the high shoreline of The Foot and the picnic area beyond, and knew it would be better to tie up there; but, like Marshall, she didn't suggest it. He knew that she knew and it gave him some hope. She knew that he knew that she knew – and still didn't say anything.

He glanced back at her. "I thought you might."

"I believe the wind will come and we'll go home."

He shrugged and again glanced at her.

"You don't think so?"

He pointed beyond the bay toward the open water, burnished silver, reflecting the sky. "The water seems flattened, pressed down by the sun," he said, and in another way, "The sea is embraced by the heat, the wind is still as dust."

"Who said that?"

"I just did."

She nodded and smiled. "You're different."

He smiled in return. "I know. I hope you don't mind."

"I don't, but I suppose it means that we can imagine our dinner. Your rather vivid imagination just might be able to conjure something up."

"As it turns out, I just so happen to have a bottle of red wine and some dark chocolate stowed down below. …I'll go get it." He didn't move but sat back and smiled.

"If you… if you really did… I'd jump in the lake right now and swim for The Foot and you'd never see me again."

"Why would you do that?"

"It would mean you set up the whole thing. It would mean you knew there'd be no wind this afternoon, and all of this would have been nothing more than an elaborate plan to trap me on the boat with you. It also means you'd be just like every other man I've met."

"Happened to you before has it?"

"On more than one occasion I must tell you."

They both laughed at the ridiculousness of their conversation.

The wind would eventually come but not until the following morning and not until after the heat lifted up into the star-washed sky, drawing the cooling winds off the lake to churn the air. The lemonade was all gone but there was water and one sandwich left, and enough veggies to last a few more days if need be. The day continued, still and windless, and they talked and laughed together as the sun turned and arced downward toward Howe Island, filling the bay with the sun's gold but without its heat. They jumped overboard twice more as they drank the water and nibbled on the veggies and talked.

Footnote by Freya Anna Bergman

Urinating… Again… what can I say? In the animal kingdom, there are examples where the male begins the mating ritual by urinating and spreading the mess in every direction, hoping to attract a lover. Please take a note, dear reader: urination may be a secret method, hitherto underutilized, that one might employ to attract that special someone. We are no different from animals in our basest instincts, after all, so in theory at least I see no reason why it may not be so.

Did you notice how my compatriot invoked almost poetic prose in his description of the landscape, the high forest reflected in the silver and golden surface of the bay, and so on? He added so much more than I gave him. It just goes to show you can work with someone day in and day out and still be surprised by them. Never give up on someone, I suppose is the lesson. Upon questioning, it turns out his family has a summer cottage on Crane Lake up in Parry Sound to which he retreats every once in a while: retreat, it is his word, not mine, and it perhaps explains a great deal as to the direction of his heart. I think he might be really getting into this finally. Perhaps we are more kindred in spirit than I had imagined. Some things never cease to bring wonder.

How Many Boyfriends?

"How many boyfriends have you had?"

She turned back to him after looking away to conceal her surprise at his effrontery. "More personal information I won't give out. The fact is, I spent most of adult life studying and men have not been a priority."

"But you dated?"

"You're nosey. Of course, I dated," she said, but then added primly, turning her nose up but smiling as she did so. "And I continue to do so you might want to know."

"I do want to know," he replied, quietly returning her smile. "It's natural I would want to know."

"But it's not polite to ask a girl such things – it's none of your business."

"Sorry."

"…What about you, then?"

"What do you mean, what about me?"

"Dating?"

"Now that's a fine turn!"

She laughed and simultaneously blushed. "You're right, sorry!"

"I date – but not very often."

"Can't afford it?"

"That's low."

"Sorry again!"

"No, it's because I just can't find anybody. The woman I am looking for is obviously very rare."

Leslie blushed. She had not expected his answer.

"But when I do… I… knock on their door. … and if they don't answer…" He shrugged.

"You're so melodramatic. You should be a playwright."

"I thought about it."

"No one would go see your plays though."

"I thought about that too."

"Except me of course."

"Why you?"

She shrugged. "I'm a sucker for the downtrodden."

He laughed. "I was thinking…" he began, hesitated, but then went back to it. "Remember I told you I could write a book about you? Well, one day I will."

Leslie found herself blushing yet again. "No way, no one can write about me, at least not right yet. Wait until I'm famous!"

"I can – and I will. I could write it tomorrow."

She looked at him oddly. He was sincere. His sincerity surprised her, not the fact he was capable of writing a book. She could already see that ability in him. "You're an odd duck. …A very surprising odd duck."

He smiled and nodded. "You're getting to know me."

"If you ever do decide to write about me, I want you to tell me."

He smiled, "Done, and as part of my research into that book, there are a few things I'd like to know."

"Like what?"

Footnote by Freya Anna Bergman

When Marshall said to Leslie, "The woman I am looking for is obviously very rare," the reality of what was in the process of happening struck Leslie like a bolt out of the blue. She hid it from him, of course, but that is how she felt. It briefly choked her up, she told me. Hitherto, she had felt, like many, that if there *was* someone out there for her, they were very rare indeed. It was natural then to be somewhat of a shock to hear him echo her feelings with almost her own words. I really do not know what to think about it, I really do not. Is it possible that, for some us, there is only one person in the world with whom we can join ourselves completely and without reservation? My instincts say no but my heart says yes.

What I feel matches popular romantic theory, possibly born out of too many silly novels, which states that the probability of finding one's so-called soul mate somewhere within the mélange of the greater population is something less than one in a million. It feels like that, I know, but it is obviously not true. The truth and documented fact is that in any random set of young people, say a thousand, half male, half female, the probability of finding a compatible mate, if you're looking for one that is, is very high indeed, better than twenty-five percent, in fact. I do believe that, having been on that side of the equation, if it was a random selection of lesbians or gay men, the probability of finding someone compatible to one's lifestyle, politics, tastes, theories of evolution, etc. is about the same, so we are not describing a corollary to one's sexual leaning at all. The statistics do not lie. They are borne out of the fact that arranged marriages work about as well those who select their mates because they are in love. It is borne out by the fact that if one spouse dies, the probability of the other marrying is high. It is also borne out by the fact that when boatloads of women went off to the New World to meet and mate, the likelihood of them finding a compatible man and a lasting marriage with some happiness was far *better* than it is today, at least on paper. Of course, the harshness of their wilderness lives was not what a modern woman would claim as ideal but that is beside the point. The fact is each and every one of those women found a man, had his children, and, while they lived, which admittedly was not very long, they were, statistically, that is, quite happy. We have their diaries to prove it. It is in black and white, my dear; go read them.

Modern women, and men, simply expect too much, I fear. There is too much silly television, and too many movies, and those impressive, but rather shallow from the perspective of character, 3D experiences that are so popular these days. Men and women should give one another more of a chance to shine. Their collective delusion is, perhaps, a reflection of the possibility that men and women do not know what love is after all; they only imagine they know. It is a mystery how the facts do not match the experience. Life is often like that.

Marshall stated earlier that he could not find someone, meaning he could not find a woman that was suitable to him. I find that interesting. It is hard to believe, in fact, because he is such a nice person, and handsome; many women would have been attracted to him. It was the same for Leslie, as gorgeous as she is and as interesting as she is. Of course, she immersed herself in her academics, as she said, but that is not why she did not go out on many dates. I feel, although she never really said so, that she was simply not ready. I suspect it was the same for Marshall. Timing is everything in relationships. When you are ready, you are ready; when you are not, you are not, and either way, one should not pretend.

As everyone who has ever ventured out to build a serious relationship with someone knows, the smallest thing, as well as the largest, can trip you up equally. The very fact one is trying to build a relationship with another is an interesting position in which to find one's self. It is like being on parade, as it were, where you are consciously opening yourself up for inspection, body and soul. My experience with men is that they are not truly interested in you as a person, at least not to any depth, at least not right away. In the beginning, they are far more interested in your body and their interaction with your body. We all understand that. It is not a mystery. Their interest in you as a person comes later, after the sex, or between the acts of sex. He knows you are right for him by the way you smile, cook his meals, fold his laundry, and the way you love him unconditionally despite all his obvious faults. He only knows you are not right for him when you do not smile, you spend too long in the shower, or you giggle too much or too loudly, you do not like hockey, or you like opera. On the other hand, you know he is right for you when he smiles, takes your hand on the path, cuddles with you instead of raping you on the spot, takes out the garbage, and gives you his paycheck. You only know he is not right for you when you discover that he does not smile nearly enough, drinks too much, has poor personal hygiene, and his passion for hockey clearly outstrips his passion for you. …Or he ogles other women… They all do, dear, they cannot help it. It is the nature of the beast so get over it. Ogle other men to get even, even if you do not feel like it. It will get his attention.

So, how rare was Leslie, and how rare was Marshall? Leslie was rare to me because I unconditionally loved her and I do not believe I have accomplished that with too many human beings. Marshall was rare for her because she could already see herself loving him. Leslie was rare for Marshall because, well, he admired her body, yes; but even within that simple conversation they were having onboard the first *The Spray* on that hot July afternoon, he could see himself loving her. So, I suppose I can tell you they were both very rare and special individuals who, by this point in their story, already existed beyond that crowd of one thousand I mentioned above. Of course, the irony is not lost on me that, for me as well as Marshall, that statistically defined person turned out to be Leslie and has only been Leslie for us both for all time. It belies all wisdom as well as folklore, I suppose. However, I still do not believe it makes the argument I made above incorrect. It does suggest, though, there might be exceptions to the rule, which, on reflection, is usually the case so I should not be too surprised. As I get older, I have determined that for some reason, life seems to be more complicated than I had originally imagined. If I knew then what I know now… We grow too soon old and too late smart… and so on.

The Scar

"That scar behind your ear."

Her hand flew up and followed the edge up into her hairline.

"An accident – my father knocked me through a plate-glass window. I wasn't too badly cut up. I went right through. It was when I fell. I sat up and had this big hunk of glass sticking out of my head. I can still hear my mother scream. After that I passed out."

"How old were you?"

"Twelve."

"Why did he knock you?"

"He didn't see me coming. His big arm came around and hit me and I flew through the glass."

"Was he drinking?"

"He was drunk again, but after that he never touched a drop. He has an occasional drop of wine now but it took him years to get back to it. He and Mom have found God too, just like my Grandpa and Grandma. It must be in the blood – but I hope not." She threw her head back and shrugged as if she was talking about the weather. "What about you? Did your parents ever beat you?" She kept her eyes on him and the smile she normally wore was gone.

"No. My father was as gentle as rain, as was my mother. They were perhaps too liberal, too open-minded. They never spanked and never seriously scolded me. If I did something wrong or inappropriate, they tried to explain, very carefully, what was wrong with what I was doing and how I could improve."

"I bet that worked."

"No, not really."

"I bet you were a real brat."

"Pretty much. I was never forced to walk the straight and narrow until I had to."

"Which was when?"

"When they died."

"...So did you take a lot of drugs, screw around, stay out late at night?"

"Nope, none of those things. I just had a mind of my own that's all. My mother always said I have my father's mind and her temperament where my father's side of me is in control."

"What did that mean?"

"It meant I sat around and read books. I was good at sports too – my mother's side – but not team sports. Skiing, skating, swimming... kayaking, canoeing, that's what I like."

"Me too. That's what I like. How about biking?"

"I like biking."

"Hiking?"

"That too."

She smiled and nodded.

"I know you like biking," he said. "I saw you with your friend, the one with the big..."

"Yes, Freya."

"Yes, Freya... If you like, after we're done with *The Spray*, we can go biking."

"Not this weekend!"

"I meant some other weekend."

"...Sure, that would be fine. But I must warn you.... I'm good."

"How good?"

"You won't be able to keep up."

Marshall quietly laughed and shrugged. "We'll see."

"Okay!"

Footnote by Freya Anna Bergman

I positively cannot talk about her scar. It is simply too much for me right now. Later, perhaps, if I can find the courage.

Also, Marshall was, indeed, a gentle man.

Marshall's Education

Marshall climbed to his feet and reached into the cubby for the thermos bag.

"I'm starving!" He handed her the bag. She opened it and pulled out the bag of veggies, half gone. They each helped themselves.

"At this rate, we'll be out of food sometime next week," Marshall offered, his mouth full.

"Don't make fun – I like veggies."

"I can tell."

"You pack a lunch next time then."

"I will."

"What would you pack?"

"Peanut butter and jam sandwiches, enough for both of us."

"That's disgusting."

"A bag of chocolate chip cookies."

"That's ridiculous! Men!"

"Water, of course."

"That's good – what about veggies?"

"No need – there'll be lots left."

She laughed and dropped her head down onto her knees as he sighed and leaned back. She glanced up. "Don't look so content."

"Why not?"

"You should be praying for some wind."

"I am – but I keep my prayers to myself."

She smiled and sat upright, again carefully watching him, her smile lingering. "How about you? Where did you go to school? …And you went to school, I can tell."

"How can you tell?"

"I just can – I won't go into it."

He shrugged. "First Queens, of course, where I studied history; four years there then the University of Toronto where I studied English."

"You didn't speak it? You sound quite fluent to me."

"Ha ha… Modern Literature. And after four years there, almost four more years at the University of Calgary where I majored in Paleontology."

"Oh yes, that's right; you're into dead things."

"Very much so."

"I suppose you collect?"

"I do. I have quite a wide collection."

'You keep it buried, do you?"

"No… on shelves mostly; the very best I mount on my wall."

"It must be something to see."

"I will have to show you someday."

"Hmmm...." She laughed. "Twelve years, that's as long as I went to school."

"Yes it is. I didn't notice until the last few years when it began to drag on me a bit. As it turned out, I didn't finish at Calgary. My parents died and I came home."

"Did your parents pay for all that education?"

"They co-signed my loans but, yes, ultimately, they did. How about you?"

"Only the undergrad; I was on scholarship for the remainder. I'm paying them back for the time at Waterloo – they haven't got much and it is a lot of money to them. Another four years and I will have paid them back. You must have had a number of scholarships."

"Why do you say that?"

She shrugged.

"Appearances can be deceiving," he said and tossed the last of his handful of carrots into his mouth and chewed slowly, watching her.

"Well, what is it?"

"One or two."

Footnote by Freya Anna Bergman

Marshall had full scholarships all along. He was recognized very early as being very clever. I think he did not want it generally known however. Sometimes, I think, his cleverness might even have frightened him a little. It is only a theory but I think it true. I say it because he rarely spoke of his years at school or his literary accomplishments later on in life, or even his position with the theater. My best guess is that none of that was important to him.

Family Love

"When your father beat you, was there any sexual connotation to it?"

"Oh my God, I don't believe you asked me that!"

"You don't have to answer."

She threw her up her hands. "It's alright… It's alright… No. No, there was nothing sexual. He never assaulted me sexually, or so much as ever looking at me in a lewd fashion. That is not my father."

"A good man, then – at least now."

"There were some issues earlier on, yes, but no longer."

"Accepting God into his life solved it for him, I suppose."

"Something like that."

"You've forgiven him then."

"Yes."

"Were they ever in love, your mom and dad?"

"I don't believe this questioning."

"You don't have to answer."

She nodded slowly. "It's hard to tell sometimes. They were very much like my grandparents. I worry about that."

"Why do you worry about that?"

"That my marriage, whenever I get married, to whomever I get married to, if I get married, may end up the same. I wouldn't get married at all if I knew I would end up like they did."

"How did they end up?"

"There's very little laughter in our home. I rarely see them kiss. I know they sleep in separate beds. That's not evidence of a loveless marriage, I know, but I can't help but feel there was no real love between them by the time they were older. That's often the way it seems to be after lifetime of marriage, isn't it?"

"I really don't think so, no."

"I'm just saying, that's all…"

"I'm going to tell you about my parents now."

"Okay…"

"I can tell you there wasn't a lot of necking going at the kitchen table. Still, they slept in the same bed, my father kissed my mother every morning upon rising: he kissed her in the afternoon… he kissed in the evening…" He began to sing, his finger clicking to the beat, following the tune made famous by the McGuire Sisters in their 1958 single hit "*Sugartime*" but changing the lyrics as his father had:

Kisses in the mornin'
Kisses in the evenin'
Kisses at suppertime

Be my little sugar
And love me all the time!

He waited for Leslie to look up. She should have laughed but she had not.

"My father used to sing that, usually on weekends," Marshall continued. "Saturday morning, it drove us crazy but, then again, my mother must have liked it. She always laughed when he sang it, letting him kiss her each time, laughingly squirming away and complaining, but not really complaining, if you know what I mean. Each time he said kisses, he'd plant a few more on her lips."

Leslie found herself blushing. She looked up. "It sounds like they were then," she said, not averting her gaze.

"What?"

"Very much in love."

"What do we know about it? I lived there and I don't know... but I suppose so."

"Take my word for it."

"Sure. Okay...." He shook his head. "I didn't realize you were an expert in such matters."

"I like to think it is one of my many talents." She smiled sadly but then blossomed and she threw her head back and laughed.

Footnote by Freya Anna Bergman

I do not know about you but I would have liked to meet Marshall's parents. His father was a schoolteacher and she was a nurse. The word was that when they died, there were so many attending the funeral that the crowd overflowed St George's. Those who could not get in clustered about the great doors just to listen; no one of importance came, just everyone came. They were well loved, those two. As were Leslie and their son – Leslie's and Marshall's funerals were crowded to overflowing, with family, friends, and almost the entire town attending. I wonder about my own funeral of course, as you, dear reader, no doubt think about your own. None of my friends will attend I am afraid. There is not one alive today; family only then. How about you, dear reader; do you know who, and how many, might attend your funeral? Do you care? I suppose not, you will be dead, after all; not much should bother you at that point. I know I shall not be bothered. They can put this old carcass in the ditch for all I care. No one will care…. I do not really believe that. The truth of it is we are more loved than we think, or often feel.

Evening Approaches

The sun was dropping, heading down along its predicted arc toward the quicksilver of the river and the irregular dark band of the far shore that was Howe Island. Lifting her face to the sun, Leslie could still feel the heat but it was diminishing as the sun dropped, mitigated as it was by the cool scented air drifting in from the forest.

"God, it's gorgeous!"

"It is that."

They listened to the sound of soft lapping water against the hull of *The Spray* as she slowly turned on her anchor. Marshall broke the silence, speaking softly, almost whispering, not lecturing, just speaking, and with wonder.

"The sun is approximately half a degree in diameter. By definition it travels fifteen degrees per hour; you can estimate how long to sunset by counting the number of suns to the horizon, at two minutes per sun."

"I didn't know that."

"Well… there you go then."

"My head hurts." She laughed quietly. "How much longer now?"

"About fifteen minutes."

"We're never getting out of here, are we?"

"No, we're doomed."

"The carrots will run out eventually."

"We'll have to fish for our supper."

"Do you have a fishing rod or tackle?"

"I'm afraid not."

"Okay… Not enough gas… No fishing tackle… A first-aid kit?"

"Okay… For the gas, I'll take a hit on that one… I have a rather extensive and recently updated first-aid kit, but as for fishing tackle, I don't fish. I think fish are under enough environmental strain as it is. More than half the male population within a one hundred-mile radius must fish these waters." He pointed, lifting his arm and dropping it back, too relaxed to make too much of a point of it. "Look at that guy over there. …One of thousands, maybe millions. …Millions and millions of fishermen equipped with hundred thousand-dollar boats, fish-finders, variable depth sonars, grenades, depth charges… sonic torpedoes… all after only a few surviving fish. It doesn't seem fair."

"Do you think we should wave to him? He could maybe tow us for a bit."

"Nope."

"Me either."

Something important was happening and neither wanted to give it up. The sun was setting, that's what it was.

Leslie pointed. "Look at the water. It's almost black, like ink." She raised herself slightly. "But if you look down, it's perfectly clear. What color would you say that is?"

"The color of mercury, burnished silver, and black."

"Ah" She looked up and squinted into the sun. "I count… about ten more suns if it follows that arc as you said. I think it's going to be a gorgeous sunset."

"*Red sky at night, sailor's delight; red sky in morn, sailor's scorn.*"

"I think red; yes, definitely, and no low cloud to hide the sun."

"It looks like we'll have to stay for the night – are you alright with that?

"No."

"Do you want to go home? We could probably figure out something."

"No, I'm okay."

"What then?"

"I want to talk."

"Okay, let's talk; I like to talk."

"I can tell."

"What do you want to talk about?"

"I'm not going to have sex with you so you can get that out of your mind right now," she stated flatly. She waited for him to turn to her. "Are you okay with that?"

"I suppose."

She shook her head, exasperated, more with herself than him. "I'm not frigid or anything but I'm not having sex until I want to. It's not you – I can tell you it's not you. ...It's a pact I made with myself years ago."

"Anything to do with the cross, black robes, white habits?"

"I'm not a nun."

They were each silent a moment, Leslie fidgeting with her fingers, Marshall remaining perfectly still.

"Don't laugh, it's not funny."

"I'm not laughing."

"What are you doing then?"

"I'm sitting here watching you... And I get it, I do. I don't demand sex or expect anything from you that you do not wish to give. I hope you would have seen that in me by now."

"You're a good guy, I can see that, but it doesn't change anything. The simplest way I can say it is that this is my body; it is the only one I have and I don't want to give it away without carefully thinking about it."

"You have a beautiful body." Marshall leaned forward in emphasis. "Do I hear a complaint that I love only your beauty? Have I nothing else then to love in you but that? Do I not see a heart naturally furnish'd with wings?"

"What's that?"

"Keats to Fanny Brawne."

"You're unbelievable..."

"I could wax on and on."

She quickly injected. "Don't bother! I don't want to hear it. It's lies anyway."

"Hey..."

She glanced up and expanded. She pointed to herself, placing a hand on her chest. "I mean, sex without the goal of reproduction is masturbation; and I would extrapolate that to say that sex without love is a type of masturbation."

"You condone masturbation?"

"No!"

"Why not?"

"You're impossible, and you're teasing me!"

"Hmmm … you're complicated."

"I'm complicated?"

"Yep."

"Not just a prude?"

"Well, that, too, I suppose… But that doesn't sound like you."

"What doesn't?"

"Invoking the word masturbation twice in one sentence... It is out of character."

"You don't know my character." She closed her eyes in frustration and made the admission. "It's Freya; that's what Freya says."

"I thought so."

"Oh, God." She opened her eyes. "Look, I won't have sex with someone until I love them. That's the bottom line I'm afraid. If you want us to move forward then that's the way it's got to be."

He nodded slowly. "Kissing okay?"

She rolled her eyes again, but laughed. "If you try anything, I'll scream!" She watched him smile and added, matching his smile, "Well, yes, then." As he made a slow move toward her, she sat back. "But not right now!"

He settled back as well. "I wasn't thinking about right now… But how about later maybe, when the moment's right and we're properly prepared?"

"When is the 'moment right' and what does 'properly prepared' mean?"

"Sunset? I'm talking about sunset."

"Hmm... Okay… We'll see."

They each laughed but their laughter was softly muted.

There was a short interlude of near silence that included only the multi-layered and complex sounds of the evening before Marshall quietly queried, "Second base?"

Leslie threw her head back and laughed. She pushed him back. "Stop!" She fell into a facetious rage, still laughing, turning her face away and talking to the setting sun. "Just stop right there!

I never have conversations like this with anyone! Not even with Freya!"

"Ah, Freya... again."

"Yes, and we never talk about things like this!" She glanced back then turned to him fully and smiled. "Look, I really like you. All I'm asking, what I'm telling you is, we need to take it slow. You and I are not, underline that word _not_, going to have sex tonight!"

"I get it □ we are not going to have sex tonight."

"You don't have to repeat it."

"You don't have to repeat it."

She reached to the side and threw a wet towel at him. He climbed to his feet.

"What are you doing?"

"I'm going to see if there's any fuel in that tank."

She tried to kick him.

He sat and laughed. "You and I are going to get along just fine."

She shook her head and laughed with him. "I doubt it!"

Footnote by Freya Anna Bergman

Sex without love is either an attempt at procreation or no more than mutual masturbation. I did say that, yes, and on more than one occasion. I am not talking about rape here; rape is something else entirely and is not really sex to my mind. It is a monstrous thing to do. I unequivocally believe that a man who rapes a woman or another man should have his manhood removed; a woman who rapes a woman is much rarer but it still happens and as such, the crime must be met with a similar punishment. A woman raping a man is almost unheard of and may not even be reported, or may instead be referred to as seduction; still, given humans are being capable of absolutely anything, I suppose that the brutal rape of a man by a woman can happen, in which case the punishment must once again match the crime. Of course, I am completely unprepared to talk of pedophilia; it is outside the scope of what I am attempting to relate, shall we say, even though I realize, once again, that human beings are completely capable of performing any act that you, dear reader, might be able to imagine. To be complete, I must mention bestiality. There is something to be said for flexibility in a species, I suppose, but, honestly, what is the point of sexual intercourse between species? The genes just got a bit mixed up, I think. If one is to experiment with gene-therapy, eradicating that rather nasty attribute might be a place to start.

On the other hand, and theoretically at least, there is nothing wrong with masturbation; it does have its place… when the spirit cannot withstand the stress the body places on it; 'The spirit is willing but the flesh is weak,' and so on. The younger you are, the more the body rules. That's simply not true, and I'm sorry I said so. We old farts are still slaves to our flesh. Only the direction is different; it is more toward the grave than procreation, I am afraid. Oh, I am completely cynical I know! Even so, I certainly do not masturbate, not that that is a particularly convincing example of what may be right or wrong. It is a matter of opinion, I know. Still, masturbation is, I believe, a narcissistic and ultimately cynical thing to do with one's body. I may be wrong there too. We are a product of our biology, after all: dogs do it, so do apes, and monkeys, and we are related to them.

I am only kidding and I am silly I know. I cannot stop from being completely cynical as well as somewhat ridiculous. My cynicism in these matters might be the result of why I do not prefer men in relationships and prefer women instead, although that could also be biological in nature, or so I am told. We are all trapped I suppose. We cannot help ourselves. You would think we could step above it though. We are after all supposed to be sentient beings ostensibly responsible for our own destinies. I wonder how much of that is true sometimes. We see through eyes that show a world colored by the heart and there is no way around that. We would have to become more like machines to see the world as it really is, and who wants to do that?

Leslie was a complicated person and definitely not a machine or a woman who let will override her heart. Like many women, she was comprised of the many dimensions and twists and turns that make up the whole woman. She was clever, yes; hard working and moral, yes; fun and full of life, yes; absolutely drop-dead gorgeous when she was young, beautiful to mid–age, and dignified and attractive up until she died, yes; but there is always some confusion, isn't there? That is *us*, I am afraid: complicated beings that are difficult, if not impossible, to pin down and explain away. Still, we all try to, don't we? Men certainly have tried to explain the female mind and heart and have largely failed. Women, too, often attempt to explain themselves. Perhaps we should just give up and accept the fact that we are who we are, and tell the rest of the world to get over it.

I cannot stop though. You cannot stop me. I must say more. There is also the rule of the *will*. An idea, a belief, can sometimes override everything but the autonomous responses of the body: mind over matter, mind over body, and so on. The type that have swung completely over to the rule of will, and there are some amongst us, I can assure you I am definitely not one of them. They are much rarer than the other type, who listen more to their hearts. Though it is never cut and dried, I think you would agree there is always a blend, always a middle ground that many walk □ and that was my dear Leslie.

Leslie refused to have sex with someone until she loved whoever it might be, and, equally, felt that he, or she, I like to think, loved her. She demanded love first and then sex, both with and without procreation in mind, I should add; but love first. In that way, she reasoned there would always be a future. We discussed this often enough, each of us trading our various perceptions of the way the world should be and never is. To her, love and life are great mysteries not to be squandered □ or so she concluded for me, pouring the last of the wine out, raising her glass and smiling into it. That is one reason I loved her so much: she was never completely serious about anything; there was always a mollifying reason not to believe in something completely.

Some people are ready for love all of the time, right from puberty, it seems. They should step back and take control over their lives, and take a closer look with eyes not so modulated by the rather confusing colors lent by their hearts. Perhaps they are just impatient, too young and stupid to know that their lives await them. What is there to lose if one should have sex without commitment, without strings attached? One's self. One's body becomes just a *thing*. They will blame others, of course, as their lives fall apart in their later years: fast cars, high-speed boats, penis enlargements…. women, clothing, breast enhancements… It is as if the only thing most of the world is interested in is *getting fucked* ☐ but life is more than just that, I can tell you.

As an aside, the above reference to fornication is not, in my opinion, dropping the f-bomb; I am not breaking any personal limits that I have placed upon myself; it is merely a replacement word for 'copulation' in this sense. Admittedly, I could have said, 'the only thing most of the world is interested in is copulation' but that would not have had the same effect. Some, including my cohort in this adventure, feel I need to be more modern in my approach. People, it seems, demand to be shocked these days. How such a short and very common word can shock one I really do not know. Perhaps it is just his rather uptight attitude toward sex and copulation in general that diverts him from seeing the word for what it really is – a short word with an amazing range of applicability in that it can be simultaneously applied as a noun, a verb, an adverb, and an adjective. Whenever I think of that four-letter word, I think of dogs in the park.

At any rate, forget the dogs. As an old woman who has had one or two lovers come and go, my best advice to those out there who might be seeking advice is that there is absolutely no point in having sex with another unless the two of you are bound by love. In other words, do not screw around unless there is a meaningful relationship that each of you believe will take you forward in time, between the acts of sex, when the sex is over with and done, and toward that end of the day when all you will have is each other. Outwardly prudish, I fear, but practical in the long run ☐ and presumably we are all in it for the long run.

Lastly, Leslie was lucky Marshall found her in the crowd, and visa-versa. Knowing it does and can happen to one fills me with the hope that there may be some mysterious force out there, Cupid's arrow or whatever, that can draw two together, and that love does not have to be so singularly one-dimensional, or such a lucky event in our lives. It is the mystery behind the glimpse, or perhaps the finger of God pointing the way, leaving us only to possess the wit and courage to turn in that direction. What the source is otherwise I do not know: intuition, another feature programmed into our biology, what one happened to consume for breakfast, anything at all really. Whatever it is that can capture two lovers and draw them together, it worked for them; and, I have to say, because I was drawn along with them, it worked for me as well. After all, I have known love, and I love, and, at the end of the day, that is all that matters to me.

Sunset Kiss

The sun was heading down through the cloud bank that hugged the horizon; as it dropped, it slipped through a break in the cloud and ballooned outward, turning the western sky to gold and red, the higher cloud catching the gold, the lower the red. The river reflected the blue sky, the band of cloud, and the red sun. The color was black and silver, blue, and fragments of red on a slowly turning surface.

"Look at that…"

"I'm looking."

"Sunset, finally."

She eyed him. "What do mean you by that?"

"I mean, the sun is the original timepiece; there is no more obvious way to measure time."

"You don't mean that."

"What do I mean then?"

He slipped across to sit next her, turning so he was facing the sun with her. Before she could reply, he said, glancing at her and then turning to her fully, "The sunset is reflected in your sunglasses; the whole panorama from one eye to the next."

She turned so she faced him completely and he gently moved her head so it faced the sun once again.

"Don't move."

"Don't you think it would be better to look at the real sunset instead of the reflection in my glasses?"

"Nope."

She reached up a hand and gently turned his head so he was facing west.

"That's better," she said.

"It is beautiful."

"Yes…"

"You sound stressed. What's the matter?"

"You're going to try to kiss me. I'm freaking out if you really want to know!"

He smiled slowly and settled back. "Let's just watch it set then. When the last of the sun slips below Howe, I'll kiss you then if you'll let me. Just one kiss; I won't get carried away, promise."

She nodded and they watched as the sun slowly kissed Howe Island and then melted into it, placing the ragged shoreline covered with tall pine in silhouette. Jet streams caught by the setting sun turned into strings of silver as the aircraft cruising high above them followed their own arcs.

"That one's going to Paris..." Marshall said, and found another "And that one, London."

Leslie pointed to yet another. The trajectory was south of the other two. "That one's going to Rome." They counted out nine jet trails and each one was assigned a different European city. The sun had long set but high cloud still caught the sun, turning into tenuous filaments and gossamers of gold the slightest wind could blow away.

Marshall turned to face her. "Okay?"

"Okay."

He kissed her, slow and sweet. "There."

"There."

He gently removed her sunglasses and then his own and kissed her again.

She pushed him back gently. "...Okay."

He sat back. "I have seen heaven in a wild flower."

Leslie laughed. "What's that?"

He laughed with her, and shook his head. "It's nothing... Blake."

Footnote by Freya Anna Bergman

God, to be young! What I would not do! Of course, if I had known what they were about at the time, I would have pushed that secret button we all wish we had, and Marshall would have exploded outward into a millions pieces never to be reassembled □ but without hurting Leslie, of course.

The Stars Above

They sat speaking in low tones, talking about nothing, whatever popped into their head, laughing and thinking about what the other had said, with Marshall's arm about Leslie so that she rested in the crook of his arm. They watched the night sky as, from the western sky to above them, it turned from light blue on the horizon to purple and then mauve at their zenith. Behind them, the sky was falling to black and *The Spray's* mast as well as the tall trees on Hickory stood in dark silhouette against a starless sky. The first bright star showed itself in the east where the sky was just turning to purple.

Marshall pointed. "That's Venus."

Leslie shifted her head in the crook of his arm; she didn't have to look up far.

"It is following the sun downward," Marshall explained, unable to stop himself. "You can't really know from looking at it, but from the orientation of its orbit, it is heading toward us. In the next couple of nights, it will seem to accelerate toward the sun then it will disappear. After that, it will only appear just before the sun rises. The sun will be following it and not the other way around."

Leslie smiled and then laughed. "You're a geek – but an interesting geek." She twisted about to look up at him and then settled back in the crook of his arm to face the planet. "I can almost see it hanging there in space between us and the sun," she said. "It doesn't look all that far away."

Marshall reached upward. "I see it that way too…" He went to grasp it. "It seems I can reach up and bring it down and hand it to you." He did so in make-believe and handed Venus to her.

Leslie accepted the planet in her open palm but left her hand open. "Put it back."

Marshall very carefully did so. "It's not right that I should have done that," he said.

"I don't know about that…"

The night settled more deeply. They spoke only a little, and only of little things. Marshall knew the names of all the constellations and many of the stars. He pointed a few out but didn't dwell on them. "Sirius, Arcturus, Vega, right above us."

"And that one?"

"That's Jupiter."

"Ah…"

"And there's my lucky star, Deneb, in the constellation Cygnus."

"Why is it your favorite?"

"As a young boy, I'd lie in the back seat and look through the rear window of our car and make a wish, and that was the star I wished upon. It's a summer star; then again, we were often if not always at the cottage during the summer months. It was natural I should select it since that time of year and at that time of night, when we were taking the ferry back home, it would have been right above our heads. I didn't know that until later. I only figured it out a few years ago."

Leslie shook her head and smiled as she shared his memory.

"What's your favorite star?" Marshall asked.

"I don't really have one. I remember the belt…"

"Orion's belt – it's a wintertime constellation."

"…up in Thunder Bay, the winter stars are so bright they almost hurt the eyes. Not like in the city. And in the summer, there are too many bugs out to spend much time looking upward, so it's the winter stars I know the best I guess. That's why I don't recognize many of these… Funny how that is… There's an explanation for everything; even the most private of things, things you thought belonged to you and you alone."

"Pick a new one tonight then; pick one you can see all year round."

"Which one do you suggest?"

He pointed. "See that … where the handle of the Big Dipper changes? That's Mizar. There are many references to it in ancient writings. The Sumerians used it for navigation. It's a binary star. If your eyes are good enough, you can see the companion."

"…I think I can!

"You okay with that one then?"

"Yes, thank you." She glanced at him and, without warning, kissed him. She settled back quickly.

"Whoa…"

"Don't get any ideas!"

"I'm good, I'm good! That is to say, I'm going to behave myself."

She smiled and lay back more comfortably. "That's good."

Footnote by Freya Anna Bergman

It was typical of Marshall that he should drop into a technical discussion of the stars and planets, constellations, and nebulae while heaven stretched out above him, and, in this case, lying, figuratively speaking that is, in his arms. He was a geek, yes, absolutely; but as Leslie said, a nice geek. Of course, that was nothing. He could invoke similar tidbits of knowledge on almost any subject. He was, indeed, a modern day '*Renaissance Man,*' I suppose. On their honeymoon, he took Leslie to see the Burgess Shale, a favorite haunt of his, to show her the creatures that lurk between the dark shale. They spent not one day but three days of their two- week honeymoon chipping away slabs of slate to find the fossilized remains of trilobites as well as a host of arthropods preserved from the Middle Cambrian, which occurred, as I understand it, about 500 million years ago. He would list them off, one for each finger, carrying onward to use his toes if need be, Marrella, Aysheaia, Canadapis, Dinomischus, Hallucignenia, Nectocaris. Lots of fun, but not something I would expect for my honeymoon: the Rockies, perhaps, yes, and the Banff Spring Hotel, and Jasper, and the Ice Sheets, of course; but not a bunch of dead things ☐ the fact the Burgess Shale *is* a UNESCO World Heritage Site notwithstanding.

For a small demonstration as to the range of his knowledge, Marshall could do something similar with the little nematodes one finds in a pond. In the middle of a hike, he would blunder into a pond up to his knees and withdraw the sample bottles he always carried with him. He would acquire a sample or two, chattering all the while about the snails, spiders, beetles, various larva, skaters, diving beetles, the common tadpole, and guppy-like fish that were swimming about his legs, as he reached back to hand Leslie the filled sample jars; she far too intelligent and careful to get her feet wet. As I said, he was perhaps one of the most intelligent men I have ever met; but on occasion, he could be somewhat of a pain. None of his children took after him, interestingly enough, at least not in that way. Nor have any of his grandchildren shown the same aptitude. The family might consider itself somewhat fortunate in that regard. However, they are all intelligent enough, particularly Geoffrey, and young Hilary, who continues to surprise us all. Dear Leslie, as much as she gained by marrying Marshall, also put up with a lot. I never heard her complain, though, not even once. Unconditional love does that I suppose.

Still, when I look up into the night, when someone is escorting me home and I happen to look up, I immediately pick out Leslie's lucky star. My eyes go right to it and I point it out to whomever I might be with. I challenge them to see the little companion star and most of them can. I am glad to say that, even in my advanced years, I can as well. Of course, I did not remember the name of her lucky star was *Mizar*; my ghost determined that. Also, and if I must give credit where credit is due, it was he who determined what stars they were looking at. That little tale about Venus? That was his as well. I rather liked it so I decided to keep it in. He seemed grateful. I do like him somewhat. I hope he is beginning to realize that. He *really* is getting into this.

Believe in God

Marshall recovered what few emergency blankets and clothing *The Spray* carried; it turned out to be one t-shirt, another long-sleeved high-tech shirt, not quite as clean, a pair of high-tech long pants, two pair of underwear, one sleeping bag good to 40 degree F, and a blanket. He lay them out on the deck of *The Spray* to air them out – they smelled a bit stale. That done, he set out the remaining lifejackets on the forward deck starboard side, and lay the sleeping bag over it.

"This is yours."

"Where are you sleeping?"

"Port side, under the jib. ...I have a blanket but it's a bit rank."

"I don't know; maybe I should just try to sit here all night."

"You'll sleep better if you lie down – it's not a plot."

It was 1 AM in the morning. The stars were full and bannered across the sky above them. Leslie acknowledged her fatigue, opened the sleeping bag, lay down inside it, and zipped it up.

"This doesn't smell so great either."

He gave her another lifejacket, covered by the clean t-shirt as a pillowcase, and helped her place it under her head, making sure she was comfortable as possible. "Okay?"

"That's better."

She lay back, looking up at the stars as he lay on the bare deck on the opposite side of the small cabin with the blanket and jib to cover him and a lifejacket for a pillow. He too lay looking up at the stars, although she could not see him; the cabin was in the way.

"Here's an inevitable question," she heard him say.

"Why is it inevitable?"

"All questions are inevitable."

She laughed quietly, feeling sleep coming. "What is it, then?"

"Do you believe in God?"

"…Yes. …You?"

"Not some old guy looking down on us… Not even listening to our prayers… but something."

"I know what you mean."

There was a period of silence between them, accompanied by the soft lapping of water against the hull of *The Spray* as it swung about on its anchor. They were each watching the dark shoreline drift by against the backdrop of stars, but each from a different perspective.

"…What about aliens?" Marshall asked, the sound of his voice indicating sleep was near.

Leslie's eyes flew open. "I don't know about that!" She sat up to find him in the dark but could just see the outline of him.

"Statistically speaking," Marshall continued, a little more alert, "there has to be alien life on one or more, and possibly a lot, of those stars. There can't be too many intelligent ones close by, though."

"Why's that?"

"We would have heard from them by now."

She lay back down and settled herself. "I'm not arguing with you; I'm too tired."

There was a long silence as before.

"It's a mystery," Marshall said finally.

"…Yep."

"The whole thing."

"Yes."

"Leslie?"

She looked over, lifting her head off her pillow. She could see his dark outline against the sky. He was sitting upright, looking toward her.

"What?"

"I can see your face in the starlight. I can see it as clear as day."

Footnote by Freya Anna Bergman

There may be no God but there are certainly no aliens, unless you include those characters I met in Los Angeles two years ago when I was with Geoffrey. Still, as one looks up into the night sky, one cannot help but think who we are, our place in the heavens, God, and so on. We are the stuff of stars I know is true; Marshall told me Carl Sagan said that first, but I also *feel* it is true as well. Every time I look up, and I do every time I am out and the stars are bright, I feel the universe spinning about me. I cannot help but feel that. More should look up into the heavens, I think; it tends to put one in one's place.

Sunday, July 15th, 2012

Preface by Freya Anna Bergman

Leslie had swallowed the proverbial pill at this point in our history but I am sure that is not what she told herself. She would have given warning to her heart, telling it to take its time and let the moment pass; after all, the next moment may reveal more for her heart to digest. Of course, even now, I can recall the green finger of jealously licking at my heart. It still does on occasion, I am ashamed to say. If I had known the details of their day, if I had known how they slipped so comfortably into one another's presence, laughed so easily together, kissed as the sun set and slept soundly side by side, I would have perfectly died. Of course, my dreams and imagination played out with much more intensity than what turned out to be reality. I had them having sex on the quarterdeck with the setting sun's glory all about them; not that there is a quarterdeck on a small boat like *The Spray* but I did not know that, did I? Up to that point, I had not seen *The Spray* or knew anything about her, other than the fact it was a boat. My imagination was taking poetic license with whatever it could conjure up from the depths of my tortured soul I suppose. My Tortured Soul …I do go on, I know. It is embarrassing, really; I have never really felt *tortured* before – beaten up, yes, but tortured, no.

Still, one can do, think, and even believe unexpected and often inexcusable things when the heart is under pressure, tortured soul or not. It is always the heart, though, isn't it? A crime committed against another is rarely an act of calm consideration. It is true when they say we are all ruled by passion and that only a very thin slice of us are creatures of reason. Because I had neither the courage nor the self-control to do so, I could not stop my imagination nor the deviousness of my mind from setting its own course until the turmoil within me was stilled, and that did not happen until I was caught red-handed. The fact is I sent both Leslie and Marshall a series of emails that disguised the owner and attempted to manipulate the recipient. Even now I cringe as I think back on it. There is no possible excuse for my behavior. My only defense, and it is not really a defense at all, is that, for those few days at least, I was under the influence of that great puppeteer called jealousy, whose strings can jerk even the most gallant of us about. Leslie told me later that she read the emails and deleted them instantly, thinking it was over between her and Marshall even before anything really had begun. I am sure she read them first, sat back from her computer in shock, and read them again as the blood drained from her face and her heart twisted within her. She probably stood and walked about the apartment, back and forth, her hands up in her hair then falling to her sides, frowning, puzzled, too upset yet to be angry, as she went over in her mind what she had read. In mid-stride, the anger taking over, she'd return to the computer and delete them. Of course, she knew they would safe in the *Trash* folder and accessible later on if she so desired. It was shocking, really, that a man would so casually dismiss her with just an email. He could have simply not called her again, or not answered her emails; she would have gotten the message eventually. 'Wait until Freya hears about this,' she'd think, preparing what she would say in her mind and then imagining telling me, expecting I would help her crucify him, and I would have, I definitely would have.

Leslie didn't know about the server; I had to go back in and delete the originals from the server later on after I had recovered somewhat, but still not so ashamed of myself that I stopped the deceit. It is one thing to listen in on a conversation but it is quite another to pretend you are someone else. The only thing that saved the situation, I suppose, is that I sent it too late, or too early, depending on one's perspective. I sent it after she had talked to him on the phone, perhaps not thinking she would call him so soon after returning. In addition, I didn't know at the time they had slept over; I thought she had been back since Saturday night. Mostly, though, I underestimated Marshall.

Desperate Times

Leslie arrived at her apartment just before 4 PM the next day, Sunday. She dragged herself the last few feet and collapsed onto her bed where she instantly fell asleep. A stiff neck awoke her. She glanced at the clock by her bedside: she had been asleep for four hours. She propped herself up and looked out the window. She had not thought to draw the blinds before falling into bed. The shadows were long and it was dark between the trees. She groaned, dragged herself off the bed, closed the blinds, and stumbled to the shower. She stayed under the cool flow longer than usual, luxuriating in the soothing spray, and then she dried herself off, went into her room, and stopped once again before the mirror. Despite the liberal use of suntan lotion, her skin was flaming red wherever the sun had touched it: her face, her arms, her legs. The red encompassed an area of milk-white that showed a perfect outline of her shorts and shirt. A curve of red swept down between her breasts but the breasts themselves were untouched, the unblemished skin carrying on downward across her stomach, hips, and pelvic area to the line where her shorts ended. She looked ridiculous, she thought. The worse was her face: it carried a violent streak across her nose and cheeks and there was a solid line across her forehead where her hat had been. By far, though, the very worst was a patch of white about her eyes that made it appear as if she had been wearing a mask. God… Her sunglasses… She looked like a raccoon.

She carefully lathered her body in lotion and dressed lightly in cotton: a single piece, one of her favorites with a cluster of roses about the open neck. It made her feel good to wear it. She pulled it over her head and let it fall easily over shoulders, down her back, lightly over her breasts, grazing her hips and settling against her legs, airy and light. She sat in her living room by the open window, pulling her legs up beneath her before settling into the comfortable chair and sighing. A cool breeze filtered in. It felt delicious against her burnt skin.

She climbed up, poured herself a glass of water from the fridge, drank half the glass then, without thinking, picked up the phone and dialed from memory. The last thing they had done was exchange phone numbers.

Marshall answered on the second ring. She didn't wait for him to speak. "Hi, it's me."

"Leslie... Good to hear your voice. I've missed it."

"Missed me?" she stumbled, not hearing him correctly. "I saw you only four hours ago."

"No, I missed your voice."

"Oh."

"...Why are you calling?"

"I'm calling because..." She couldn't think why she was calling and she faltered, feeling the heat of embarrassment rush up into her face. "...I just wanted to say what a wonderful time I had. ... I really did." She almost hung up in embarrassment. She had caught herself completely off guard. She should have thought about she wanted to say before calling, now she sounded like an idiot. Sweat began to form on her forehead and a small trickle formed along her back.

"I did too."

"Oh, okay..."

"We'll have to do it again someday."

"I don't want to go sailing... I mean, I do... again... sometime; not just next weekend."

"Okay, I understand: bike then?"

"No, I can't... I'm busy... I have this paper to write and I have to get it done." Before he could say, 'Well, why did you call then?' she quickly injected, "But I was thinking maybe you could come over here afterward on Saturday. I could make you... dinner. Yes, dinner. Dinner would be good. I could put something together."

She felt him smile at the far end of the line.

"That sounds great. I'd like that. I'll starve myself in preparation."

"Okay... You would have to catch the last boat home."

He quietly laughed. She could barely hear his laughter but it was there. "I get your drift," he said; she could hear his smile then too. "But you do realize the last boat leaves at 2 AM?" he added.

"No, that's no good... I mean, that's too late. Is there an earlier boat?"

He laughed outright. She had seen him laughing the same way on the boat. He was not laughing at her. "How about the 11:20PM?" he suggested.

"I guess that's okay…"

"What time should I arrive and what can I bring?"

"How about just after six?"

"I'm sure there's a boat for that – and what can I bring?"

"Nothing – maybe some wine if you drink it."

"Oh I drink wine."

"Me too."

"Red or white?"

"It doesn't matter."

"I'll bring a bottle of both."

"I'll only have a glass or two. You can drink the rest if you want – as long as you're on that boat I don't mind."

He laughed again. "I don't drink that much!"

"Only one bottle then."

"Red then; it will be dry and something from Ontario."

"That would be fine."

She felt incredibly stupid. Her hand was grasping the receiver so hard she imagined she might break it. "That sounds perfect," she said and hung up, pressing the button and holding it down, not waiting for him to respond further, imagining as she did so Marshall holding the receiver at arm's length and peering at it, wondering where she went.

She tapped her forehead with the receiver and slowly placed it the cradle. She threw her arms up and let them fall to her side. "Now look what you've done!" She inwardly cringed but then laughed and began to pace about the room, replaying their brief conversation over and over in her mind until she realized how ridiculous she was and forced herself to sit down. It took her a few moments to calm down but she did. She finally sidled up to her laptop and opened one of the papers she needed to review for the next day. It was difficult for her to concentrate but she managed to get through it.

At about the same time as Leslie was settling in for the evening and getting her clothes and books ready for work the next day, Freya was sitting at her computer, composing and recomposing a series of emails targeting first Leslie then Marshall. She did not intend to send them but there they were nonetheless on her computer screen, side by side. A simple click of her mouse would send them zinging through the ether like an arrow launched at close range or a sniper's bullet fired from the high ground. She had complete access to Leslie's account and had temporarily modified her own to use the same fonts and style as Marshall had in his earlier emails. It was very clever, really, and she liked the cleverness of it. It was an act of desperation, she knew. She would never think of doing such a thing if she was not desperate.

She realized she had no idea what exactly had transpired between them but she did know Leslie, and she knew her friend would be cautious. It was logical then that this rather insipid backhanded approach of hers might actually work in that it just might turn an undecided mind in the desired direction. Leslie would never know from whom it truly came; but if there were any suspicions at all, Freya would only have to deny it. Leslie, of course, would believe anything she said. Freya would not have to lie like that, though; it was all so perfect.

While composing Marshall's email, she tried to recall how he spoke, his selection of words, the cadence. She knew something of his personality – his cleverness and his inherent ability to turn a phrase. Leslie had told her what little she knew about him on the phone the other day after they had finally made contact. Freya had remained silent as she went on and on, every word hurting, causing Freya to worry all that much more and ultimately prompting her to do what she was about to. She knew she could not be too specific; after all, she had no idea what, exactly, had been exchanged between them after a full day of sailing together. She knew she didn't have it perfect but it would have to do.

> *Leslie,*
> *I thought I'd head things off with an email rather than call you. You know how much I hate calling on the phone. It is hard for me. The fact is I like you a lot – you are wonderful and beautiful - but we are, sadly, just too different. What can I say? A glimpse on a ferry, a pleasant conversation over a coffee, and a fun day in the sun does not guarantee a future □ just a friendship, perhaps. It is my fault. I admit it. Even so, I don't really see a point in carrying on since the type of relationship I'm looking for is just not*

possible with us. Maybe I'll see you and your friend on the ferry again someday.

> *It was a good day sailing and I had fun.*
> *Marshall.*

After Leslie's was gone, Freya then sent a similar email to Marshall, knowing her friend's tone and sentiment much better:

> *Marshall,*
> *I want to say what a great time I had sailing with you this past weekend and what a nice guy you are. But after thinking about it at length, I'm not quite ready for a relationship with anyone. I'm not picking on you, and I hope you realize that. Right now, though, I feel strongly that I need to concentrate on my career. It has been a long path to where I am now, and the position I'm in was hard won and I do not want to be diverted from it. I hope you understand. Maybe with any luck I'll see you on the ferry someday and you'll be with someone else. I hope so anyway.*
> *Leslie*

As it turned out, Leslie did not see her email until later the next evening, and Marshall did not see his until late Thursday morning, almost four days later. He was never one for checking on emails.

Footnote by Freya Anna Bergman

I am not proud of it. It was wrong of me.

SEASONS' LIBRARY

July 16th through 19th, 2012

Preface by Freya Anna Bergman

There is nothing more beyond the sins of manipulation and deceit that I have not already admitted to. It reminds me of a scene from Hamlet where Marshall of course is Hamlet and I am Guildenstern. Hamlet asks Guildenstern, referring to a musical instrument like a flute he carries in his hand, "Will you play this pipe?" and Guildenstern answers he cannot. Hamlet rejoins with something like, "Why, look you now, how unworthy a thing you make of me! You would play upon me... Do you think I am any easier to play?" I am haunted by that. I love Hamlet. I often quote him. I quote him almost as much as Marshall does in fact. Well, not quite. In the end, though, how am I, Freya Bergman, any different from Guildenstern, that well-meaning gentleman? I cannot play. What made me think I could?

I recognize, too, that I have sinned greater than Guildenstern, not that Guildenstern sinned at all; he was just caught out, I would say. But I have sinned. I played with two hearts, while true to form there is not a musical bone in my body. Even so, I am often swept up by music, and sometimes tears well upward as the music swells. I only mention that because I do not want you to think I do not feel anything or know anything about how Leslie and Marshall felt after fate intervened and they discovered the truth of what I had done. If our lives are complex instruments that resonate with music then although I may not be able to play, I can still hear and be swept away, just like you, I suspect. I hope you can agree that, while I am an admitted sinner, I am also redeemable.

Intervention of Fate

The next four days were intermediate days perhaps, but one cannot say that nothing happened in those very important in-between days; after all, all throughout that time, hearts were broken, built back up, and fortified.

Monday began well enough. It was a good day. The day had a particular color to it and a brightness, accompanied by a musical score, that had not been present the week before. Leslie moved through it with a light heart but when she read the first of Freya's emails late Monday evening, she read it first with shock, then disbelief, and finally anger. She had, of course, no doubt that it came from Marshall; but why would he agree to come to dinner and then send that, she asked herself. It made no sense. It was not like him; although, she had to remind herself, she did not know him at all really. Her instincts suggested something was not right so she decided not to reply right away, and instead stewed about it. It began to eat her from within. Never one with high confidence but still faced with the raw evidence, she eventually began to believe the contents and assumed she was simply not attractive enough for him; why else would he 'throw me away like that?' She was physically too large – not that she towered over him or could wrestle him to the ground, but she had none of that feminine delicacy that men seemed so attracted to. She ran over the events of the day on *The Spray* in her mind again and again. She did not know how he could pretend such familiarity and such closeness so easily and so casually, and grew angry thinking about it. She had imagined he was growing to like her, and like her a lot. It had been a mirage then; a delusion of her making. It just goes to show that what you think is being said, or what you might think is being felt, is nothing like what it really is. God, he was a *sonofabitch* to mislead her like that and to smile and smile and mean something else. She anguished about the possibility it might be because she had not put out, but he had seemed to accept that condition readily enough. Perhaps by that time he was not all that physically attracted to her so it had not mattered. God, she was a fool, then, to have let herself feel what she had. "Never again then; never again!" she told herself. What she felt was really not all that much different from anyone who has ever been rejected by another, not for something they might have done but simply because of *who* they are or what they *look* like. It is not fair, it is not right, but it happens all the time.

She did not sleep well Monday night. She tossed and turned, and got up at 3 AM to sit in her living room to stare out at the lights along the path leading into the park, her mind empty and tired and her heart twisting inward. She went back to bed, finally, got up late from a dreamless sleep, and had to rush to get to class. It was a class of graduate students, there for the summer, and they didn't like to wait. They'd give her five minutes and then they'd go.

All day Tuesday Leslie walked about as if in trance. Her heart ached but she would not allow herself to dwell on it. She threw herself into her research and into her classes but at odd times of the day, the feeling would rise up unannounced and it would instantly stop her from what she might be thinking or saying. She would steel herself, it would sink back down, and she would hold it there. It was agony. On Tuesday night, she cried for the first time. She was preparing her evening meal, chopping the vegetables when it struck her. It was sudden and unexpected. Catching herself, she angrily brushed the tears away and continued to chop until she could go on no longer and slammed the knife down. She walked out and down the street to the University Quad where she mixed with the summer students. She sat on a bench and watched them cross back and forth to and from the medical residence until she calmed. As night fell, and the student traffic lessened, she returned home, gathered up the half-chopped vegetables and stored them in the refrigerator for the next day. Just before going to bed, she replied to his email.

I don't know why you agreed to come to dinner then. That was not right.
Leslie.

She sent it flying off with a click of the mouse and went immediately to bed. She slept better that night in that she did not get up but she tossed and turned nonetheless, unable to get Marshall and their day and night on *The Spray* out of her mind. The conversations they'd had, the images of the silver river, and sun heading toward the horizon, playing itself over and over in her half-asleep and half-awake state like a broken record.

Freya had managed the account so that it was offline and, unknown to Leslie that night, her response remained undelivered.

Instead, Freya, surprised that they had arranged to meet for dinner, composed what she imagined might be an appropriate reply from Marshall and sent it Leslie.

It was very wrong of me, I know. Again, I apologize.

She had him not sign it; it would give Leslie a sure sign that things were over.

Leslie read it the next morning and immediately composed her response, her fingers flashing over the keyboard in anger.

You're a sonofabitch!

But she didn't send it. Because it wasn't sent, Freya never saw it; if she had, it may have given her more confidence and perhaps lessened the torture she suffered inwardly. Leslie deleted it after letting it sit up on her screen for a half a day on the Wednesday. She wouldn't stoop like that, she decided, and felt herself shrink inwardly as it disappeared into *Trash*. She felt like crying but she wanted to scream.

Wednesday was a repeat of Tuesday with the exception that after school, she rode her bike over the LaSalle Causeway up the hill leading the fort and about Fort Henry and back, all the while lying flat along the length of her bike and pushing the speed up as fast as her strength could endure. She returned home exhausted, managed to finish chopping the vegetables, watched some TV, and went to bed, sleeping soundly for the first time since Sunday afternoon.

On Thursday morning, Marshall finally read his email. Reading it, he immediately composed a response. He was more direct.

Please, please, please, Leslie, give us a chance! What could change your mind so quickly? There's lots of room for your career. Please rethink it. Keep Saturday. I'll be starving by then. :>)
Yours,
Marshall.

Freya intercepted it just before noon. She knew Leslie would be at a faculty meeting, always held on Thursdays at noon, so she would not have seen it. Freya felt lucky and immediately deleted it.

Leslie was stiff from overextending herself on the bike the day before but Thursday seemed easier. By this time next week, she would be completely cured, she hoped; it would be as if it had never happened. Classes and her reading went by quickly. In the evening, she returned home to find a bundle of flowers leaning against her door. She put her pack aside and gathered them up. The assortment was not one a florist would typically arrange. There were yellow and white lily's mixed with pink peonies and blue iris's as well as clusters of black-eyed Susan's, all fresh, all very beautiful. It was bundled in a white plastic grocery bag with the stems wrapped in a water-soaked paper towel and again in plastic and tied off with an elastic band. There was a card. She hastily opened it and read:

Dear Leslie,
These were overflowing my garden and needed to be trimmed, but rather than put them in a vase and stare at them myself, I thought you might like them. I hope you like flowers. You never said.
Always,
Marshall.

PS:
I know Saturday is off but I hope we can start again. Call me, please. There's lots of room for your career.
M.

She called him ten seconds later. There was no answer. She put the phone down and stared at it. She put her hands through her hair and continued to stare at it. Thirty seconds later, it rang. The call display said it was M. Davenport. She snatched up the receiver.

"Hello?"

"Hi, it's me."

"Hi."

"I saw you called. You found the flowers?"

"I did."

"...Okay."

"They're beautiful, thank you."

"That's good... I keep the gardens up. They were my mother's. You should see them some day."

"They are beautiful..."

"What's going on, Leslie?"

"I was going to ask you the same."

"What do mean by that?"

"Your email."

"My email? What about your email?"

"You're the one who broke it off □ not that there was anything to break off. We're just friends... We just met..." Leslie walked over to her computer and flipped it open. She selected Freya's email and brought it up. She read from it, "The one you said there was no point in carrying on... I'm looking right at it. It was time-stamped Sunday night 10PM."

"What?"

"The one you said there was no point in carrying on... I'm looking right at it, time-stamped Sunday July 15th, 2012 at 10:11PM. It's from you."

"... I know nothing of it. But I know of yours..." He read it back to her but from memory. "I didn't see it until this morning. I should check more often."

Leslie gripped the receiver. As he quoted back the email she had not sent, she pressed the receiver against her face and squeezed her eyes shut. Her mind was spinning. "I don't believe this," she said finally, her voice breaking.

"Nor I."

"We need to talk."

"Okay."

"Face to face."

"You tell me when and where and I'll be there."

To say Leslie was upset would be a complete understatement.

Footnote by Freya Anna Bergman

Thank God Marshall sent the flowers.

Friday, July 20th, 2012

Preface by Freya Anna Bergman

It took a while for them to determine I'd sent the emails. Leslie thought at first it might have been one of her graduate students; but on second thought, none of them knew enough about her private life to have sabotaged it so successfully, or I should say so *pointedly*. She forwarded a copy of her email from Marshall to one of the faculty members in the Computer Engineering School at Queens, and he quickly identified that the originating IP address was from the Toronto area. Leslie only knew one person from there and, of course, that was me. She did not call me right away. She atypically stewed about it. She tried to rationalize it, I suppose. Was it a joke in rather poor taste? Had I been drinking? Why would I want to see the end of a relationship that really was not yet a relationship at all, just the promise of one? She knew I could not read her mind, or her heart in this matter, but she also knew she had told me enough of how she felt that perhaps I could piece things together, and then perhaps expect the worst, if beginning a relationship with someone new was the worst. It did not make sense to her, I am certain. It haunts me even now how Leslie must have anguished and it is amazing to me even to this day how she quickly forgave me once the truth was out. I am not certain I would have been so magnanimous if the situation was reversed. I like to think I would have been.

There is another thing about which I should be completely clear. I did have other relationships with other women after Leslie. I forced myself to. Forcing one's self into a relationship never really works out, at least not in my experience. I should have known better. I barely recall their names now. They were all my age, or younger, and generally proud of their status as lesbians. Not that I was not. I was just not so obvious or public about it, I suppose. It was all a sham for me, really. We participated in our mutual masturbation and pretended we were in love but it was no such thing. Months later, I found myself once again by myself, in

love with Leslie and wanting no other. To love only one person...
It is a shock, really; one does not really expect or even believe it.
As I have said before, common wisdom has it you fall in love, you
fall out of love, and you fall back in love again. Not for me,
apparently. I have only ever had one love in my life, and I am glad
of it. It took a while to learn that, years, in fact. It was as if the
passion within me had to drain away first. After that, it became
easier for me not to confuse passion for love I suppose.

Alisa, yes, Alisa... small, dark, petite... double-jointed...
Gorgeous, beautiful, fun, full of life... not particularly bright
though. God knows what Marshall thought about her. He never
said. I remember now – her full name was *Alisa Elizabeth ... Craig*,
or something like that. A nice Italian girl, she was... Marshall's
joke... She was the only one I ever introduced her to Leslie and
Marshall. Now that I think about it, we had dinner together, the
four of us, Leslie, Marshall, Alisa, and I, and it went well. There
were lots of laughs. Leslie, of course, said she was lovely, which, of
course, she was. Alisa and I drove up and stayed in the Holiday
Inn near the ferry terminal and we had dinner at Chez Piggy's. I
had roast duck with an exquisite orange sauce, if I recall. It was
delicious. Oh yes, now I remember; Marshall did have something
to say about her after all. He and I found ourselves sitting alone
for a few moments. Leslie and Alisa had headed off to the Ladies.
I had already gone, and I could not help it as I leaned forward and
asked him what he thought. He said something to the effect,
"Alisa should speak more with an indoor voice while indoors,"
before sitting back in his chair and smiling as he does. I choked on
my wine. I thought it hilarious as well as perfectly true. I told him
as much and we both laughed. By the time Alisa and Leslie
returned, I had dried my eyes and wiped up the spilled wine and,
of course, did not mention it, nor did Marshall.

Four months after that little showcase event, Alisa and I
had a row and that was that. I called Leslie and told her all about it
and I am sure she told Marshall. Our demise had something to do
with vacation time, if I recall, when and where we should go, who
with, and so on. It was stupid, and possibly just an excuse to make
the point we were not really made for one another. Anyway, she
left in a huff of tears, saying something about Leslie and me, and I
never heard from her again. It was just as well; it never would have

worked. She did speak rather loudly under all conditions and wherever she might be. I did find it jarring and annoying. She was not the last of my flings, but pretty close. After that, there was only Leslie and Leslie only. Of course, I had to share her with Marshall but that was not so bad as it turned out.

Meeting at Ferry Dock

Marshall agreed to meet with Leslie the following evening at 7PM at the ferry dock, Kingston side. Leslie decided at the last moment to ride her bike and was waiting for the 6:30 PM boat. There was no sense in having Marshall waiting by the jetty until 7.00, she reasoned. Besides, her mind was in turmoil and she couldn't sit about any longer. She had been sitting about all day.

He was up on the upper deck, scanning the crowd as the boat came in. He saw her right away and waved. She waved back and watched him slide down the ladder and jump to the gate, waiting for it to drop. When it was down, he was the first across, his long strides bringing him right to her. He reached out a hand as he approached and she took it.

"Good to see you," he said, not letting go right away.

"Good to see you too."

She released his hand and took an unconscious step backward, which he noticed right away. She knew what she wanted to say but even thinking about it all day, rehearsing one approach after another in her mind, she could not start.

"Listen...," Marshall began.

"No, I want to start..."

When she did not, he again reached for her hand, taking it in his. She let him hold it. She looked up but found she could not meet his frank gaze.

He offered, "Shall I say some weird shit's been going on here and maybe we should talk about it?"

Leslie finally smiled. "I suppose you could say that;" but her smile quickly disappeared as she shrugged and spilled out what was foremost in her mind. "I just want to say that I'm sorry. It's my fault."

"How is it your fault?"

"I know who sent the emails."

"Who?"

"My friend Freya."

"Do you know why?"

"I'm not sure… It's not like her."

"Jealous, maybe?"

She glanced back at him. "Maybe."

Marshall could clearly see the turmoil within her. "Have you talked to her?

"I called her… no answer. I'm going down tomorrow. We'll have to cancel our dinner."

"That's okay… But not forever, though, right?"

"No, not forever; when I get back, I'll call you – no emails next time."

Marshall smiled, wanting her to see his smile, and when she would not look at him, he gently touched her arm and she looked up. "That's better."

"What's better?"

"You're looking at me."

Leslie smiled, closed her eyes, and shook her head then opened her eyes and widened her smile. She threw her hands up in exasperation and laughed lightly. "I can't tell you what I feel, how this really bothers me," she explained, her laughter and her smile quickly disappearing.

"I can see it in you. I understand."

"How can you understand? You know nothing."

"I don't need to know anything about you and your friend. It's enough to know you will be coming back, and one day soon we're going to have dinner."

"What about after that?"

"Who knows? Early days yet."

She nodded. "I know."

"But…"

"But?"

"I've got a good feeling about this one," he said, and he laughed, as did Leslie, finally released.

"How many have you stacked up there?" she asked, smiling still, feeling her eyes fill, quickly turning her face to the side and wiping them clear.

"A gentleman doesn't say... but I'll let you in on this one...
There's only one so far."

Leslie's smile widened and she could not help but laugh
aloud. She turned away and then quickly back to him with the half
smile she wanted him to see. "Okay..."

He laughed and lifted her chin and kissed her briefly on
her lips before running back onto the ferry to catch the return trip.
The ferry had been waiting for him, she noticed. The crew
manning the gate was standing on the deck with their hands on
their hips, while the captain and the mate were up on the flying
bridge, leaning against the rail, looking down at them. She waved
up at them and the captain and the mate quickly returned to the
bridge. Moments later, the gate lifted back into position, the sound
of the engine picked up, and water churned and frothed at the foot
of the jetty as the ferry backed out, heading back again to the
Island.

Saturday, July 21st, 2012

Preface by Freya Anna Bergman

Leslie did call that Thursday night and later again Friday and again in the afternoon. I ignored them all. I knew what she wanted and I knew I had been caught. You can only imagine what I might have felt: the guilt, the shame, the horror. I imagined, and felt, it all. While she was talking with Marshall by the ferry dock, I was scrambling to think of some excuse, my heart, my head, and even my body in complete turmoil. The body follows the mind, it always does. Some might be able to hide that fact but I am not one.

She called me again while still on the jetty. I could hear the ferry pulling away. I confessed everything right away. I just blurted it out, crying all the while, I think. God, I was a wreck. It was as if I was drowning. Yes, it was exactly as if I was drowning. When I was a child, my mother made me take swimming lessons. I was an overconfident eight-year-old and I was in the deep end. Some of the older children decided to cannonball me, one after the other. To them it was a game but I did not think so. Several hit me and I found myself on the blue-tiled bottom, the shimmering and broken surface filled with swimsuit-clad torsos and kicking legs. I kicked up and off, but was hit yet again; a foot was planted on my shoulder and I was pushed downward as the owner went for the surface. All the air from my lungs suddenly burst outward, and suddenly, beyond panic, the world about me became very quiet. I began to drift, the pool and the shimmering surface above becoming very bright but as seen through a narrow tube. It is not something one forgets. Someone, one of my friends, a giggly girl with blonde curls, Rebecca, I think, even suggested I might have been dead for a short while but I do not think so. I would know if I had been dead. Someone pulled me up, one of the instructors, I think. He tossed me rudely on the tiled deck, face down. I recall brown tiles, small, half-inch square, one chipped. I threw up, pool water mostly. It was gross, I remember, because there was some of my breakfast mixed up in it. I had had kippers for breakfast, which made it particularly nasty. Kippers second time up one does not forget, no matter how long one might live.

What I know now is that that sense of drowning was exactly what I felt as I waited for Leslie to come down from Kingston and walk through my door to save me. It felt just like that. Mostly, I remember from the experience of nearly drowning the luxury of breathing; I will never forget that. Breathing again after thinking you never might was how I felt after Leslie forgave me and kissed me the way she does now, holding my face in her hands and kissing my cheeks and eyes in turn and always in the same order: my left cheek, my right, my eyes, left and right. The first time she did that was that very night when I could not explain nor stop the tears. After that, I told her everything. After that, I was more or less out of the closet, one might say, and I was glad of it too. There is nothing like holding back one's true self. It is like constantly lying. The truth shall set you free, it is said, and so it does. It was not Christ who set me free, though; it was the only one who could, Leslie. I weep still with the memory of it, and the sadness and the relief.

Showdown

Freya watched Leslie park her new Subaru on the street below beneath a streetlight that dropped a ring of blue-white light against the concrete curb and asphalt, casting into stark relief a lone maple with its plastic bag-wrapped trunk. She watched her friend climb out, reach back in and grab her knapsack, shut the car door, carefully and consciously press the key to lock, shoulder her bag, and walk the short distance across the parking lot to the front door of the complex. On the way across, she glanced up to find her window and, finding it, quickly looked away and stepped out more quickly.

Freya let the blinds fall back into place. She walked across to the hallway and stood before the intercom. It buzzed. Her voice: "Hi, it's me." "Okay…" She immediately hit the button, allowing Leslie into the building then returned to the living room and sat. Unable to remain sitting, she stood and again began to pace the room, wringing her hands, wrapping her arms about herself as if she might be cold, returning to sit, and up again. Her friend would be on the elevator, tenth floor, the door would be opening, she'd turn into the hall, all the way down on the soft carpet to the very last unit. Freya moved to the door and placed her hand on the handle. There was a soft knock and she opened it. Leslie's hand was raised to knock again. Freya stepped back to let her in. "Hi…" "Hi…" Leslie did something unexpected. She dropped her bag, and wrapped her arms about Freya and hugged her, pulling her inward and holding her. Freya pushed back and turned away, her hands up over her mouth, keeping her back to Leslie, stumbling into the room. Leslie followed her in. She removed her light coat, set it over the edge of the chair, and followed her in.

"You sent those emails," she said.

Freya did not turn back or answer.

Leslie sat on the edge of the chair and faced her. "Why?"

Freya still could not answer or turn to look at her friend.

Leslie prompted her again. "Freya, you know I love you. You are my best friend. Why did you do it?"

Freya still would not answer. She remained turned so that Leslie would not see the tears that poured out of her eyes and, by this time, coursed down her cheeks. Leslie saw a slender body that was rigidly still.

"…It's all right now. There was no damage done," Leslie offered.

Freya's first words, "I can see it's okay."

"…I had some bad days though."

"I'm sorry."

Freya used the tissue she had in her pocket to blow her nose, and then the cuffs of her blouse to wipe her tears, and then finally turned to face Leslie. "I can see it's okay," she repeated, staring at her friend, her face empty.

Leslie climbed to her feet and stepped toward her. "You asked me to come and I am here. You owe me an explanation."

"I have no good excuse, I'm afraid; I'm just stupid."

"We know you're not stupid, don't we?"

Freya nodded and again turned away. She walked over to the window and pushed aside the blinds. She looked outward but instead focused on her own reflection. Her hair pulled severely back, her eyes sunken and wet; and then behind her, the lights in her apartment, and then Leslie, her face creased into a frown and deeply shadowed.

"What are you looking at? Are you expecting someone?"

"No…" She turned back. "There's nothing out there. No one's coming; all are mustered and accounted for." She returned and sat at the far edge of her couch, settling back in the cushions. Leslie returned to the chair and sat facing her.

"What's going on, Freya?"

"I love you."

Leslie was momentarily taken aback. "I love you too."

Freya looked at her directly. "I don't mean it like that. I mean, I love you."

Leslie caught her breath but said nothing.

"And I'm scared now. That's why I sent the emails. I was trying to stop the two of you from getting together. It was wrong of me."

Leslie was in shock. She was catching up. "It was very wrong of you."

"I could see right away, as soon as you walked through the door, that…"

Leslie pushed up off the chair and went to her side. She sat next to her.

Freya continued, following her with her eyes as she sat and took her hand. "…you found somebody." Leslie kissed her hand. "The first time on the ferry I knew there might be a problem, and the way you talked about him afterward, confirmed it. I couldn't have that."

"You love me, Freya?"

"Yes, I do."

"How long?"

"Since Uppsala."

Leslie squeezed her eyes shut. She shook her head as understanding dawned. She slowly opened them. "Are you…?

"Yes, I'm gay. I've always been gay. …You must have suspected."

"No…"

"I can't believe that."

"Okay... I noticed some things."

Freya nodded, her head lowered. She was staring at her hands and Leslie's that was tangled in with hers.

"I'm not," Leslie added.

"I know."

"But I love you."

Leslie placed her hands carefully about Freya's face and kissed her slowly on each cheek, and then eyes, and then lastly on her lips. She stood. "I've got to go. I can't stay."

Freya jumped up and followed her to the door. She could see Leslie was confused and she could see she was crying but trying to hide the fact. Leslie picked up her coat as she passed by the chair. "Don't go! You just got here!"

Leslie turned slowly back. She had difficulty controlling her breathing, Freya saw, and now she was crying outright. "He's right for me. I don't know if it will ever end up anywhere, but he seems right for me."

She stepped around Freya and grabbed her pack. She placed her hand on the door handle and opened it a crack but then turned and held Freya again. She held her and kissed her. "We'll talk about this again... but I can't talk about it right now." She opened the door and stepped through, not bothering to close it behind her but running toward the elevator.

Freya remained in the open door, her hand on the jam. She heard the elevator door open and then close. Only then did she glance down the hall. It was empty. She slowly shut the door, walked again over to the window, and peeked out through the blinds. She watched Leslie run to her car, climb in, and drive off, the car accelerating around the corner, the tires squealing.

Freya's hands were shaking. She held them up and watched them vibrate as if they had a life of their own. Her entire body was the doing the same. She managed the couch, fell onto it, threw her head back, and stared at the ceiling. Her hand was by the phone. Her fingers trailed on the coiled plastic cord. She dropped her eyes to it, and picked up the receiver. She knew his number. He had it listed. She dialed. Marshall answered. She said, "Leslie just drove off. She'll be back in Kingston in three hours. You should meet her there."

"Freya?"

"Yes, it's me."
"This is Marshall Davenport. You know me then?"
"I know you."

She hung up, unplugged the phone, layback, and fell asleep, not waking until the following evening.

Footnote by Freya Anna Bergman

As it turned out, it was late enough that Marshall had to take *The Spray* across to Kingston. When I called him, it was about 10 PM, and Leslie was not due to arrive until 1 AM Sunday morning. The last boat back to Marysville is 2AM; it gave him an hour, which he did not think would be enough, so he sailed *The Spray* over. It was only twenty minutes from his 'settlement', if I may say, to where *The Spray* was tied up, and it was another thirty minutes across. There was no wind so he needed gas. He had not bothered yet to top up the tank, given the expense, as well as the fact that the possibility of being stuck windless like that again was, by his determination, quite low. He had not considered this particular turn of events, I am sure, or he would have topped it up. Instead, he siphoned off what remained in the almost-full tank of his ride-on John Deere, and a bit more from his decidedly dilapidated Subaru, and hoped he had enough. As it turned out, it was. Remarkably, from the time I called him from my apartment to the time he managed to get to Kingston, only one hour and twenty minutes had elapsed. He also had the foresight to take his bicycle along, which shortened the time it took him to go from where he tied up *The Spray*, which was adjacent to where the ferry tied up, to Leslie's apartment. As it was, though, he waited over two hours for her to make an appearance. She had stopped just outside Trenton for coffee and a pee break and so she took a little longer than I had originally estimated.

He climbed to his feet when she approached. She did not see him right away but when he stood, she saw him and froze in her tracks. He walked up to her, his arm extended out to her, but she would not take it. He told her I had called and had asked that he please be waiting for her when she arrived, and that was why he was there. She nodded and kissed him briefly, and without another word, walked past him through the doors leading to her apartment, leaving him where he had been waiting. The entire rendezvous had lasted no more than thirty seconds, Marshall later told me. He could see she was upset and that she didn't want to speak about it and he wasn't about to force it. As she walked past, he quietly asked her if she was okay and she replied that she was fine, although he could tell she was anything but. She was exhausted, he could tell. "I'll call you," was the last thing he heard her say as the door swept shut, separating them, he on the darkened street and she beneath the glare of the lights in the foyer of her apartment building. He watched her take the stairs and she was gone. He said he felt empty after that, as if I had won, he said later.

He did not hear from her for another three weeks. All the while he waited, he said, it was like walking on glass. He would toss and turn at night, as Leslie had done earlier. It was very unlike him. He later admitted to me that even in those early days he realized that Leslie was for him, and he was going to do everything he could to convince her that he was for her as well. "Love at first sight?" I asked him. "Something like that," he had intoned. "It took me almost a year before I knew I loved her," I once admitted. He picked up on it right away. He looked at me curiously and said, "It doesn't make your love any less so." Marshall is a good man, as I have repeatedly stated. I love him as well; not in the same way as I love and will always love Leslie, but deeply nonetheless. Like their children, although not like that either. Every love, and reason for loving, is unique, I suppose.

I do have some idea what went through Leslie's mind during those three weeks. She, of course, eventually explained it me. She didn't tell me until many, many years later when we were both in our fifties and the children were almost all out the door, and our so-called passions were somewhat damped with time. Still, we did not laugh about it; not all that much time had gone by. She could only speak about it then because *enough* time had gone by, she said. She told me that she had spent the three weeks debating about the only thing she deemed truly important in life, and that was love. It is very typical of her, I must say, and I had no difficultly believing it. Inwardly, I hoped she had been wondering if my love for her, a true thing she must have known, was enough for her; love is love, after all. At the time, what was Marshall to offer other than that, she had undoubtedly asked herself. One should not forget that, in the times I am referring to, Marshall was nowhere near what one would believe to be a sure bet. To reject me, to throw me away, as it is often said, would accomplish nothing; it would only leave her with a world as cold as it had once been, and she would not have wanted that. God, I could almost have won, I thought, simultaneously feeling the irony and tragedy.

I might have let that perhaps delusional version of my state of mind slip out once. She glanced at me, shocked, but then threw her head back and laughed. Sufficient time had gone by for that at least. She stopped our progress along the path and kissed me. "You could be right!" She laughed and took my arm and held it close to her side as we continued. We were walking through the Old Commons, now that I recall. She was wearing that red cap of hers and the scarf Marshall had bought her in Paris the year before. It was a cool fall morning; as the wind touched the trees, the leaves fell about us in cascades, spinning downward and settling into drifts across the path, and skittering about our feet.

Some people do not believe that, I know. For them, the important thing in life might at one time have been love but that was perhaps when they were younger and more foolish. Later they might believe it is their family, then the children, or perhaps their career; and, later still, as they grow older, perhaps it is their health, and their ability to enjoy what life they have remaining has to offer. But for Leslie, even past her middle age, she believed it was love. I am humbled by that. I can also only agree. That is perhaps why we remained as lovers for our entire lives. No, I do not mean sexually; I mean we were lovers in the purest sense, without the sex, but with every other aspect of love fully intact. God, I do not know how that could have happened; I do not feel I deserve that depth of happiness.

That was our life together; I shared her with Marshall, and Marshall, being Marshall, understood completely. He told me so. It took many years but he told me. Of course, by then I had no doubt, but I did appreciate him saying it. He said, taking me back to my apartment after Christmas was over and there was a foot of snow on the ground and I didn't feel like driving myself, "You know we all love you, Freya," and he kissed me goodnight. I think I was sixty-three at the time, making him sixty-seven. He was at the peak of his career at the Festival. We lived in Niagara-on-the-Lake, of course. Geoffrey pretty much told me the same thing and almost in the same way. It was if he had heard his father say the same thing and wanted to repeat it for the family. Of course, there never has been any doubt how Marcia feels, or Alice. I am blessed, I know.

Leslie eventually elaborated further and told me that she had thought long and hard about what to do. The fact I loved her the way I said had floored her. In some ways, she said, my love for her might have been enough; she knew it was true and she knew it would not fade. Still, she was not gay and had never even entertained the possibility that she might be. Marshall at that point was a great unknown, but she had a good feeling about him. Her instincts told her to follow through with him, even with the outcome being uncertain. She could not stop that. She had to see it through, despite how I might feel. In the end, though, she told me she decided that, no matter what happened between her and Marshall, or any other man that may show up in her life, she was not about to leave me behind. In the end, she told Marshall she wanted both him and me in her life, and he agreed. As I have said before, I have loved and I am loved and, in the end, that is all that matters to me.

After I wrote this, I cried myself to sleep and I dreamed of Leslie. When I awoke, the sun was high in the sky and I felt a deep peace. I did not move out of the position I awoke in for quite a while even though my eyes were open and I heard the day beckoning. I so wanted the feeling to last.

Sunday, July 22nd, 2012

Preface by Freya Anna Bergman

I suppose it is now time to tell you of the scar. I have been putting it off, but not because it represents a particularly tragic episode in Leslie's life, though she did not like to talk about how she acquired it; her scar was more a birthmark, an identifier that was exclusively her own. When one saw the scar, seeing nothing else of her, one knew it was Leslie. I saw her scar last when the nurse pulled back the sheet covering Leslie to show me her sleeping form. She was dead. I do not know how nurses can immerse themselves in situations like that day after day; they must have wonderfully strong hearts in them or perhaps no heart at all, although that does not seem at all possible.

She had acquired it by crashing through a plate-glass window when she was twelve years old. It was presumably an accident. Her father, it was said, had accidently knocked her and she went flying. A large piece of glass lodged deep into her skull and surgery was required to remove it. Her mother told me the glass actually cut into her brain so they had to leave her skull open until the hemorrhaging subsided. She was in the hospital for almost two weeks, a long period of time even then. She was very lucky. There was no permanent damage, just the scar itself, which later made it appear as if she had narrowly missed losing her ear. One imagines her ear bloodied and dangling, with the flesh torn back from her skull as she stood up crying and in shock, although as I understand it was not so. There was just the shard of plate glass sticking out at a right angle and very little blood at all. The scar begins just below her earlobe and reaches up into her hairline, where it disappears. Her hair is very thick so most of it is nicely covered. She showed me how it went on for almost two or three more inches into her hairline before it abruptly ended. I suppose she could have had it removed or the rather noticeable weal mitigated somewhat by plastic surgery, but she never did. By the time she was a young woman, it did not look all that bad actually.

One had to look to find it, or she had to turn from you in such a way you would see it; it did not just jump out.

The troubling aspect for me is not the scar itself but the memory of it, the small things, the daily things, building right from the moment I met her. A good memory can be a curse sometimes and mine is certainly excellent. Testing has shown I have the memory of a forty-year- old. It is those little white pills they give you these days. They help with the memory, prevent Alzheimer's, and senility, hardening of the arteries, one's sex life, and so on. The tiny little thing that is one of those miracle drugs takes generations to develop and costs billions of dollars. Everyone asks the same thing. We are all so similar in the end; we think and reason in the same way. "What would happen if I took the entire bottle all at once?" we all ask, with each one of us continuing with, "Would I remember everything?" The answer is no, of course. Taking the entire bottle all at once, we are told, would lead to a rather severe brain hemorrhage. As explained to me by the nurse who presented the first of many to me, and who was also polite enough not to roll her eyes or sigh as she answered the same question posed to her by almost each and every one of us, that, basically, one's brain would explode. I must add, however, that living where I do, and at my age, I suspect it has been, at least in the past and no doubt will continue to be so in the future, a preferred method of checking one's self out of the premises for good. It somewhat guarantees you will see your life flash before your eyes before all turns to white. Of course, they do not ever give you the entire bottle; you get one pill a day in that little white cup they bring about, although if one is clever, one can stockpile them I suppose. I also understand that it is not only the pill that makes the miracle happen; there is an entire cocktail of things we all take, some of which is mixed into our tea.

I recall her scar from our Uppsala days, lying next to Leslie in bed and watching her sleep. Once I reached out and touched it, feeling the hardened, and surprisingly velvet to the touch, edge. It woke her. She turned her head on the pillow, looked at me, and asked what I was doing. I told her. Her hand reached up beneath her ear and she touched it herself. She smiled, turned, and presented her ear to me. "Go ahead..." She held my fingers and traced it for me up into her hair and then she told me the whole story of how she got it, her voice still heavy with sleep, saying with her eyes closing what a close call it had been. I withdrew my hand, tucked it up beneath me, and watched her fall back into sleep. The sun was just rising; the room was filling with the colors of dawn, red and gold, silver and blue. I wanted to kiss her scar, to make it go away... I do not know... I don't know if that's what I was thinking or feeling. I was just beginning to know how much I loved her and so I was feeling a great deal, including some confusion about what I was feeling. I closed my eyes and when I awoke, she was up and about and the morning was well on.

It was a constant within her; it never changed, although she aged beneath it as we all age. I would catch sight of it at the oddest times, and each time it would draw me back to that time in Uppsala. The last time I saw it, as I said, was in the hospital in St Catherine's with her head on the pillow, appearing not so unlike the morning in Uppsala, with her eyes closed. Marshall was with me. He was standing right next to me with his arm about me. He saw me reach out to the scar and he held my shaking hand and guided my fingers along its edge, as Leslie had. He did not say anything. He kissed Leslie and then me and then we walked out of the room together. Marcia was there, and Alice; Geoffrey was in the air, apparently. God, I... I can't think of that anymore...

Anyway, it was sudden. She died in her sleep. It was the morning of their 66th anniversary; she never got to see it. Marshall woke up next to her. He knew instantly she was gone, he said. There was no autopsy; she was, after all, ninety-seven years old, and one expects the cleaver of death to come down at any moment at that age. She did not suffer, that was certain. I had seen her two days earlier for our 'constitutional' as we called it; everyone calls it that, a slow walk about the park beneath the trees that are older than our ages combined. We talked of nothing really: the children, mostly.

I always like to talk about Hilary and her comings and goings because she is the youngest and, as I have mentioned before, she was born the same day I was and she carries my name, *Hilary Freya*... The fact her last name is Patterson really matters little. Alice and Douglas separated; if I were Alice, I would change my name back to Davenport; in fact, I never would have changed my name in the first place. None of this applies to Hilary, I suppose; she is a Patterson and there is not much she can do about it. I am glad that Douglas has pushed off, though; I never really liked him. I never thought he was good for Alice. He was always so smarmy and ingratiating in his manner. Leslie, of course, would not give her opinion but I could tell she agreed with me, at least in part. "We can be thankful for the musical talent he gave the children," she said. "It must have come from his side since there is none in ours." I suppose that is true, and I agreed to that much at least. She was always like that; she always managed to say something positive about someone, no matter who they might be. At any rate, we then went to her place and had tea in her garden, and later Marshall drove me home as he usually does.

If I had known that would be the last time I would ever speak with Leslie, I think I would have taken the time to revisit our days in Uppsala together; but, then again, perhaps not. Those were the days before Marshall. She always said her life really did not begin until she met, first me, and then Marshall. I think instead I would have revisited the days I am writing about here, and let her relive the excitement of falling in love with Marshall for the first time, and for the rest of her life. After all, any last conversation I might have been able to arrange through the grace of God should be more about her than me.

There is irony here, everywhere. I believe it is in the garden where we last had tea. That is where Marshall had his last moments as well. He died exactly one year to the day that Leslie died. That is, he also died on their anniversary, what would have been their 67th. It is somewhat bizarre to think of it. One almost thinks there was some kind of purpose, or plan, behind it, as if Marshall had to stick around for some reason, perhaps to say goodbye for both him and Leslie, I do not know. It is hard to imagine what it could be otherwise. The only thing I can think of is that Marshall, devastated by the loss of Leslie, and who barely throughout his year alone could get up in the morning, somehow *willed* death to bear down on him, picking out the actual date for the *symmetry* of it if nothing else. That is particularly hard to believe though. Once again, God moves in mysterious ways. Or perhaps God does not have any plans for us at all but merely observes, I do not know.

Hilary and I found him. Poor Hilary, it was one of her first times driving about on her own, having just acquired her license. She came by to pick me up for a morning outing. We drove along the parkway to see the river and then out and about in the rural countryside to view the ripening rows of grapes. We dropped by to see her grandfather who, we both knew, needed company. We came around the back of the house into the garden and found him in one of the white wicker chairs, chin on his chest, arms to his side. I froze when I saw him. I would have collapsed but young Hilary kept me upright and then sat me down. She walked over to her grandfather, quite dead in the chair. I could not stay seated, and joined her. The child was crying. I was crying. I wanted to throw up. I could barely stand. I could barely look. On his lap was a cut rose. It was red and a perfect specimen. It was Leslie's favorite flower; she tended her roses every day. "If God placed the perfection of the rose within the rose, He did so with the expectation that it takes loving care to bring it forth," she used to say. The cut rose on Marshall's lap lends one to believe he was thinking of Leslie when he died. We all believe that now. I certainly do.

I often wish I had gone first but, then again, if I had, I would not have been able to write this all down and then, perhaps, no one would read it, and then no one would know. There are a thousand million lives out there that have been lived and no one remembers. It is some consolation, I suppose, that for the very short while this book remains in print, the lives of the two people I loved the most in the world, Leslie and Marshall, shall be known and remembered.

Nothing Happened

I realize that it is a ridiculous thing to suggest that nothing happened; still, the events mentioned above are outside the scope and intent of the biography as it was originally intended and as I was commissioned to write by Geoffrey Davenport. I realize, too, that this work has become *more* than originally intended, and therefore nothing is 'beyond the scope' any longer. I do not know where the story may be going from here, only that there is one major part to Leslie's and Marshall's early days that has yet to be told. We will endeavor to get there. …And, by the way, I do *feel* a lot for them. They were very lucky.

Sunday, August 26th, 2012

Preface by Freya Anna Bergman

After three weeks of pondering what she should do, Leslie did eventually call me. She called me before she called even Marshall in fact. She said, simply, that we were best friends and that she loved me. She did not say anything about forgiveness, not at first; she did repeat the fact she is not gay and that the love I was possibly looking for could not happen. Her voice was so soft when she said that I could barely hear her. I pictured her standing at her window, looking out at the night and the lights of the city and the shadowed park below. It was almost midnight when she called. Normally she would have long been in bed; she always went early to bed, it was a habit of hers.

The time between her normal bedtime and the time she did finally call was must have been occupied by something other than staring into the distance, or making her lunch for the next day. She was no doubt debating, even up to the last moments, what to say exactly. In fact, she had undoubtedly been preoccupied with that same debate for quite some time, days probably, weeks also likely. What could, or should, one say when one's friend confesses undying love? I am certain it has ruined many friendships, between men and women; between men, one of whom imagined they were best friends; between women whose special girlfriend could not imagine she was more than just that. I have a number of friends at work I see socially, and even from my schooldays in England and Sweden as well, and if any of them confessed to me what I had confessed to Leslie, I am unerringly certain I would be completely shocked, horrified even. I would no doubt run the other way and possibly would never talk to them again, although, on the surface, I would have been openly sympathetic and pretend understanding. Such is my hypocrisy. No matter the degree of my hypocrisy, or the depth of my sympathy, they would have crossed a line and it would never be the same. That is what I feared would happen between Leslie and I, only it was I, of course, who had done the confessing. I cannot tell you what that felt like, to possibly lose a friend and a lover all in one grand sweep of so-called confession and revelation. I can only say as a way of giving you some idea of what it might be like that right to my very core, and within every bone and cell of my body, I was pervaded with a deep and irreconcilable sadness that was like a dark and impenetrable cloud within me. I felt cold when the room was warm; nothing could warm me, no hot bath, no shower, no other lover.

Even so, and to give me some hope, Leslie's heart was bigger than most hearts. She said at the end of her call that she would call me again in a week or two, and then, perhaps, she asked, I could come up to Kingston. I agreed, of course, and without hesitation; but I was deathly afraid of seeing her again even so. I did not know if I could handle it if it was not to be the same, or nearly the same, between us; and I felt it could not possibly be. I had stepped over the line and had said the unforgivable. The act was forgiven, yes; but forgotten, no; not by her, and not by me.

It did not turn out that way, of course. Leslie... Well, Leslie would not *allow* that. As I said, her heart was too big, and I know now that she loved me at least as much as I loved her, although she could not express it in the way I needed her to.

When she did call me two weeks later, the tone of her voice was quite changed. It was lighter, happier, although I imagined, as I listened to her laugh at the far end of the line, that I could detect a lingering reticence. She called me around dinnertime when she knew I would be in, and, as she said she would, invited me up to Kingston for the coming weekend □ but to stay at Marshall's place. She made a particular point of saying it was not her necessarily inviting me up, but Marshall. I could hear her smiling when she said that, although the smile on her face would have been careful.

"I suppose that means the two of you are together."

"We are."

I heard the pitch of her voice change as she said, '*We are*'; it held excitement in it, and a touch of wonder too. It hurt, it definitely hurt, but I was beginning to deal with it. I did say that, if

Marshall was inviting me, why did he not call? Again, I could hear her smile. "He's chicken," she said and laughed.

She said she would email me the directions, or Marshall would. When she mentioned 'email,' I immediately cringed and I imagined I heard her voice crimp as well. I said I would come and hung up, and immediately began to wring my hands together in trepidation. I did not fear facing Marshall; as I said, it was Leslie I feared.

That was then and now is now and, looking back, I can see now how generous they both really were; Leslie, of course, but also Marshall, who had the most to lose since he was potentially inviting up a rival. He did think that, and he told me as much years later. Again, it was the largeness of his heart, as well as his love for Leslie, that made it possible for him to overcome his fear in this regard. He was not unlike Leslie in that way. As I say, he was a most wonderful man. I definitely can see what Leslie saw in him.

I can look back now, sixty-six years later, with a certain amount of detachment I suppose. Jealousy does not cut quite so deeply, and my eyes are that much less clouded because of it. As such, it is now possible for me to postulate the next days and weeks of their time together. I am talking about sex here, admittedly: when they first had it, how many times after that. It is all about the where, when, what, and so on. As I stated flatly earlier, it is disgusting to think of such private things but I simply cannot help myself thinking. Even so, I shall not be getting into any *great detail* on the subject, and I expect and demand that *what's-his-name* will not add a section on this, mainly because, being male, he would completely misrepresent the facts, I feel. I fear he would titivate the truth and put something out there that may be quite misleading. Still, it is worth saying something, I suppose; but I do reserve that right solely for myself.

I imagine, then, that Leslie called Marshall the day after she called me, which would have been the Thursday, their conversation probably something like as follows: "Hi, it's me, Leslie." "Hi Leslie." "I said I'd call you back and here I am." "I'm glad." "Dinner this Saturday then?" "That'd be great." ...Or something to that effect... Boring stuff, and hardly relevant, really.

What is relevant is that Marshall must have gone over to Leslie's place the following Saturday for dinner as originally planned. He would have brought a bottle of red wine, of course, and only one bottle, as I said; and he no doubt brought along another bundle of newly cut flowers from his mother's garden to replace the first bunch, which had, by that time, withered away. Leslie could only cook one thing to any level of competency in those days, so she must have served him lasagna with a Greek salad, and jello, and chocolate chip cookies, which she knew he liked, for dessert.

They sat at the table in her small, rather sparsely furnished dining room and listened to some classical music as they ate. What they talked about I do not know, but I expect I was on the top of their list. In fact, the following day, I received an email from Marshall, formally inviting me up to his place and giving me the directions, which meant that whether or not I was to be invited up was openly discussed, and a conclusion was subsequently reached, with the responsibility of actually inviting me up passed on to Marshall. Of course, he emailed me the invitation. I'm certain he sent an email on purpose rather than call me, no doubt smiling to himself as he sent it, savoring the irony of it, hoping, of course, that I would understand his intent. They talked of other miscellaneous and unimportant things besides me, no doubt, but I imagine that, overall, it was an awkward affair. One just cannot jump back into a relationship as if nothing at all had happened, particularly after something, after all, had happened: *relationship-interruptus*, so to speak, where the *interruptus* was all my fault.

He kissed her goodnight as well I am sure, in an attempt to bring things more into alignment. I am also certain they did not have sex, not on the first night; and I have absolutely no doubt Marshall made the 11:20 PM ferry that night. It was a start, though; and it is not particularly a surprise that by the time I met them at Marshall's place two weeks later, they were definitely having sex. I could tell. One can always tell. A simple glance at the couple does that. The look on Leslie's face was, well… one I had not seen before; and Marshall, only the second time I had seen him in the flesh, looked pretty pleased with life I must say.

My imagination will not stop there, as no doubt your own will not. Leslie did fill in a few more details as girls, and grown women too, do when they really do not want to tell everything, but want and need to say something. I imagine it was like this: there was some rather intricate and somewhat delicate precursory activity leading up to the final *denouement*, if I can use that word. *Denouement* is a better choice I feel than, "when she was deflowered", or "when they consummated their relationship", or "they copulated', or "made love", or finally managed the "full monty." Or from those who simply like to believe they are more accurate on these and other matters and therefore believe they speak with some detachment, which of course they do not, and I can't stand people like that they're so *contrived*, "the first time they experienced sex." I would like to know what the attitude of those overtly detached and pretentious lovers might be; I imagine, like all of us, they saw something rather like the Veil Nebula the first time they came off their high. It does not require drugs or the Space Telescope to see the Veil Nebula, just first-time sex with someone you love or care a great deal for. I will not beleaguer you, dear reader, with yet another lecture on masturbation. Even so, I am certain Leslie did not simply jump into bed with Marshall at the very first opportunity. Knowing Leslie, the main reason she finally surrendered herself to him was because it was no doubt becoming increasingly uncomfortable to make out on the couch, or on the floor, or the front seat of her Subaru; or, and I hesitate to use such a word in this context, the *cockpit* of *The Spray*. All of those physically awkward places lead to stiff necks and sore backs, which are to be avoided at all costs and are not normally experienced in the confines of a comfortable bed.

I am being unfair, and I am perhaps being a somewhat coarse in my description of a rather delicate matter, but that does not change the fact that, all the while Leslie was falling in love with Marshall and he was falling in love with her, sex, in the form of kissing, touching, and finally intercourse, played a pivotal role. Their relationship, the closeness that began to develop between them, would not have developed without it. Sex, when there's love involved, is about intimacy; and without that kind of intimacy, there will always exist a barrier between lovers. Well, I should clarify that. It is possible for two lovers to be fully committed and loving to one another without the intimacy of sex to reinforce it;

Leslie and I are, after all, living proof of that. Still, I feel we may be an exception to the rule.

At any rate, Leslie did manage to tell me about the cheese, and the candlelight, and sitting up in bed passing crackers topped with cheese back and forth, and the glasses of red wine carefully sipped and somehow managed not to spill. I imagine there was more to it than that although she did not elaborate. Of course, I do not believe their first night together ended by sweeping aside the cracker crumbs, capping off the wine, blowing out the candles and lying down to sleep side by side without *something* happening. Of course they had sex! My mind, and any decent mind, simply will not go there. It is a private thing. I honestly believe that one should place limits on one's tendency to want to know it all, right down to the final thrust, so to speak. It may be titillating but it is also a type of voyeurism in that one is creating a secret image of a couple having sex. It is a type of pornography with the lines written and staged solely by the imagination. One breaks a barrier when asks or demands to know the details of such intimacy. It is like insistently enquiring about one's bowel movements, also a very private thing, I'm sure you would agree.

I am really off topic, I know. I do apologize. I somehow ended up with a discussion of bowel movements while I only wanted to relate a sense of how they fell in love. It is very easy to digress, particularly when broaching such a sensitive subject. It is the romance between the two I wish to emphasize, and not bodily function. At any rate, Marshall is a romantic, and I know he is expressive in his love, as is Leslie. For all their lives, whenever they met after being apart for a while, like coming home after work or in the morning as they awakened, they just did not kiss one another in greeting, they embraced and kissed. I never saw them do anything else. It was a particular affection reserved only for one another. All those who love one another have something similar, and likely unique, between them: a touch, a look, something said, it does not matter. What matters is that it is there and it is shared. That, dear reader, is far more important in a long-term relationship than the, at first, perhaps hourly, then daily, then alternate days, then weekly, finally monthly, then never, ten minutes of heated, hormone-induced sex, the passion of which is over in the seconds following.

Footnote by Commissioned Author

I am not an idiot, and although I cannot be identified for contractual reasons, I do not like to be referred to as *'what's-his-name.'* I am not a *'titillator,'* whatever that is. I consider myself sensitive as well as possessing some understanding. I can then, and will, make an attempt at describing the love that had grown between the two □ and with somewhat more brevity and focus, I might add. They deserve that much at least. I dare Freya to delete it.

The Denouement

Leslie swung her bare feet up and onto the bed and turned in the candlelight to face Marshall. The light from the candles bathed her in gold. She tucked her feet beneath her and sat upright so she rested on her knees. She was wearing a t-shirt that billowed off her and a pair of shorts that rose up on her thighs. Her blonde hair was brushed back behind her ears. The scar was just visible in the dim light. She had a few crackers topped with cheese laid out on her open palm, and another cracker, similarly capped, in the other. She popped it into her mouth and offered the others to Marshall. He carefully set one of the glasses aside, lifted one of the crackers off her hand, and set it in his mouth. Marshall was dressed as he usually is, in t-shirt and shorts. He was resting against the back of the bed; his long legs extended outward, his muscular thighs and ham muscles emphasized in the candle light, the same steady light that bathed Leslie fell across his face. It was a long and thin, a strong face, and the light deepened the dark texture of his hair, which was combed back.

"I hope you like cheddar."

"I love cheddar. I hope you like Pinot Noir."

"I love Pinot Noir."

"What kind of cheddar is it?"

"Very old, from Perth..." She leaned across with the remnants of the cheese and cracker she had been eating on her lips and kissed him. Done, she remained leaning toward him, smiling.

"Ah, very old indeed..."

He kissed her back and, as he did so, lingering on the kiss, set the glass aside and wrapped his arms about her. Still in the kiss, they fell back onto the pillows. Marshall ran his hand up her shirt, and she up the back of his. He held her breast in his hand and then moved his hand around and undid the clasp of her bra, which fell away. She had her hand down the back of his shorts and slipped them downward. He removed her shirt and then his own, dropping his face between her breasts, his hand along the elastic of her shorts maneuvering them downward as she removed his, all the while not breaking the kiss.

Footnote by Freya Anna Bergman

I agree he is not an idiot. I am sorry if I gave one the impression that I might have thought so. As for what was written above, it is completely fictitious and, of course, is based on pure speculation. He did get the cheese right if nothing else; and we all know the ending, after all. That is why I truncated it. If you, dear reader, were hoping for more, I do apologize, but I will not have my friends *exposed* on these pages like that. I hope you understand.

Still, it has been a revelation for me to think they were both virgins at that point in their lives. That is the story, anyway; at least according to the both of them. Not that I asked, and not that they came right out and said so but one does get the sense of it by the way they blush and glance at one another whenever those days are mentioned. It could all be in my mind, I realize; still, I like to think it did not happen in the way described above at all but was rather a bit more hesitant. I much prefer a version that includes a little nervous groping beneath the sheets that ultimately led to some rather awkward moments that were eventually resolved.

I can still feel a trill of jealousy and a clutching at my stomach. I doubt it will ever go away. It is like a permanent scar within me. I should not think of it as a scar; Leslie owns a scar, and it is a real one. I should say *wound* although I am not *wounded* in any way. The worst of it is, perhaps it was as my fellow author suggests after all. I know he wrote it that way on purpose, knowing it would get to me. He can be an asshole, I know, but still, I believe he is much more *sensitive* now than he was when we began. I think he now truly appreciates who Leslie and Marshall were as people, as well as the love they shared together. God knows what is going on inside his head, or how he feels. I may have underestimated him again, I fear.

Despite what I might feel, it comes to mind that if I had had the imagination to picture such a scene and, unfortunately, I do but only with those I do not know or do not know very well, I doubt very much I would have made an appearance at Marshall's place that afternoon. I would have felt that I simply could not compete, and therefore I would have felt that much more out of place. Then my world would have been very different, as would their own. It turned out the way it should have turned out, I suppose, which again gives me some consolation that our lives may be mapped out to some extent and we are not just doomed by the randomness of life as well as our own inconsistencies.

Marshall's Place

It was one of those rare Sundays in August that crop up occasionally after two weeks of suffocating heat. It was not like August at all. It was more like mid-September when the nights are cool but the days are sunny and the river remains warm. It had rained the night before, a gentle rain that had begun in the early hours but had dispersed by the dawn. The sun rose to clear skies and glistening leaves with a quickly dissipating layer of mist hugging the low ground and settling along the banks of the river. The river looked as if it was moving from left to right as a gentle wind came up the channel off the lake.

Leslie opened her eyes. It was 7 AM almost exactly. Her alarm normally went off at that time, but there had been no alarm set for that morning; she awoke out of habit. She turned her head slowly on the pillow and saw that Marshall was still asleep. He was turned facing her and he had thrown his arm about her. He was breathing gently and evenly, deep in sleep. She smiled and kissed him quickly, waking him, and swung her feet off the edge of the bed. She stood and turned immediately to the window. She leaned forward against the sill, her forehead against the glass, looking out. She could hear Marshall stir behind her and called back over her shoulder without turning, "It's a glorious morning." She straightened and glanced back over her shoulder. His eyes were open and following her. She realized then she was naked. She blushed, found her chemise at the foot of the bed, and swung it about her shoulders, covering herself. He saw her in silhouette, her beautiful body outlined against the window, the blue sky, the draping limbs of the fruit trees in the garden, the shifting river, and the morning sun filtering through the light fabric of her gown as it fell about her. He closed his eyes and opened them. She had moved off the window and was smiling back at him from the hall.

"Later…"

"Promises, promises…"

He closed his eyes looking for sleep, and could hear her laugh. He stretched out to his full length, luxuriating in the sensation and the coolness of the sheets while listening to the sound of her bare feet on the hardwood floor, water running, the kettle placed on the stove, and the *click, click, click*, as she turned on the element and set the flame. The home was full again. There was not just him and the shadows of the past.

On the outside of the cottage were his mother's gardens, carefully built up over time and faithfully tended by her for thirty years or more. Marshall attended them now; it was a daily chore. He saw his mother in every flower. He knew it was a way of keeping her alive not only in the living flower that came back each spring and summer but in his mind as well. In the days when she lived and he was a boy, it was one of his chores to help weed the garden and help move the heavier things. She had him bring up some of the flat stones from the river to make a path; the stones were still there, grown around now with wild phlox and sedum. It was a wild sort of garden, populated mostly with wildflowers and flowers that had filled gardens across generations. There was nothing engineered in a hothouse or purchased from a nursery. They were mostly perennials, or flowers from the bulbs his mother had placed in the ground years ago, and which had now spread. In the spring, crocuses led to yellow bobbing daffodils, to swaying rows of red, yellow, and white tulips. Later, the tall strands of wild lily originally from the ditch, and then long rows of purple iris, red amaryllis, blue allium, hyacinth, dahlia, and, of course, a hedge of red and white peonies, some of which had self-hybridized and were now pink. Her prize flowers were the roses that grew up over the trellis that opened to the garden. She had tended to them daily and was often found talking to them, so they would know how beautiful they were, she said, or so that they knew what they could do to improve their beauty.

The grass was uncut. His father liked it that way. He liked the way the birds, the finches, and warblers, red-winged blackbirds, and even the robins nested in the high grasses or in the limbs of fallen trees scattered about the acreage. He had made birdhouses for the swallows and bluebirds; these Marshall continued to maintain by emptying them out each March so they would be fresh and ready for the new occupants when the spring came. As he thought of his mother in her garden, he always thought then of his father. Of course there were wide paths cut through the high grass that led up to the cabin and about the barn but, in general, the yard was uncut, and in the spring full of wildflowers, including wild daisies, buttercups, and wild rose. This time of year, it was purple asters and Queen Anne's lace.

The first time Leslie saw the garden, the grounds and accompanying cabin and outbuildings was the weekend Freya had predicted, the weekend following her phone call to Freya and, the next day, her phone call to Marshall. It was the weekend of the 11th of August. Three weeks had gone by since the showdown with Freya and, after deciding to call Marshall back, she was on her feet again, and on that uncertain path that she was determined to see to the end.

The phone call Leslie made to Marshall was brief and to the point. She reissued her invitation to dinner and he readily agreed. He was there on time and he brought a bottle of red wine. He couldn't tell her enough about how wonderful the lasagna she served was; how perfect the sauce, how tender the noodle, how delicate the meat. The Greek salad she made, too: the crispness, the tomatoes, onion and pepper, , the tang of the dressing, the subtle taste of olive oil, absolutely perfect. He ignored the wine, a dry Valpolicella that he could tell she really didn't like, but then went on about the jello at which point she put her foot down.

"The lasagna was good but the jello is just jello."

"I know."

"And the wine isn't all that bad – it's a bit dry."

"I'll do better next time."

They looked at one another over their plates.

Leslie nodded slowly, "Okay…"

The stereo was playing Vivaldi, 'The Four Seasons'; the music peaked, the violin cascading downward then upward, once again peaking, in complete contrast to the stiltedness of their conversation.

"I love Vivaldi."

"I do too."

"It is very beautiful."

"Yes."

"Inspiring."

"Yes, it is."

Marshall sat back, putting his jello spoon aside and scratched his chin. "Look…"

Leslie shrugged, not looking up at him. "We don't have to carry on, if you don't want to," she managed.

Marshall sat forward. "I want to."

Leslie managed to smile. "Okay…"

The level of conversation did not improve but they were more relaxed with one another. They arranged to meet again that Saturday. On the way out, the dishes done, dried, and put away, Marshall turned at the last moment and kissed her, holding by the shoulders, and then stepping back.

"You are a very beautiful woman, Leslie."

She smiled.

"Come to my place tomorrow." He had gone to great detail telling her what it was like and where exactly it was on the island, but he had not invited her yet. "You need to see my place. When you see it, you will know a lot more about me."

"What will it tell me?"

He touched the tip of her nose with his finger. "It will tell you that we are made for one another."

She laughed and pushed aside his finger. He kissed her again. She agreed to come, blushing deeply, and he ran to catch the

10 PM ferry; she closing the door behind him and he leaving an hour and thirty minutes earlier than they each had planned.

The next day, she drove to the ferry and came across with her new car, turned left at Marysville, and followed his directions until the beginning of his laneway and there she hesitated. It was clearly marked: Davenport. It was narrow and graveled as he had said, and overarched with trees putting the lane into deep shadow. "Okay, Krueger…" She slowly went up the lane, potholed and pitted, the graveled surface overgrown in places with weed, and in some places no gravel at all just the forest floor and a set of tire tracks made the day or so before; his tracks from yesterday, most likely. The lane turned a corner and rose up then flattened and dropped down toward the river that had suddenly appeared through the trees. She turned the corner and she saw Marshall's place for the first time; the whitewashed buildings with the steel roofs, the open and uncut field, and the colorful gardens, and in behind the river itself. She turned down his drive and followed the curve through a tunnel of red maple beyond which were the fields of high grass swaying in the light breeze, and the long stalks of the daisies with their white and yellow heads in synchronized motion, and the purple asters. She stopped before the barn. There was no sign of livestock; she found out later it was only for tools and the tractor. She climbed out. Marshall was nowhere about. She wondered for a moment if she had the right place, but then she saw his car and knew by his description of the gardens that this was the place.

The path that led up to the small house curved though the gardens, following a path of flat stepping-stones at the end of which was an arbor overflowing with roses. She stopped by the arbor and smelled one. It was warm from the sun and the scent was as full and as vibrant as the color. She turned back to look upon the garden she had walked through. It was wild, in some disarray, but perfectly tended. It was, as it was no doubt intended, natural and tended at the same time. She heard the birds, then; hundreds of them flying in and out of the grasses and the trees. She didn't know why she had not heard them before, the sound was almost deafening. It was full of energy and life, as if the birds had been just born and were seeing the world for the first time.

She stood, unable to continue but not because the path did not. She marveled. He had done this.

A sound behind her made her turn. She turned slowly about. Marshall was on the steps, leaning against the frame of the house. He had been watching her. When he saw that she saw him, he smiled and waved, and approached her, taking the steps one a time, slowly and deliberately.

He reached out his hand. "Hi."

"Hi."

"Welcome."

"It's very beautiful," Leslie offered.

"Thank you."

He kissed her quickly and then led her down toward the water, placing his hand on the small of her back to guide her. There was a rudimentary stone pier and a floating section; he led her out onto it. It wobbled unsteadily and swamped a bit with their combined weight. He pointed out over the water. The river was wide and blue; across was Howe Island. She recognized it and said so.

"How's *The Spray* doing?" she asked after a while, smiling shyly up at him, finally letting their eyes meet.

"She's afloat."

She laughed and they walked side-by-side back up to the house. Marshall served her a lunch of hotdogs cooked on an open grill, mustard and relish, and a can of coke each. Leslie hardly noticed; she was too overcome by the splendor of the place and the knowledge that Marshall was responsible for making it so.

The ice was broken between them. From that point onward, their lives opened. It was just one-step-after-another; that is all it took, that and the sunshine, the resplendent gardens, and the warm days that followed. Who knows when they became lovers? The best guess is around the 18th of August, the weekend following that one, and one week before Freya arrived. Leslie called her on Wednesday, the 22nd of August, and Freya arrived on the Saturday the 26th to a day very much like the first day Leslie had experienced, full of sunshine and easy warmth and beautiful gardens.

Freya parked next to Leslie's new Subaru. She had decided to rent a car for the trip and had driven up from Toronto that morning, catching the 12:30 PM boat, the last car on. She took her time once on the island, her hands sweating on the wheel and her heart beating faster as she neared, her stomach clutching. She climbed out and stood as Leslie had, facing the path that wandered up through the garden. Leslie and Marshall were waiting for her at the far end, beneath the trellis of roses. They had their arms wrapped about one another. As Freya approached, her heart flying, Leslie broke away and met her half way. She held Freya's face in her hands and kissed her: her cheeks, her eyes, then held her for a moment. She stepped back with arm about her and turned her to face Marshall.

"Freya, this is Marshall... Marshall, Freya."

Freya blinked her eyes clear. He extended his hand, waiting for her to take it. She grasped it with her left, stepped in, and quickly kissed him on his cheek before stepping back. She was shaking and barely contained. Marshall had not let go of her hand. He nodded solemnly and then smiled before he returned it. Freya looked as if she might collapse as Leslie stepped in close, held her up, and kissed her again. "I want to show you the garden, and then the waterfront □ and then the house, it's pretty cool too."

Freya nodded. She stood tall and proud but tears were streaming down her face, which she did not attempt to conceal. Leslie, drying her own eyes, led her through the garden as Marshall followed, slipping his arm about Leslie as Leslie slipped one arm about Marshall and the other about Freya. "There is no you without him, and there is no him without you," Leslie quietly said, whispering into her hair as they walked through.

Freya nodded and wiped away her tears with her free hand. They stopped their progress along the path as the two women gathered themselves together. Marshall dug into his pockets and produced a handful of folded napkins he had picked up off the dining room table on the way out; "Just in case," he said, as he handed each of them a handful. He smiled as they dried their eyes and blew their noses, and then laughed as they laughed, and then turned with them as they turned and continued onward with the tour.

Footnote by Freya Anna Bergman

On the rare possibility that some may be curious, Leslie had prepared a lunch of pinto bean salad along with some oven-baked bruschetta, a cup each of tomato-basil soup, and a lovely Pinot Grigio from one of the newer Niagara-on-the-Lake wineries. For dinner, Marshall brought out three thick steaks that he cooked to perfection: that is, rare for Marshall but medium rare for Leslie and I. We had the remainder of the pinto bean salad accompanied with a wine I brought along, yet another Niagara-on-the-Lake wine, a rich Cabernet Sauvignon from Inniskillin. I have to admit, too, and somewhat sheepishly, that at the end of that meal, Marshall produced a plate of leftover cheddar and, because the Cab-Sav was quickly drained, a bottle of Pinot Noir from Peller Estates not even half consumed. I know what you are thinking. It probably *was* leftover from the previous evening. I did not think about it until many weeks later and only after Leslie mentioned the wine and the cheese that led to… well, she would not specify but we all know, don't we?

Lastly, for completeness, I did not stay the night. That I could not do. Instead, I headed out late and stayed at Leslie's in Kingston. She gave me her keys and instructed me to leave the door unlocked when I left, which I did the next morning about 10 AM. It was strange to be in her apartment without her there amongst all her belongings. They seemed not to belong to her anymore, and nor were they mine. It seemed very dislocating and odd, as if someone had died, although no one had. In fact, it was the opposite. The love of my life had been reborn.

Last Word by Freya Anna Bergman

My so-called co-author has departed these shores so to speak. He bowed himself out with some grace, I have to say, saying something to the effect that the book was about three people and not just two and he hoped his contribution was appreciated. I told him I did very much appreciate his efforts. I sounded very sincere I thought. He went on to explain that he had sent an email to Geoffrey explaining his position, and he hoped that I would not be in any sort of 'deep ka-ka', his words. That's a laugh, I tried to explain to him; I had practically weaned Geoffrey. I had certainly changed enough of his diapers, I went on to say, adding that if there was any ka-ka I had cleaned it up long ago, trying to make light of the situation. Before I managed to get that far, though, he had disappeared. He practically tiptoed from the room, blushing on his way out. I am puzzled but not upset. As a way of concluding my thoughts of the young man, I can only say I hope he has a young woman waiting for him somewhere. He certainly deserves someone. Perhaps that is why he left in such a hurry. He might be one of those that drop everything for love. Perhaps his efforts in getting this history told taught him that, I don't know.

At any rate, he did, as his last contribution, manage to spark a memory within me about Geoffrey. It was the day he was born. I recall it as if it was yesterday. The phone rang… Marshall had called me, panic in his voice, and said that Leslie was going into labor and could I possibly go over to the house, call 911, whatever it took, and get her to the hospital? He was in Toronto. He had not wanted to go since he had been worried that his wife might go into labor earlier than predicted but there he was anyway, at least one hour away, with his wife about ready to drop. I ran over of course. I had put off all my flights overseas until after the birth since I was not about to miss it, so I was only sitting there waiting in any event. It was not a burden on me, certainly. I had been present for the births of both Marcia and Alice and Geoffrey was, in my mind, yet another in the string so I was quite prepared to do whatever it might take, including substitute for Marshall if that was what was needed.

I found Leslie on her front porch, wrapped up in blankets. It was a colder than normal November that year; in fact, both Leslie and I had practically succumbed to the cold during the Remembrance Day ceremonies the day before, and so we were both quite prepared. She was very calm. I entered through the screen door and as I entered, she smiled and gave me her hand. The contractions were coming every five minutes at that point and because it was her third child, I called 911. It was fortunate that I did. Geoffrey was born within the hour. Marshall had just run in, throwing on the gown, I looked up, Leslie gave one last push, screaming at the top of her lungs, and Geoffrey popped out! Marshall ran right to Leslie, apologizing over and over, kissing her face and eyes and hands. He was quite beside himself. Little Geoffrey, all wrinkled up, was placed across Leslie's breast, breathing his first lungful of air. Marshall saw it was a boy. He gently caressed the bald and still slimy head with the tips of his fingers and named him on the spot, Geoffrey Edward Davenport. Marshall was weeping for joy as he turned to Leslie who, holding and kissing her child but already falling toward sleep, tried to calm him down. I cannot imagine how he drove the last little bit without wrecking the car. The nurse picked up Geoffrey and turned him over for inspection and, oddly, and the only time this happened for all the children, when the doctor was done doing whatever they do to check over a newborn, the nurse handed Geoffrey, all wrapped up, directly to me. I was the first one to hold him and look down into his eyes. They were a striking blue, as they are today, and very clear. I, of course, immediately offered him to Marshall but he would not take him right away. Instead, he put his arms around the child and me and drew us to Leslie. The four of us huddled together, each of us taking turns kissing the baby's warm face and looking into his eyes as we all cried, each marveling at something that is always so amazing, the birth of a child.

As an aside, they no longer put that *stuff*, that silver nitrate solution, into the eyes of newborns, unless they feel they should. None of the other children needed it; they all came into this world with their eyes wide open, looking curiously about them. I always thought children were born into the world all squinty-eyed and rheumy but it is not so.

Geoffrey, today, all grown up, is a very influential man. He can sometimes be a card, though, by habit and necessity, I suppose, he always puts on the airs of calm and thoughtful consideration. He is very politic and a very handsome man. He looks like his father, and even has some of his father's sense of humor, though he is not quite as subtle as his father often was. He is a very commanding man. One of his vice presidents once leaned into me and said that Geoffrey is responsible for a budget that exceeds that of the Province of Ontario, but I rather doubt that. If he had said Prince Edward Island, or Saskatchewan, I might have believed him, but not Ontario. I think that VP of his rather liked me. I could never really seem to get away from him that trip. I had to keep shooing him off.

It is somewhat refreshing, as well as liberating, to put down on paper whatever I feel like putting down. There is only one more thing I would like to say and that is perhaps personified in the youngest child in our family, Hilary. I have made no bones about it; she *is* my favorite. It is not right to have favorites but one simply cannot help it. Those who have grandchildren and say they do not, are lying for the sake of those they have no intention of hurting. Having a favorite is not wrong but, for the sake of fairness, one just cannot be too obvious about it.

Hilary was born eighty-two years to the day I was born. She is being raised in a completely different world to the one I was raised in; she is tall while I am short; her hair is darker while mine was very blonde; she is young, just leaving childhood, and I am old with one foot in the grave; and yet I feel we are kindred spirits. It might have something to do with the fact she looks exactly like Leslie, or will when she gets older; but I really do not think it is that.

By the time one gets to my age, one tends to think a great deal about death. I am the only one left of the three of us. All those years we shared are behind us: all the love, and tears, joys, and tribulations. I do not believe in an afterlife. I believe when you are dead, you are dead: when your body dies, your mind, your memories, and your soul, if there is such a thing, die with it. The hard truth is our only bequest to the future is the genetic material we pass on to our children. I do not have any children, and when I die, Freya Anna Bergman ends with me. It is true that we live on in the memories of others but after a generation or so, that too is gone. The catacombs beneath the streets of Paris include walls made of human skulls stacked one upon the other. The first time I saw that I was shocked to my core. 'Alas, poor Yorick; I knew him well, Horatio, a fellow of infinite jest…' We are flesh and bone from the beginning to the end, and then dust; the rest is all vanity, as it is said. Those are the facts, and that is what I believe; and yet, it does not completely ring true, does it? I cannot explain why it does not; perhaps it is one of the many delusions that keep us from simply killing ourselves when the facts of the matter are finally believed. I don't know. I don't.

Oh, I am a perfect ball of joy, am I not? I sometimes have to shake my head to remove the dark shadows that haunt me, and no doubt haunt us all through the various stages of our lives, in one way or another. We quite often talk ourselves into our gloom. It is equivalently true though that the world is simply not like that. It is not black, white, or gray; it is a kaleidoscope of truth and delusion, hope and despair, in a spectrum of color.

I have a story to tell you, which I hope will make my point. It is about the future, and there is a future, dear reader, that may not include us but is still wonderful even though you sometimes may not think so. Hilary was fourteen. It was our birthday. We were at Alice's; Leslie was there as was Marshall. The lace curtains covering the large doors to their garden were drifting in and out with the soft breeze. It was a gorgeous May. One may experience only a handful of such days throughout the course of one's life. It was a perfect spring day of sunshine, warmth, and new life. Tulips were just opening, soft grass tickled the bottom of one's feet, bright new leaves were dancing in the sun, and a host of birds flittered back and forth singing their hearts out, almost mad with all the excitement. The cycle and promise is never ending but nor is it quite ever the same. There is grandeur in this view of life that includes us, dear reader; take my word for it.

Hilary had promised she would play for me. Alice gathered us all about and the child sat at the piano. "This is for my Aunt

Freya. Beethoven wrote this for Guilietta Guicciardi," and she pronounced the Italian woman's name perfectly, "a young woman he fell in love with but could not have." She looked up, found me, and smiled. "It reminds me of you, Auntie," and then she played. She is such a gifted child. It was Beethoven's 'Sonata for Piano, Number 14' and she played it perfectly. It was sad and joyful. The music swept us all away. I cannot say what it was truly like. I, of course, cried my eyes out. I was quite beside myself, I do not even know why. The music just swept me away so. I glanced over at Leslie; she was wiping her eyes as well. She looked and smiled when she noticed I had turned and was watching her. The child finished and sat back. No one spoke, we were so stunned, I suppose, by the beauty of the moment. She said in the midst of the stillness, the curtains sighing downward, "Happy Birthday, Auntie." She stood and, as the curtains again billowed inward, revealing the day outside, she swept around the piano, came up, and kissed me. There was not a dry eye in the place I am sure.

I do not quite know what to make of it. It was one of those moments that stay with you. It will stay with me until I go. I do not know how it will rest in Hilary, but I imagine she will always remember it, and have others like it, I hope. There is no conclusion, or final words to set the point, even if a point has been made. There has been a history. All I can say at this point, dear reader, is that life is not about you and I, it is about all of us.

One Last Thing More

Oh, there is one last thing. It is something I had forgotten until just now. I do not why I just thought of it. Memory is funny like that; the past does not come back all at once but in dribs and drabs. In this particular case, it is more like a piece of a puzzle that has slipped behind the cushion; you find it and it fits perfectly where it belongs, somewhere within the puzzle that has been sitting for months on the dining room table just waiting to be completed. It was something Geoffrey said while I was in his office. We had just finished discussing that framed photo on his wall showing his mother and father swinging out on *The Spray's* rigging, their life, their love, their youth, their children, Geoffrey himself, all in the future. It was the time he suggested I write this book, suggesting I would be perfect for the task He said he would arrange for help if I needed it. I should have said then that I would not need it. It would have saved me a great deal of trouble I must say. We then talked about the possibility of getting it published but that will never happen as I look at what this is now. I agreed to the assignment, of course, and began to move away. He could see I was quite overcome. He placed his arm behind me and led me over to the large plate-glass window overlooking the Colorado foothills. It was a magnificent view. It took my breath away. Of course, I had seen it coming into the office, and I had also seen the mountains from the aircraft as it came in; but it is not quite the same as being shown. Why that is I do not know. At any rate, I calmed and wiped my eyes and blew my nose, and he handed me his handkerchief since mine was already completely done. 'Blubbery old fool that I am,' I said. I glanced up. Geoffrey was watching me. He looked away and settled his arms on the railing but then looked back. I could see there was something he wanted to say and, still wiping my eyes, I nodded for him to continue.

"You took the picture."

"Yes, I did. It was just before they were married."

He turned to face me more completely. "I can't ever remember a time in my life without the three of you." I nodded and smiled. It was true. I was looking up at him, seeing the boy in him, I suppose. "Thank you, Auntie."

"Whatever for?"

He smiled and put his arm around me and drew me to him. He had turned into a big man; not unlike his grandfather whom he had never met and was otherwise nothing like.

"...For everything."

It started my eyes watering again I am afraid; it is a curse of the old and infirm to let go sheets of water at the simple drop of a hat. I was embarrassed but could not help myself. He let me cry myself out and then we went to lunch.

Addendum

As I mentioned in the preface, I tacked this on at the last minute. It is a laugh, really. Marcia brought it over. She slapped it down in front of me and laughed, pointing her finger at me exclaiming, "You did this!" I did not think she or anyone would suspect I had written it. I like the idea of some anonymity. I had written it almost a year ago and had it posted in the local rag as well the St Catherine's *Standard*, and the Kingston *Whig Standard*. I also think I may have put it in the *Globe* and *Mail*. Of course, it was Marshall's funeral notice.

She sat down across from me. She looked so much like Leslie, with some of Marshall, too. "We originally thought it came from someone attached to the theater but when I found it hidden beneath some papers on my bureau this morning and read it again, I just knew it was you!" She laughed, still pointing her finger.

I smiled and admitted to it as she smiled back, pleased with herself. I shrugged. She then sat with her arms crossed over her chest and waited for me to open up as I normally do. I stared her down for a while but ultimately told her everything. It took me quite a while to write it, I explained; the problem was I did not know quite what to say since everyone in town knows who Marshall was, and Leslie too for that matter. I just wanted to be certain that what needed to be said was said, I explained. I do hope it was okay. In the end, I thought it perfectly fine, I told her; in fact, I was rather proud of it.

What I did not expand upon was what a frustrating struggle it was, not only write it but to organize things and be sure that I got everything I wanted. There were a lot of phone calls to those pompous know-it-alls in City Hall, but all I had to do in the end was remind them of who, exactly, Doctor Marshall Davenport was and what he meant to this town. The flowers, too ▢ I was certain they would be in fine abundance but I simply had to add my own, even though I did not want anyone to know they came from me. Marshall preferred peonies of all flowers. Peonies were

impossible to get that time of year but roses are available almost all
year round, and Leslie loved roses. Her garden; God, her garden!
So I purchased exactly one hundred and three roses, one for each
year of his life, and included one white rose representing Leslie
and one yellow rose representing myself. I imagined many might
not make the connection. They might expect three yellow roses,
one for each child, and yet another color for the six grandchildren.
Admittedly, the concept did cross my mind. Ultimately, though, I
thought it somewhat *out of scope*, shall we say, in that their time will
come.

Right after posting it, I had called Marcia to let her know I
could not possibly make the funeral, decrepit old body that I am.
Her mother's funeral the previous year was bad enough, and I
could not possibly bear this one. She was somewhat put out but
knew me well enough, I suppose, not to make a scene or argue
with me, at least not right away. She would recall the scene I made
at her mother's funeral when I passed out and had to be dragged
out of the church, lifted bodily and then carried to the gravesite.
Besides, I told her, I can see the doors to St Mark's from my room
and, further on, the old cemetery grounds where their cremated
remains will be laid to rest. She would have nothing to do with it,
of course; none of them would, and an hour before the funeral,
they sent Geoffrey up to rush me down. I had already drawn my
chair up to the window and was quite prepared to watch from my
perch but he would have none of it and one cannot argue with
Geoffrey, everyone knows that. He was forced to *carry* me down to
St Mark's, actually, since I would not go of my own accord. I told
him I could barely walk and I *was* upset, after all. It was
embarrassing, yes; but he did set me on my feet so I could walk
down the aisle under my own steam.

I am glad I went in the end. I sat next to him and all the
children. Anne was there, and even Catherine; I had not seen
either of them for quite a while. Afterward, we went back to the
old house, strangely empty, and had tea and sandwiches. It turned
out to be quite a nice day. One does not think of the dead when
one is eating cucumber sandwiches and drinking Oolong tea in the
backyard with the garden overflowing with flowers and family and
friends. Their photos were everywhere, their lives laid out; but still
I was not thinking of them, not at that point at any rate; later yes,

of course. At the time, I was more interested to hear about Eric's new gig in Toronto, and Hilary's first recital to be held at the Queens's Parade Park in the Gazebo next week, and Catherine's acceptance into the Harvard Business School. Marcia's children are much more academic and I hardly ever see them since they are always at school; but I saw and talked to each and every one of them, Elizabeth, Laura, and Robert; it was very pleasant. They are studying hard but seem to be having fun as well, which of course is very important.

I do not know what they ultimately did with all those roses I sent. Marcia, Alice, and Geoffrey brought the three up to my room; one of the red, and the white, and the yellow, so they all knew they came from me in the end, I suppose. They did not ask, and I did not even suggest that I might have, but I am certain they knew.

After everyone had gone home, I sat alone in my room with the roses. I returned to my perch and looked out. It was very quiet then. Alice had asked if I would like to sleep over but I had said no, I was fine. St Mark's was very quiet, there was not even a car parked along the road. The old cemetery beyond was so deep in shadow I could see nothing at all but the darkness. I knew exactly where they were though. I would have no trouble finding them in the dark. When my time comes, I will be lying right next to them. I can wait, I suppose. Time is nothing to me now. Besides, if the forecast for this coming winter is anywhere close to being correct, it will not be long. Perhaps a good bout of pneumonia will speed things up.

In Memoriam

Marshall Eugene Davenport.
April 12ᵗʰ, 1978 to August 26ᵗʰ, 2080

Doctor Marshall Davenport, the well-known and respected writer, playwright, philanthropist, and director of the Shaw Festival for over 20 years, died yesterday of complications due to pneumonia at the respectful age of 102 years. He died peacefully in his sleep at his home in Old Town, Niagara-on-the-Lake, Ontario, Canada. A longtime resident of Kingston, Ontario, Doctor Davenport and his wife Leslie moved to Niagara-on-the-Lake upon his acceptance of the Directorship of the Festival 23 years ago. He was predeceased by his wife of over 60 years, Leslie Marie Davenport, nee, Krueger, PhD, who died exactly one year ago to the exact date, and of whom it has been said she was a woman unparalleled. She has been very grievously missed by all who knew her, including, of course, her children and grandchildren; but, most particularly, Doctor Davenport himself as well her lifelong friend Freya Anna Bergman, also a longtime resident of Niagara-on-the-Lake, who has never ceased mourning her loss. Services will be held in the old St Mark's Anglican Church in Niagara-on-the-Lake, this Saturday at 10 AM; Interment in the old grounds and light refreshments to follow, rain or shine. For those interested in attending, it is strongly suggested to come early since seating will be limited. Overflow seating will be provided, however, in Addison Hall immediately adjacent to the church where closed-circuit video of the service will be provided. Finally, the Niagara-on-the-Lake Town Council has magnanimously offered to waive all parking fees within the area of the cathedral one hour prior, during, and immediately following the service.

In Memoriam

Freya Anna Bergman
May 22nd, 1982 to April 26th, 2081

In memory of Freya Anna Bergman, the generous-hearted, high-spirited, talented, deeply lamented lifelong friend of Leslie Marie Davenport and her husband Marshall Eugene Davenport, novelist, playwright, poet, and director of the Niagara-on-the-Lake Shaw Festival for over 20 years. This matchless woman died in her sleep to the exceeding grief of the Davenport family, children, and grandchildren, on the 26th day of April, 2081 at the age of 97 years.

"No woman has loved more. No woman was more loved."

One More Last Thing

Preface by Hilary Freya Patterson

Dear reader, while going through my auntie's papers I found this additional hand-written note on her desk. It was right on top so I know she meant me to find it. I think it was meant for the book she was working on, which I know was about my grandma and grandpa. She let me read some it and I thought it quite good. It appears she might have forgotten to add it. It's not very long and I thought it should be included and so does my mother and Auntie Marcia and Uncle Geoffrey. It's about a joke my grandpa used to tell all the time. It really *is* him. Everybody always really laughed when they heard it. I don't know if it was because of the joke or because he seemed to be having so much fun telling it. You wanted to laugh because he was laughing. Both my grandma and grandpa were like that, and so was Auntie Freya after she relaxed a little. I really miss her. I hope you don't mind that we stuck this on.

Marshall's Joke

There is one more thing I need to say since I did promise it. Marshall, as I said, has quite a sense of humor. The time I am thinking of was their 60th wedding anniversary. We rented Addison Hall for the occasion and everyone was there, all the family, friends such as were still alive, some of Marshall's colleagues from the theater; even the mayor of Niagara-on-the-Lake and his wife attended. They lived next door, by the way; one simply could not invite them. The neighbors on the other side and across the street also came. I even had some of my friends from what I like to refer to as "The Home" tag along – they knew Marshall and Leslie as well as all the children from all their visits to see me. The place was simply packed. The doors were all open and every window. It was a very warm day and Leslie could not abide air-conditioning, and nor can I, leaving Marshall with no choice in the matter. In the end, though, it was turned on full with the cooler air mixing with the summer air outside, making it quite a pleasant experience for everyone. I do the same in my small room: windows wide open and air-conditioner on full. I will not have it any other way, although I realize it is quite a ridiculous thing to do; one cannot cool the entire planet.

We sat up at the head table, Marshall in the center, Leslie to his right, and me on his left, followed by Geoffrey, and then Anne at the end. Marcia sat next to her mother, then Neville, and, then Alice, followed by Douglas at the very end. I do not mind Anne so much being at the head table but I could have done without Neville or Douglas being up there with us all. They seem like such outsiders even after, in Marcia's case, thirty or more years of marriage into the family. Neville, who Marcia refers to as "Nev", is not so bad, I suppose; he is somewhat witty and good for a laugh now and again; but Douglas, referred to as "Dougie" by Alice and almost everyone else except for myself, is a real stick in the mud. I think Eric would have been a nice replacement; I rather like the young man and he is next in line, after all, in Douglas's line of succession. Still, if I had had my way, I would not have had any man at the head table whatsoever, except Geoffrey and, of course, Marshall

It was, however, a grand affair, and lots of fun. All the children had a speech prepared. Geoffrey's, in particular, was the most polished. He talked about their days on *The Spray*, his sisters, but mostly how much his mother and father loved them, and unconditionally so. It was very moving. Marcia, though, could hardly get through hers; she could not stop from crying. I had to stand up and hold the paper for her, and as she continued to bawl her eyes out, I put my hand on her shoulder to calm her, and she managed to get through it. It was a lovely speech, though, and from the heart. Alice's was also beautiful, and from her heart, too. She never lost a beat getting it out there. It is funny, really; it was if they had reversed roles. Normally, Marcia is the calm and controlled one while Alice is the one who can sometimes take flights into emotional fancy. I suppose one never knows what is completely in one's heart until there is an occasion to pour it out.

At any rate, Eric played his guitar, George Harrison's 'My Guitar Gently Weeps.' He was brilliant and there was a standing ovation of course. Hilary recited a poem by e. e. cumming's, 'i carry your heart'; she could have played a piece, there was a piano available, but she decided not to. I was very surprised she did that but the effect she wanted she obviously achieved. The poem is very beautiful and very powerful, and the way she read it was just so heart-felt that there was barely a dry eye in the place. I, of course, choked up like everyone else; I could not speak or even look up for several minutes after she sat down. I didn't want to embarrass myself up at the head table so I did finally manage to still some of the water-works I seem prone to. Elizabeth and Laura had organized the large-scale 3D image projector that was set up in the corner and from which selected moments of the family's history were recreated to the extent that the images seemed almost real. I have to say I was well represented throughout. It was embarrassing really. I had no idea I was so *prevalent* in their lives. Oh, and Robert stood up and recited a rather off-colored anecdote I would rather not mention ☐ something about when they were children listening to their mother and father making love in the back bedroom. We all could have done without it.

At any rate, I am once again digressing and I wanted to tell you about Marshall's joke. He stood up and took the podium seemingly in response to Robert's ill-phrased humor. I really do not think that's it though. He just decided to deliver his favorite joke and that was as good a time as any, I now believe.

He stood up and admitted to chuckles all around that he and Leslie did indeed have at one time a rather robust sex life; but no longer, he conceded, triggering a wave of understanding and smiles. He proceeded with an anecdote that he claimed to be a confession of sorts. On the occasion of his 97th birthday, as a treat and as a way of hoping to mitigate the rather sad state of affairs that his sex life was now all but nonexistent, a number of colleagues of his from the theater arranged for a hooker to show up at his front door. She was a well-known actress from the theater, in reality. Thank God Leslie was not home, he said. It was late at night, and rather cool, and it was raining outside. He opened the door to a scantily clad and well-endowed young woman who, despite the fact she was shivering with the cold and was being soaked with a cold early spring rain, immediately came out with a bubbly, "Hi! It's Super Sex!" He thought long and hard about it, he said, the door open, droplets of rain dusting her hair and shoulders and bare breasts and ultimately spotting the toes of slippers. It took him a while to absorb the situation, he said, but he finally made up his mind. Since Leslie was not home, what would it hurt? "I think I'll take the soup," he said.

He had them spilling their drinks and falling out of their chairs. Hah! I laughed until my sides ached. What a laugh!

FAB, Niagara-on-the-Lake, Ontario, April 1st, 2081

Acknowledgements

I would like to thank Neil Bobroff for his wit, insight, friendship, and support. Don Flemming, Sarah Reid-Yu, and Arnold Davenport for their technical assistance, good advice, and longtime support. All my friends at the Applied Physics Laboratory who support me. My family, particularly Alison, Sarah, Mitch, Barb, Mike, and Jude who have encouraged me, and Patti Reid for her continuing encouragement, and who taught me all I know, or think I know, about love. Finally, I would like to thank Mary Alice Marsh, also known to me as Grandma Beckett, for setting me upon this road.

About the Author

j. d. Reid lives an eclectic lifestyle immersed in isolation, beautiful views, dark skies, and a deep passion for writing the best novels he can. He likes physics, mathematics, music, art, literature, astronomy, paleontology, anthropology, entomology, geology, even religion — but finds the human mind and heart the most interesting and often the most perplexing of all. He has a degree in physics, and owns a kayak. He has a cabin by a river and wonderful friends and family, without whom he wouldn't bother to write. What would be the point? Besides writing in the morning and late at night, kayaking beneath gentle rain, he likes to hike in the mountains of British Columbia or canoe in the back country of Algonquin Park. He has holed himself up on Wolfe Island where the Great Lakes merge into the St Lawrence River, and takes close-up pictures of wildflowers when he's not writing or trying to keep up with those around him who take up his time but only because they care. He is a Canadian and a proud American. He has English roots, some Scottish peat in his blood, and even a tingle of the Irish. He has a lot of good stories in him.

He can be reached at jdreid1p0.com

Author's Note

There were two women on the Wolfe Island Ferry on the morning of July 8th 2012 who were young, beautiful, and ready to set out on bike-ride about Wolfe Island, Ontario. This novel takes its inspiration from them, wherever they are, whoever they are. The few places mentioned about Kingston, Wolfe Island, and Niagara-on-the-Lake, are also real – they are nice places to visit and you should do so.

Soup and Sex

I first heard the joke "Soup and Sex" from Dr. Robert McHarg, also known to me as, "Uncle Bob", who's unflagging sense of humor as well as his friendship for our family I shall never forget.

About the Cover

The front cover is a 'cartoonification' of the Wolfe Island Ferry en route to Wolfe Island, Ontario, from Kingston, Ontario, Canada as has been modified from the original photo kindly provided by Will S. and is currently posted on this Flickr site: http://www.flickr.com/photos/wiless/5243407918/

Wolfe Island and Kingston are located where Lake Ontario turns into the St Lawrence River near the internationally known Thousand Islands, an archipelago of 1864 islands that straddle the Canada-US border. It is a beautiful part of our planet and well worth the visit.

Made in the USA
Middletown, DE
27 May 2017